I0691001

CAN YOU FEEL THE MAPLE TONIGHT

LOVE IN MAPLEWOOD

BIX BARROW

Cover designed by Morningstar Ashley Designs

Cover image: Depositphotos

Proofreading by Lori Parks

eBook ISBN: 978-1-964616-11-7

Print ISBN: 978-1-964616-14-8

BOOK AND SERIES BLURB

Catching feelings for my friend with benefits? Surely there's a song about that...

When my musical mentor asked me to help his old buddy put on a music festival in Vermont, I thought it'd be a nice break from my regular life. Not that my life has been regular lately. My twin left to go be an actor, and I'm not on tour for the first time since I was a kid. Working on a project like this is just what I needed.

But I'd barely arrived in Maplewood when I almost ran over a teenager, heard about a local cryptid, and got shouted at by a fanny-pack wearing, floppy-haired, thirty-something veterinarian named Finn. Who was adorable. When he wasn't yelling, of course.

This being a small town, I keep running into Finn no matter how I try to avoid him. Only, as much as he rubs me the wrong way, I wouldn't mind him rubbing me the right way, if you know what I mean.

Turns out he feels the same, so we agree to stop bickering and start lick...er-ing. Whatever. You get my drift. It's all just casual, friends-with-benefits fun, a physical release. And that's all it can be, because I'm only in town until the festival is over. Then it's back to my regular life.

But someone should've warned me that Finn's actually sweet. He's always doing thoughtful little things for me, and he's so supportive of his teenager. How can I keep things casual in the face of all that? But it's way too soon for either of us to be having "feelings". Maybe I can find an excuse to stick around a little longer....

Can You Feel the Maple Tonight *is a low-angst, small town contemporary MM romance with an age gap, a single parent, musical interludes, something strange in the woods, a giant tortoise, hats for every occasion, and a murder chicken.*

With the highest percentage of LGBTQIA+ residents in Vermont, Maplewood is a town where everyone belongs. And with festivals year round, there's always something fun happening! This multi-author, low-angst queer series features ten standalone romances—each set against the backdrop of a different festival. Come for the celebrations, stay for the happily-ever-afters!

AUTHOR MISCELLANY

AUTHOR'S NOTE

If you find any typos or continuity errors in this book, please email me at bixbarrow@gmail.com. Reporting errors through Amazon does not trigger an alert to the author.

ACKNOWLEDGEMENTS

Thank you to the members of my Facebook group, Bix Barrow's Boom Boom Room, who voted on which side character from my Bent Oak, Texas series they most wanted to see get his own book. I hope I did Drake justice for you!

Many thanks to Elizabeth D., ARC reader extraordinaire, who won the opportunity to name Charlie and helped me with some of his behaviors.

Thank you so much to Lee Blair and Riley Long, who organized the Love in Maplewood shared world, and to my other fellow Maplewood authors: Ana Ashley, Rhys Everly-Lawless, Amy Aislin, Chantal Mer, Jeff Adams, Beck Grey, and Susan Scott Shelley.

A round of applause for Morningstar Ashley, who nailed my beautiful cover on the first try!

Thank you to Amy Pittel, my amazing professional beta reader and editor!

Thank you to Beck Grey, DJ Gainer, and Lee Blair for beta reading. Y'all are the best!

Thank you to Lori Parks for proofreading!

Love as always to the Sparrows!

CONTENT WARNINGS

- A main character is attacked by a bird
- A main character recounts being emotionally and financially abused by a parent
- Multiple mentions of the deaths of parents caused by cancer, car accident, and drugs.
- Brief mention of a pet dying of unspecified causes and another pet dying from cancer, both happening prior to the start of the story
- A side character recounts being chased through the woods by what he believes to be a locally legendary monster
- Brief mentions of a side character losing weight and maintaining a low weight for an acting role

CAN YOU FEEL THE MAPLE TONIGHT

SCHOOL

ICE RINK

TO MOON MEADOWS
MAPLE FARM

FORBIDDEN
MAPLE

NORTH →

SPARKY'S

SPARKY'S
DINER

TOWN
HALL

VET CLINIC

HARMONIC
CIRCUS

SCOOPS ON
MAPLE

THE HONEY
SPOT

SPECIAL
BLEND

WILD
PALETTE

Wild Palette

CLOVER STREET

MAPLE STREET

THE STRIPED
MAPLE

Striped Maple

MORGAN STREET

FIREHOUSE

MAPLEWOOD CITY PARK

PLAYHOUSE

THEATER

LIBRARY

GARNET DRIVE

RED'S RESTAURANT

RED'S
RESTAURANT

TO FESTIVAL GROUND
AND FOREST

RED CLOVER
INN

Maplewood

VERMONT'S
QUEEREST TOWN

TEXT CONVERSATION MONDAY, 3:22 P.M.

FINN:

Everybody, Charles went missing from Mom and Dad's house. They don't know what time exactly, but at most an hour or so ago. His phone's going straight to voicemail. Can you please help look for him?

ADDY:

Shit. Getting in the car now. I'll start from Mom and Dad's place and do a spiral

ADDY:

I asked Nate if he could search the woods behind the house, but he's too far away to get over there before dark

FINN:

Dad said he went into the woods about fifty feet in a few areas but didn't see any sign of him

ALEX:

I'll swing by the park and the high school. Did you contact the police?

FINN:

No. I will if he doesn't show up before it gets dark.

MICKEY:

I'm stuck at the diner. Do you want me to let everyone here know to keep an eye out for him?

FINN:

Not yet. I don't want to embarrass him if I don't have to. I'll let you know, thanks.

ANDRE:

He's not at the library

SAM:

Did you check with Roy at Harmonic Circus?

FINN:

Yeah, he hasn't seen him

SAM:

Okay. I'll drive around too. Addy, I'll call you to coordinate

JASON:

Me too

ADDY:

Roger that. Finn, stay strong. He's a good kid. Even if he's acting out, he won't run away.

FINN:

I hope you're right

CHAPTER 1
DRAKE

Monday, nine days before the festival

"And you would not believe the food! Dude, they put every kind of food out all day long, as long as we're filming. I'll never go hungry again."

I snorted. "Be careful. Don't you have a shirtless scene coming up soon?"

Dirk's groan echoed through the SUV's speakers. "Don't remind me."

I laughed. As much as I had mixed emotions about my twin discovering a passion for acting—something we did *not* share, thank you very much—I was happy he was getting to follow his dream. His first role, a tiny part in an indie film last year, had led to the offer of this much larger role in a movie with a few more zeroes in its budget.

But it meant he and I weren't working together anymore. Weren't even living together anymore for the most part. Sure, all of his stuff was still in the condo we shared in Texas, but he'd be on location for filming for the next few months.

Which was why I'd jumped at the chance to come to Vermont, even though the music festival I'd be helping with didn't start for a week and a half. Zeke, the guy in charge of putting on the event, asked me to arrive early if I could. Apparently our mutual friend, Jake Lord, had told him I had time on my hands.

It's not like I was unemployed, though. I was a songwriter these days. The ultimate in a flexible schedule, work-from-anywhere job. Too bad I wasn't allowed to visit Dirk on set. He was also in New England, only a few hours away from where I'd be staying for the next couple of weeks.

So far my impression of Vermont was... green. Spring was in full swing, and trees lined the highway as far as the eye could see. Trees, trees, trees.

But were trees supposed to... move like that? Like they were being shoved aside so something could get through them? I took my foot off the accelerator while I squinted to get a better look at the sloped forested area about half a mile ahead on the right. The road curved here, and I didn't want to veer onto the shoulder.

"Drake?"

"Huh? Sorry, it's just.... It's weird. It looks like there's something big moving through the forest. It's coming toward the highway." I slowed the car further, my hands tightening on the steering wheel. I hoped my dashcam was recording this.

"Bro, you haven't even been in Vermont an hour. Are you already sampling the local product?"

"Shut up. I don't know how else to explain it. It's about to reach the edge of the forest right up ahead and—*Shit!*" I spun the wheel toward the shoulder as an unexpectedly human-shaped form ran out of the woods and leaped, trying to hurdle over the guardrail along the highway. Instead they caught their foot on the metal edge and fell, landing terrifyingly close to where my car might've been if I hadn't slowed down.

"Fuck!" I pulled the SUV to a stop and set the parking brake. My hands were trembling.

"Drake! What's happening?"

"Sorry, I'm okay. I'm okay." I rubbed my chest, trying to calm my racing heart. "A guy tried to jump over the guardrail onto the road in front of me and fell down. I'm gonna go help him."

"I'm staying on the line," he said grimly. "It could be one of those insurance scams."

"Yeah, of course." I remembered to turn the car off and grab the phone from its holder before I opened the door with my still shaking hand. I'd never been in a car accident before. I hadn't hit the guy, but he wasn't getting up. Shit, shit, shit.

I jogged over to the guy—kid, really. Maybe a teenager. He was curled into a fetal position clutching one arm, with his upper body on the road and his lower half on the dirt of the shoulder. He was wearing a battered black leather jacket, jeans, and dirt-caked Nikes. I was relieved to see I'd avoided him by a good twenty-five feet at least. Things had seemed much closer from the SUV. "Hey, are you okay? Do I need to call an ambulance?" I looked worriedly up and down the highway. I hadn't seen much traffic today, but it always showed up when you didn't want it to.

The kid groaned. "Fuck. Finn's going to kill me." He writhed on the ground a little bit, his black leather jacket protecting him from the grit and small rocks.

"Um, maybe we could talk about that after we get you moved away from the road? I don't want you to get run over by a car."

He scoffed. "Like there's that much traffic in this town." He turned slightly onto his back, and I could finally see his face. He was probably fifteen or so, tall with gangly limbs, pasty skin, and messy brown hair.

"Yeah, maybe, but it would make me feel better."

He sighed dramatically, which I took to mean he wasn't seriously injured, and rolled fairly smoothly to his feet, still cradling his right arm. The rest of him was dusty from the road but appeared uninjured. He was breathing pretty heavily, and his face was flushed.

I led him over to the passenger side of the SUV, opened the door and got him seated. "My name's Drake. What's yours?"

"Charlie—sorry, I go by Charles now. Nice hat." He squinted at my fedora before frowning down at his arm.

"Okay, Charles. You want some water before I check out your arm?"

He shook his head. "It's fine. I just bruised it." He carefully straightened his arm and turned his hand over. He didn't have any abrasions on his palms. Based on the dirt ground into his sleeve, he must've landed on his elbow.

I grimaced. "That must hurt like a bitch." I winced. *Don't curse in front of the kid, Drake.*

Charles laughed. "Yeah." He let me help him out of his jacket. Underneath he wore a short-sleeve t-shirt. His elbow was swollen and red.

I sucked in a breath. "Ouch. Um, I'm not an expert, Charles, but I feel like you need an x-ray."

"Noooo! Can't I put my jacket back on and we pretend you never saw it? Please?"

I looked into his pleading eyes and frowned. Dirk and I had always been the youngest of anyone in our acquaintance, so I had zero experience determining whether Charles was trying to avoid ordinary parental punishments or if he was truly worried for his safety.

"What will happen if, uh, Finn, did you say? What will happen if Finn sees it?"

He huffed and stared down the road in the direction I'd been coming from. "He'll make Brad and Janet feel bad. I was supposed to spend the afternoon at their place, but they both fell asleep, so I went outside." He shrugged without looking at me. "They're nice. I don't want them to feel like they did anything wrong."

My phone vibrated in my pocket. Dirk had probably needed to get back on set.

"Okay, well, unfortunately if Finn is responsible for you, he'll be the one to decide whether you need to go to the doctor. I can't take you myself without raising a lot of eyebrows."

He nodded miserably. "Okay."

"Would you rather call Finn now, so he'll know you're safe?"

He shook his head. "I left my phone at Brad and Janet's, and I don't have Finn's number memorized."

"I see." Bro obviously hadn't grown up a Derry like me and Dirk. He needed to work on his lying skills. His phone was in his back pocket. "Okay. Let's head to wherever Finn is. Can you get your seat belt on?"

He swung around in the seat and pulled the seat belt across, clicking it securely. I shut his door, then stopped on my way around the car to get a bottle of water out of the cooler in the back.

Dirk had messaged that he had to get to work. I'd have to call him later with an update.

I handed Charles a water bottle and put my phone back in its holder on the dash. "Right. What's the address?"

Charles blinked. Then he looked between the phone and my face. Twice.

Dude. Just no.

I sighed and held up a hand. "How do you want to do this?"

"Can you drive, and I'll tell you where to turn?" He turned puppy dog eyes on me.

Fuck me. "We're going to Maplewood?"

"Yeah. Downtown." He was definite on that, thankfully.

Maplewood was a small town. He wouldn't get away with hiding his destination for long.

I took a deep breath and put the SUV in gear. This would be interesting.

According to the sign we passed, we were only twelve miles from town. I wondered how long Charles had been running through the woods when he'd emerged.

"Hey, what were you running from anyway?" Because he was too small to have been what had made the trees move so strangely. But I wasn't about to be the first person to mention it.

"Huh?" He jerked his head around from where he'd been teenagering intently out the window.

"You ran out of the woods, and it seemed to me you meant to keep running across the road. Did something scare you?"

"Oh! Uh... I... it was creepy in there, and I thought I heard an animal or something." He kept his face fixed toward the windshield.

Uh huh. "Oh, yeah. That makes sense, because the reason I was going so slow was I thought I saw something big moving in the trees, but I couldn't make out what it was."

I made sure to glance at him right as I finished speaking, and he flashed wide eyes at me. "You did?"

I nodded, turning back to the road. "It was almost like the trees were being moved out of the way of something, but it was just more green." I shrugged. "Not sure." I signaled, even though no one was behind me, as I took the exit for Maplewood.

He cleared his throat. "There's, uh, a town legend. Not that I believe it or anything."

"Okay?"

"It's called the Maplewood Monster, but the locals say her name is Mabel."

"Mabel the Maplewood Monster?"

"Yeah. She looks like she's made out of leaves. She's really tall and her arms are, like, long." He held his arms out in front of him. "She gets mad if you litter or damage the forest."

"That sounds creepy. Do you think Mabel was what was following you?"

Instead of answering, he pointed. "Turn there."

I gave up. After I dropped Charles off, I was headed to a compound owned by Zeke Knight, the guy I was helping with the festival. I'd only spoken to him on the phone once, but I'd bet my last hat he'd have all the stories about this Mabel.

Downtown Maplewood was exactly as quaint as I'd pictured. Lots of little shops and businesses with a big park in the middle, and people walking around at a leisurely pace.

Charles had me turn a couple of times and then, with an aggrieved sigh, he pointed ahead and told me to pull into the parking lot for the Maplewood Veterinary Clinic. Why I couldn't have put this in the GPS, I would never know.

"Your... uh, Finn is a vet?"

"Yeah." His tone made it clear Finn had chosen his profession solely to irritate Charles.

As I pulled into a parking space, he groaned. "Brad and Janet are here. Fuck." But when I turned the car off, he didn't hesitate to unbuckle his seat belt and get out.

I let him lead the way into the clinic. I pulled my fedora off as I looked around. The lobby itself was empty, with no one waiting and no one manning the reception desk, but several raised voices were coming from somewhere in the back. Charles used his good arm to push through a set of swinging doors to the left of the desk, stomping resolutely down a hallway toward the cacophony.

"I don't know how to find his phone! I don't think we ever... linked them? I don't remember doing it. Does it require a special app?" The light baritone seemed on the verge of tears.

Charles' shoulders hunched.

"Well, when he turns up, we'll make him link his phone with yours first thing." This was an older woman.

"I still think we should call the police," an older man announced. This led to more shouting.

We turned a corner and an open doorway to the right showed a sort of break room with a table and chairs. Only one person was sitting—a thirty-something guy wearing blue scrubs. He was hunched over with his elbows on the table and his hands in his hair, staring down at his phone. The other three—an older couple and a tall woman a few years older than me covered in tattoos and piercings—were standing around gesturing at each other while they loudly debated the merits of bringing in the cops.

Charles hesitated, and I didn't blame him. This entire scene gave me flashbacks to loud arguments in my family when Dirk and I were in our early teens. My back clenched into a knot of tension.

But Charles hadn't seemed frightened of returning to his family, more like he just didn't want to get in trouble, so he'd have to deal. I clapped him on one shoulder and pulled him with me into the doorway. "Hey, there!" I said in as cheerful a tone as I could manage.

The guy at the table—who must've been Finn—glanced up first. His eyes were red-rimmed, but they filled with absolute joy when he saw Charles. "Charlie!" He jumped out of his chair and ran over to us. The others finally noticed and added their voices to the cries of relief.

I stepped back to allow Charles to hug Finn. The older couple threw their arms around both of them. I met the younger woman's eyes over their shoulders and waved. She waved back but that was all we could do with the others blocking the doorway.

My movements must've caught Finn's eye. His happy smile vanished, and his eyebrows met over his nose. "Who's this? Is this who you've been with?" He didn't wait for Charles to respond, just dropped the hug and stalked over to me as he looked me up and down. He was bigger than he'd seemed sitting at the table. He had a good two to three inches on me, and his shoulders were much wider. His scowl deepened, but his threatening demeanor was undermined by the black fanny pack around his hips. "You're not a teenager. What were you doing with Charlie? Statutory rape charges apply when the minor is a boy as well as a girl."

My eyes went wide, and I held my fedora up like a shield as I took a big step backwards. "Whoa—"

"Finn!" Charles grabbed him by the arm with his uninjured hand. They were definitely related, with similar features, and the same floppy hair. Brothers, maybe, though there was a huge age difference. "This is Drake. He rescued me. He brought me here so you could check out my elbow and see if I need to go to the doctor."

I straightened my spine and nodded. "We met not even thirty minutes ago, I swear." My heart was pounding.

Finn spun back to Charles. "Your elbow? What happened?" He held out his hand as if expecting to examine it right then and there.

Charles huffed and cupped his injured joint with his other hand. "It's probably fine. It's a little swollen from when I landed on it. I tripped. No big deal."

"Sweetie, where did you go? We were so worried." The older woman, who must've been Janet, kept lifting and then dropping her arms like she was restraining herself from pulling Charlie into another big hug.

Charles sighed and looked between her and—I assumed—Brad. "I'm sorry. I didn't mean to run so far, and I got turned around. I promise, it won't happen again."

None of them seemed relieved. Finn slid his eyes to me and back to Charles. "We'll talk later. Why don't we get a look at your elbow, Charlie—Charles." He grimaced, then he turned to me. "Um, sorry, I didn't catch your name."

I smiled and turned on the Derry charm, low-wattage version. "I'm Drake. Nice to meet all of you." Not that I'd actually met any of them except Charles. I mentally shrugged. Would I ever run into these people again? No. "Charles here told me all your names, so no need to introduce yourselves." The girl in the back coughed a laugh, but I kept my gaze on Finn's. "He was real worried about upsettin' y'all." I tried to minimize the Texas twang—I wasn't wearing the right hat for it—but unfortunately it tended to make an appearance when I was stressed, much to Dirk's everlasting amusement. Right now I was only stressed about how to extricate myself from this family drama and get to where I'd be spending the night.

Finn seemed like he was trying to figure out a reason to get pissed at me again, so I turned to Charles and smiled. "Time for me to get on with gettin' on." Oh, god. I needed to get the fuck out of here. Dirk would bust a gut when I told him. I focused solely on speaking in my regular voice. "Y'all take care now, and I'm glad you're okay, Charles." Mixed results, but I'd take it.

I took a step to the side in preparation for turning around, when I noticed the younger woman in the back holding her phone up, looking between me and the screen. Yep, time to go.

Charles' face fell. "Do you have to leave? I feel like I owe you dinner or something for rescuing me." He gazed earnestly up at Finn. "It'd be the nice thing to do, right?"

Finn eyed my fedora suspiciously. "Um...."

I held up my hands again, ready to make my excuses. My phone buzzed, and I grabbed it gratefully from my pocket.

"Please?" Charles had some killer puppy dog eyes.

"Um, hang on. This might be important." It was Zeke, my soon-to-be host. Probably not *important*, per se, but whatever the reason for the call, I could turn it into an excuse not to have dinner with Charles and his family.

"Zeke?" I walked back to the empty lobby.

"Hey, kid, I heard you're at the vet clinic." His voice was raspy, as if he'd smoked and sang his way through life.

Wait, how did he know? "Yeah, I'm here. I had to make a stop, but I'll be at your compound in a few." It was none of Zeke's business why I was here, no matter how he'd found out about it.

He grunted. "That vet-boy's good people. You could do a lot worse. And his get's livin' with him now, right? Have them come out for dinner tonight. My tortoise needs seein' to. I got a casserole and homemade maple butter bars. Tell that niece of mine to tag along." He hung up.

MAPLEWOOD MATTERS BLOG, MONDAY 7:42 P.M.

Things were tense around the vet clinic late this afternoon, as the whereabouts of our youngest recent transplant to Maplewood were temporarily unknown. The troops were rallied for the search, but in the end it was a handsome stranger who saved the day and brought the errant teenager home.

Who is the man in the hat? MM is on the case.

CHAPTER 2

FINN

Monday, nine days before the festival

The very pretty, but very young, stranger, who was apparently named Drake—and who saddles their kid with *Drake*?—frowned down at his phone. I felt bad about all but accusing him of kidnapping Charlie for sex, but I still didn't want to have to invite him for dinner. Charlie and I needed to talk.

But Charlie—Charles—was determined to get his way. "Well? Will you have dinner with us, Drake?"

The guy had been trying to get out of it earlier; I'd seen it in his face. But his current expression was more confused than regretful.

"Um, that was Zeke—Zeke Knight. He wants you to come out to the compound and look at his tortoise?" He turned to me for confirmation.

Well, fuck. I sighed and nodded. "Dolores." She was a 90-plus year-old giant tortoise who tended to get shell rot when we had a lot of rain. Though it'd been dry lately. But Drake knew Uncle Zeke? I frowned at Nova, who'd been busying herself at the reception desk shutting everything down.

Drake blinked. "Um, okay. He says he'll feed you dinner.

Er, both of you." He glanced at Charles, who almost exploded in his excitement.

"Really? We get to have dinner together?"

"Seems so. Out at Zeke's place. And he mentioned his niece?"

"That's me. I'm Nova." She waved. "Sorry, I told Uncle Zeke you were here."

Drake's earlier dig about not needing to be introduced to anyone came back to me, and I cringed. "Um, sorry. I'm Finn. These are my parents, Janet and Brad." I gestured for them to come over.

Mom headed right for Drake. "Thank you again, sweetie, for rescuing our Charlie." She enveloped him in a hug, and he patted her awkwardly on the back with one hand, holding his Indiana Jones-style hat with the other.

"It's Charles, Janet." The put-upon teenager rolled his eyes.

She released Drake and blew Charles a kiss. "Yes, hon. I'll try harder to remember."

I put my hand on Charles' shoulder. "Let me look at your elbow. Um, Drake, if you want to go on ahead, I'll let Zeke know if I have to take Charles to urgent care. If that happens, I'll stop by tomorrow to see Dolores."

"What? No! I don't need to go to urgent care." He dropped the hand he'd been using to cradle his injured elbow. Nice try.

Drake nodded solemnly. "If it needs to be checked out, you don't have a choice, Charles. But if I don't see you tonight, I'll see you tomorrow, okay?"

Charles grumbled but walked Drake to the door so he could leave. Nova took off too, wishing Charles good luck.

After I sent a quick text to everyone who'd been searching to make sure they knew Charles was found, the four of us walked to the back of the clinic. Charles carefully took his dad's leather jacket off, and I noticed it had a lot more scratches and scrapes on it than when I'd seen it this morning. Had he been running through the woods?

His elbow was swollen, but nothing seemed broken. "Okay, we'll ice it down when we get home tonight, but unless the swelling is worse in the morning, you don't need an x-ray."

Charles cheered and put his jacket back on.

Mom and Dad opted out of going to Uncle Zeke's. They preferred to go to bed at a reasonable time. So did I, for that matter, but Charles hadn't met Uncle Zeke yet, and he was certainly keen to spend more time with Drake. If I were a better parent, I would probably keep Charles home to punish him for leaving Mom and Dad's place this afternoon without telling anyone. But he was stuck with me, a poor substitute for the real thing. So instead, his punishment would be an unpleasant conversation in the car on the way to Uncle Zeke's compound.

I'd been ready to leave but Charles informed me that, even though Zeke wanted me to look at his tortoise, it would be "cringe" for me to wear my scrubs to dinner. Fine. I ran to the house—conveniently located behind the clinic—and changed into jeans and a t-shirt with a flannel over it. At least I could remove the flannel if Dolores got it dirty.

Eventually, just as the sun was setting, Charles and I were in my SUV heading to the east side of town. I cleared my throat and ignored the sweat suddenly springing up under my arms. "Tell me about this afternoon." That was neutral and non-accusatory, right?

He froze, his phone clutched tightly in one hand, water bottle in the other. "You won't believe me." His voice was low, his tone defeated.

Fucking hell. Was there a teenager how-to book? "You don't know that. Try me."

He darted a glance at me then stared out the windshield.

After a minute he cleared his throat. "Um, what do you want to know?"

"Well, can you start with why you left Mom and Dad's house?"

He blew out a breath. "I didn't mean to go beyond the backyard, I *promise*. I was feeling... antsy. I'd finished helping Brad clean out the garage, and he was napping in his chair in front of the TV. Your mom went in the bedroom to lie down for a few minutes. You know, next time maybe I could borrow your car? Then I could come home if I wanted to."

"We can discuss that later. Go on."

He huffed, but it was mostly under his breath, so I ignored it. "I went out to the backyard, but you know how it's open to the woods?"

I nodded. I'd grown up in that house, after all.

"Yeah. I thought I saw something moving in the trees, so I went to check it out."

I stared at him for a little too long, given I was driving. "You... you know there are bears and other dangerous animals in those woods, right?"

He waved this away. "It wasn't a bear. It was too tall. Lonnie at school told me about Mabel, the tree creature that's supposed to live around here, and I thought it'd be cool if I could say I saw it."

I bit back the urge to tell him popularity wasn't worth putting himself in danger. He was a teenager, and he wouldn't listen. Instead I breathed in and out, then I said, "Okay, so you went into the woods. What happened?"

He squeezed the water bottle, making the plastic click as it crumpled. "Um, I—I think I actually did see it."

I glanced over at him, my eyebrows high on my forehead. "You did?" I'd lived in Maplewood my entire life, and even though dozens of people swore they'd had close encounters with Mabel, I'd never seen any sign of it.

He nodded but kept his eyes on the passing scenery. "It was, uh, tall, and looked like it was made of leaves mostly. Or like branches covered in leaves I guess. But with eyes?" He shivered. "It, uh, moved. Like, it walked toward me. So I ran." He put the water bottle in the cup holder and wrapped his arms around himself.

Whether this was teenage histrionics or not, he seemed legitimately freaked out. Maybe I should have Nate take a walk around the woods behind my parents' house. I put a hand on his shoulder. "That sounds pretty scary. Did you get away from it?"

He shook his head. "It followed me for a while. I'm not sure how long I ran, but I ended up at the highway. You know where it curves for a few miles before the exit to Maplewood?"

I gaped, glancing between Charles and the road ahead. "I'm sorry, *what*? You ran from Mom and Dad's house to the fucking highway? Through the woods?" It was easily four or five miles if he'd run in a straight line. No wonder his jacket was all scraped up. Wait a minute. "And then what happened? You said Drake rescued you?"

He shivered. "I didn't really realize I'd left the woods, but suddenly I was at the road, and I tried to jump the guardrail, but I tripped and fell."

My heart seized up. "At the road? You mean you fell down on the *highway*?" We were about to pass the feed store, so I pulled into the parking lot and stopped the car. I turned to Charles and grabbed his hand. I barely restrained myself from running my hands over his head and chest to check for injuries.

"I'm fine." His tone was dismissive, but he didn't pull his hand out of mine.

"Tell me what happened after you fell."

He shrugged. "I didn't hit my head or anything, just my

elbow." He frowned down at himself. "And I fucked up Dad's jacket pretty bad."

I ignored his language, but this time I didn't stop myself from running a hand over his head. "I know your dad would be pretty damn happy the jacket kept you from getting more severely injured."

He chewed on his bottom lip as he regarded the leather. "Probably."

"So, you fell...?" Teenagers were incredibly frustrating, I'd been learning over the past couple of months.

"Yeah. Drake saw me fall, and he pulled over and got out of the car."

I closed my eyes against the lightheaded feeling coming over me. What if Drake *hadn't* seen Charles fall? What if he'd hit Charles? I shuddered. "He helped you up?"

"Yeah, and he made me show him my elbow. He was worried I'd have to go to urgent care."

I swallowed. "I have to point out that you shouldn't get into cars with strangers."

He didn't roll his eyes, but I got a strong feeling that he wanted to. "I'll try to remember that the next time I need a ride from the side of the highway."

I stifled a sigh. "You were lucky he was driving by."

"No joke. We didn't see another car til we got off the exit to town."

I took a moment to get my breathing under control before I put the car back in gear and returned to the road. "I'll have to apologize to Drake for yelling at him earlier."

"Yeah. That wasn't cool, Finn."

I nodded. *Dammit, Noelle, why'd you have to die and leave me with this kind of responsibility? This wasn't the fucking plan!*

When we turned onto the driveway to Zeke's property, the

gate opened for us. He must've been watching his security cameras. I pulled around behind the house to park.

"That's Drake's car." Charles pointed at the first cabin, which had a Porsche SUV parked beside it.

I squinted at it. "Is Drake some sort of rock star?" He couldn't be more than twenty-five at most. That wasn't a car most people that young could afford, but if he was staying with Zeke, he probably worked in the music industry.

Charles shook his head. "I don't think so. I didn't ask though."

We got out of the car. Zeke's back door banged open, and he stomped out onto the porch. "Took you long enough! Dolores is on the verge of expiring." He pointed at the tortoise, who was crouched in her pen next to the house, chewing contentedly on a pile of spinach leaves.

"Oh, cool!" Charles trotted over to the pen. "Can I pet her? I mean, sorry. Hi, I'm Charles."

I sighed. "Zeke, this is Charles. Charles, this is Zeke." I got my medical bag out of the back seat.

"Call me Uncle Zeke, kid. And, yeah, you can pet her. She likes to be scratched on her neck." He clomped down the steps as Charles reached over the low fence and stroked Dolores gently.

I opened the small gate and went into the enclosure. "What symptoms are you observing?" I couldn't see a thing wrong with Dolores. Her shell appeared uniform, with no discolored areas. Her eyes were clear, she was holding her head up to be petted, and she'd been eating when we arrived.

Zeke didn't answer, so I looked around for him. He'd walked over to Drake's cabin, where he proceeded to go around to the far side, which was where the door was, facing away from Zeke's house. We heard him bang his fist against it. "Hey, Derry! We got company, so get your ass out here."

He came back around the side of the cabin and stomped

toward Dolores' pen. "Young 'uns these days." He shook his head. Then he caught me staring at him, and his expression became almost panicked. "Not that he isn't an adult." He hiked a thumb over his shoulder at the cabin. "Wouldn't be here otherwise."

Um, what? I opened my mouth, but the sound of the cabin door opening stopped me from asking.

Drake came around the cabin. He'd exchanged his Indiana Jones hat for a black beanie, but he was otherwise dressed the same as earlier. He scanned the parking area before sauntering over to Dolores' pen. "You bellowed, Zeke?" I blinked. I'd gotten the impression Drake hadn't met Zeke before today. He gave me an up-nod. "Hey, Finn. Charles."

"Drake, get in the house and help Nova with dinner. Finn here's gonna make sure Dolores doesn't die on me tonight, then we'll be right in."

Drake saluted. "Sir, yes, sir." He gazed down at Dolores as he walked past her pen. "I'm not a tortoise expert, Finn, but she looks a little depressed to me. Have you considered pet massage therapy?" He didn't wait for a reply, just jogged up the steps to the porch and breezed inside.

My gaze was drawn to his ass, and I jumped as the door shut behind him. Shit. I jerked my eyes back to Zeke, who had an oddly smug expression on his face.

Dolores was still allowing Charles to pet her. I stared Zeke down. "What symptoms is she having?"

He rubbed his chin. "You know, Drake might be on to something. What if she's depressed?"

We both looked at the tortoise.

I gritted my teeth. "What behavior have you observed to make you think she's depressed? She seems to be eating."

Charles took his hand away, and Dolores nudged him to get him to pet her again. He scrunched his eyebrows. "Maybe she's lonely. Have you thought about getting her a friend?"

Zeke grinned and walked over to clap Charles on the shoulder—fortunately it wasn't the arm he'd injured. Charles made an *oomph* sound and stumbled forward. "Good idea, kid. You ever thought about going into animal medicine like Finn here?" He didn't wait for a reply. "Think I'll get Drake on finding Dolores a companion." He spun around and headed for the house. "Y'all come on in when you're ready." In seconds he was inside the house.

I shook my head. "He never said what was wrong with her."

Charles furrowed his brow. "Did he think he needed an excuse to invite us for dinner?"

I sighed and picked up my medical bag. "We'll probably never know. I'll put this in the car, then we can go in."

TEXT CONVERSATION MONDAY, 10:39 P.M

DRAKE:

Well, I had an interesting evening

DIRK:

Do tell. The guy in the middle of the road
sounded young, from what little I caught.

DRAKE:

Yeah, he's a teenager. He was running from
some sort of local forest monster he swore
he saw

DIRK:

That's different

DRAKE:

And then he had me take him to the vet
clinic where this guy Finn works. I'm still not
clear on their relationship, but they're
related somehow. Finn accused me of
kidnapping Charles – the teenager – for sex

DIRK:

Excuse me??

DRAKE:

Don't worry. Charles set him to rights. But I was sweating for a minute there.

DIRK:

Damn. Hopefully you won't have to see them for the rest of your trip.

DRAKE:

About that...

CHAPTER 3

DRAKE

Monday, nine days before the festival

Nova was checking something in the oven when I walked into the house. "Hey, Zeke said I should come help you. It smells amazing."

She shut the oven and rolled her eyes. "It's a chicken casserole, and Uncle Zeke made it. He just likes to pretend everyone else does the work."

I raised my eyebrows. "Well, you're the one who helped me unload the equipment from my car, not Zeke."

She shrugged this off. "But Zeke's the one who made sure your cabin was ready for you, and he manufactured this little dinner party. Here. Pull out the big bowl in that cabinet. You can make the salad."

Zeke slammed the back door open and thumped inside. "I'll be in my office. Yell when the food's ready." He turned a corner and vanished.

Nova shook her head as she pulled glasses out of an upper cabinet. Once I'd washed my hands and had all the salad ingredients lined up to chop, I asked, "Why did you say he'd 'manufactured' this dinner?"

She threw a glance out the window, where Finn seemed to be putting his bag back into his car. "He gives most guests a list of the diners and pubs in town, and they're on their own. But you're friends with Jake Lord, right?"

I nodded. Jake Lord—real name Wesley—was a retired rock and roll legend who lived in my hometown of Bent Oak, Texas. We'd met five or six years ago when Dirk and I had moved back to be closer to our brother Steve. "I know Zeke and Jake go way back."

She gave me a significant look that I couldn't interpret. "I'm pretty sure they've been making plans."

I jumped when the back door opened again. Charles was rattling off a monologue about Dolores needing a friend. Finn dragged him over to the sink, where they both washed their hands. Charles didn't stop talking the entire time. "I did a search on my phone, and tortoises get along well with a few different animals. But cats are hit or miss."

Finn filled the glasses with ice and water before making Charles take them to the table. He knew where everything was, but this seemed to be Charles' first time visiting.

Maybe one day I'd learn their story.

In contrast to his frazzled and irritable demeanor at the vet clinic, when Finn had been talking to Zeke about Dolores, he'd had that quiet competence about him people get when they're sure of themselves and what they're doing. It was compelling, and I'd had trouble taking my eyes off him.

Nova lifted the casserole out of the oven. It appeared to be heavy, but I didn't make the mistake of asking her if she wanted help. I'd already gotten my head bitten off when she'd taken the instrument cases out of my SUV earlier.

Finn, Charles, and I got the table set with three place settings on one side and two on the other. Nova positioned the casserole and salad in the center before yelling, "Uncle

Zeke! Dinner!" Then she walked to the table and took a seat on the side with three places.

Shrugging to myself, I sat next to her, with Finn and Charles opposite us. Zeke emerged from wherever he'd been and thumped down into the seat next to me. "Well? What're y'all waitin' for? Let's eat!"

Finn and Charles looked uncertain, and Zeke wasn't reaching for the food. Internally rolling my eyes, I grabbed the salad bowl and put some on my plate. I passed the bowl to Nova on my left, then I scooped up some of the casserole before handing the serving spoon to her.

Since Zeke had instructed us to eat, I forked up some casserole and put it in my mouth. It was actually pretty good, cheesy with potatoes and chicken. "This is delicious. Thank you for having us to dinner." My mother would've been proud.

Zeke grunted as he finished dishing up his own plateful of food. "Can't have you goin' to a diner your first night in town. Might find yourself signin' up for an allegiance you didn't mean to."

I waited, but he didn't elaborate. Charles nodded. "Finn told me when I moved here. You gotta make sure if you go to one, you go to the other one within a couple of days. Otherwise everyone in town will know you're on team Red's or team Sparky's, and they don't let you change."

"Uh. Okay?" Somebody had said something about a pub, which sounded like the safest bet.

Finn smiled at Charles. I hadn't seen that expression on him yet, and it made my breath catch. Damn, he was one good-looking man when he wasn't being an ass. He turned to me. "How long are you in Maplewood, Drake?"

"Through the music festival, so two weeks."

Zeke set his fork down. "Stay as long as you like. Jake said you got nothin' scheduled this summer. The cabin's yours if you want it."

I fought the urge to scowl. Certain people should know to keep their mouths shut. I'd already figured out that helping Zeke with the festival was an excuse to keep me occupied while my twin was off starting his new career. In the end I managed a semi-polite, "We'll see."

"Charles." Zeke pointed his fork at his next victim. "Roy at Harmonic Circus tells me you're pretty good on the guitar."

Charles flushed and looked down at his plate. "I don't know if I'd say I was *good*."

Finn straightened in his chair. "Hey, what little I've heard when the door to your room is open sounds great." He turned to me. "He can sing too."

Charles regarded him in horror, and I could tell he'd be making sure his door was shut tight going forward.

I cleared my throat. "What style of guitar are you learning? Right now I'm trying to teach myself blues guitar, but there're so many different flavors of blues, I can't decide what to focus on."

Charles goggled at me. "You can play guitar?"

Zeke clapped me on the shoulder, almost sending me face-first into my plate. "Drake, you should give Charles here some lessons. Supplemental-like."

I smiled at Charles. "I don't know if I'm any sort of teacher, but I'm always up to practice together." His face lit up. "We can play out here, so you don't have to worry about anyone listening in."

"Really? That'd be so cool."

Oh, shit. Was I supposed to ask Finn's permission first? I gave him a quick glance, but he was smiling. Whew.

Zeke pointed his fork at Charles again. "You know Kirk Barbour?" He glanced at me. "He's taking lessons from Roy too."

"Yeah, he's in some of my classes, and I see him at the music shop sometimes."

Zeke looked thoughtful, as if this was new and fascinating information. "Roy and I tried to convince Kirk to play in the amateur competition at the music festival, but he doesn't think he's ready." He pointed his finger at Charles. Uh oh. "You know, kid, *you* could enter the amateur competition yourself. We need some young blood. Those old biddies'll probably win again this year, and only a few of the entrants so far are under the age of forty."

Charles' eyes went wide, and his expression was panicked. "Uh, I don't think—"

"No need to decide right now." Zeke shook his head. "Maybe Drake here can tell you what he thinks after he's heard you play."

Fuck me. I glared at Zeke. "I'm supposed to be one of the judges for that contest."

He waved a hand in the air. "We can work around it."

"Hold up!" Charles gaped at me. "You're a judge at the music festival? Are you famous or something?"

I chuckled. "Obviously not very."

Nova, who'd been very quiet since we sat down to eat, laughed. I made a face at her.

Zeke leaned back and whacked me on the shoulder with his big hand again. "Don't be shy, ki—uh, Drake." He looked at Charles and Finn. "This here's Drake Derry, originally of Melodious Moon." Their mouths fell open, and I rolled my eyes. "He and his brother Dirk also made an album by themselves—won some awards too."

"Just for songwriting," I muttered at my plate.

"Which is what you've been doing since then, right? Dirk's off *acting*." He spat the word like it was one of the worst life choices Dirk could've made.

"He's pretty good at it." I kept my tone positive.

Zeke wasn't buying what I was selling. "He left you high and dry."

I sat back in my seat and raised my eyebrows at him. I'd spoken with Zeke on the phone exactly twice, and today was the first time I'd met him in person. He'd started ordering me around right away, and I'd sassed him back to remind him I didn't actually work for him. But this wasn't anything he had a right to speak to. I kept my voice calm but firm. My twang didn't even try to make an appearance. "I don't know what you and Jake have been talking about, but I agreed to come here to help you with the festival, not to hear your opinions on my life or my brother's choices."

Zeke narrowed his eyes at me, then his face creased into a grin. "I like you!"

On my other side I heard Nova moan, "Oh, fuck, there's no stopping him now."

I jerked around to face her. "What do you mean?"

She shook her head and stood up, starting to clear everyone's plates.

Zeke stood too. "Afore we have dessert, we gotta feed Dolores and Mabel."

Charles and I both froze. I found my voice first. "Mabel? Like the tree creature I heard about?" I carefully didn't look at any of the others.

Zeke nodded as he put his plate in the sink. "Yep. Critter's gotta eat, just like everybody else."

"And you volunteered to feed... her?"

He shrugged. "I'm feeding somethin'. I figure, might be Mabel, might be a bear or whatnot. Either way, getting rid of my leftovers don't hurt nothin'."

He opened a cabinet under the counter and pulled out two bowls, one small and one very large, bigger than the one I'd put the salad in, and made of sturdy stainless steel.

I gave Nova a wide-eyed look, but she just smiled and went

back to stacking dishes. Finn was gaping at Zeke but didn't comment.

Charles, however, seemed as disturbed as I was. "Uh, Uncle Zeke? Where do you feed Mabel?"

Zeke pointed vaguely toward the back of the house. "As far away from the fairground as possible. Don't want any humans runnin' into her, do I?" He looked over at me. "That reminds me. You'll need to check out the fairground in the mornin' so you can get familiar with it. There's a gate at the south end of the compound. I gave you access to it on the lock app." Zeke's property was set up with a phone app that allowed keyless entry to the driveway and my cabin. He'd added me as soon as I'd arrived, muttering vague curses about technology the entire time.

He dumped the salad leavings into the smaller bowl and put the leftover casserole into the large one. Mabel must not be a vegetarian. He then rummaged around in the fridge and brought out a couple of potatoes and a cucumber, which he tossed in the large bowl as well.

"Alright, come on. Drake, you need to learn how to do this. Charles, you can come too."

"I-I'm pretty tired. Um, Finn, is it okay if we go home?" Charles's face was pale.

Finn nodded decisively. "Sure. You had a stressful day; I shouldn't have made you come out here with me."

Zeke made a production of packing up several maple butter bars for them to take home, then we all walked out to Finn's car to see them off.

Before I could escape to my cabin, Zeke put his hand on my shoulder and steered me toward Dolores' pen and the dark, creepy woods. "Time to feed Dolores and Mabel!"

ZEKE:

Don't forget to check out the fairgrounds
this morning.

ZEKE:

After that, can you call around and order
twenty or so portable toilets? Last year the
festival restrooms backed up and we didn't
have any portable ones on standby

ZEKE:

Don't forget about teaching Charles to play
the guitar. Roy says the kid's got talent!

I groaned and rolled over, pulling the covers over my head.
The bed was surprisingly comfortable. I liked the cabin itself,
too. It had one decent-sized bedroom plus a smaller one with a
desk and a twin bed. There was a full kitchen, and the living
area featured a fold-out couch, two armchairs, and a fireplace.

But it was barely after 6:00 a.m. Even before he'd texted
me, I'd heard Zeke outside banging around in Dolores' pen. I'd
swear that man only had one volume setting: loud.

Fuck it, I'd never get back to sleep now. I threw back the
covers and hauled myself out of bed. It took me a few minutes
to figure out the coffee maker, but I had enough in the pot for
a cup by the time I got out of the shower.

I wasn't ready for breakfast, so after I got dressed, I put on
my beanie from last night, then I took my coffee and my
phone and went to look at the fairgrounds per Zeke's
instructions.

There was a walking path that split into three directions
just past my cabin. That was too complicated this early in the
morning, so I checked where the sun was and went in a
southerly direction, walking across the grass until I ran into
the wall around Zeke's property. I followed it until I ran into
the gate. The wall was high, but it wouldn't keep out the most
determined of music fans. Poppy was headlining the festival,

and she was supposed to stay in the cabin behind mine. I put a note in my phone to warn her security detail about the potential for unauthorized entry.

The gate seemed sturdy, and it had an electronic deadbolt lock. But, again, it wasn't stalker-proof.

I let myself through into the festival grounds, verifying that the gate shut and locked behind me. Then I panicked slightly until I tested the phone app to make sure I could get back in. Walking all the way around would be a fucking pain.

The festival grounds were huge, maybe three-quarters of a mile long. I'd been expecting something a lot less... permanent-looking. At the far end to the south was a large amphitheater, with smaller stages on each side about halfway down. There was a large barn-like structure on the west side, and an open-air pavilion on the east. Signs indicated food courts and vendor booths down the center, with permanent walls and tent tops in place. The whole thing was a big oval, with wide aisles on the east and west sides, and paths to cut over here and there.

Damn, Maplewood must make all its revenue from festival tourism.

Movement caught my eye, and I saw two guys jogging toward me along the east side aisle. They weren't running with purpose, like a security team would've been. No, they were dressed for their morning run, like they jogged through here all the fucking time. Damn it, the fairgrounds should've been fenced off and locked up. I'd have to walk the perimeter and figure out where all the holes were.

That was going to suck.

My phone chimed with a text, and I idly kept my eye on the runners as I thumbed it open.

STEVE:

Good morning! Gamora and Mantis wanted to say hi! [photo]

Awww. Steve's husband Baz was face down in bed, and my and Dirk's pet rabbits were sprawled across his back. Steve and Baz owned Gamora and Mantis' mother and one of their siblings, so he was our go-to pet sitter whenever we left town.

"Drake?"

I glanced up to see the joggers were getting close, and one of them was Finn. Well, hell. I could've done without knowing how toned his legs were, and how his chest filled out that tight t-shirt. The fanny pack was along for the run, but he probably didn't have room for pockets in those compression tights. I dragged my eyes over to his companion, who was shorter, with dark hair and a trim, muscular build.

"Hey." I nodded as they slowed to a stop a few feet from me. "Hi," I said to Finn's friend—or whatever their relationship was. "I'm Drake."

"Drake! Finn told me you helped Charles yesterday. I'm Alex." He blatantly eyed me up and down.

Finn waved a hand in my direction. "Drake's staying at Zeke's."

I cocked my head. "Zeke wanted me to check out the festival grounds. You mind telling me how you two got in here? Is it not locked up?"

They looked at each other and made identical grimaces. Finn rubbed the back of his neck. "Uh, we've been running here a few days a week since back in high school. There's a gap in the fence if you know where to look." He held a hand up in a placating gesture. "We never use it during the festivals. We always pay for tickets." Alex nodded frantically.

I scowled. "How many people know about this gap in the fence?"

They glanced at each other again, both shrugging. "We've never told anyone." Alex frowned. "You're the first person we've ever seen in here. We avoid it during festival prep times, and of course during the festivals themselves."

I resisted the urge to yell at them. "Poppy is coming here next week. *Poppy*. You know, the multi-platinum, sold-out arena superstar? Do you know how many fans will be trying to find a way in here?" I rubbed my forehead. "I need you to show me this gap." I held up a hand to their protests. "I'll talk to Zeke about letting you have access to the compound so you can park there and come through the gate to jog here in the mornings." I glared at each of them in turn. "But if you don't show it to me right now, I'm still going to find it. It's getting blocked either way. You can help me and keep running here, or you can get shut out forever."

"Holy shit!" Alex stared at me wide-eyed. "That was so hot!"

Finn punched him softly in the shoulder. "Shut up." He sighed. "We'll show you."

He started walking back the way they'd come, so I followed.

Alex fell in beside me. "You're in town through the music festival? Any chance you'd be up for dinner *or whatever* while you're here?" The innuendo in *whatever* was unmistakable.

I hesitated. I guessed this meant Alex and Finn weren't together. And ordinarily I'd be all over Alex, with his soft hazel eyes and square jaw. Unfortunately I'd rather climb Finn like a tree.

Before I was forced to respond, Finn rounded on his friend. "Alex!"

He scowled. "What? I can't ask him out?"

Finn sputtered, "Uh, I, uh...." He turned bright red.

Alex was apparently able to interpret this. "You didn't call dibs. Plus, it's up to Drake, right?" Alex maneuvered around me so he was on my right and Finn was on my left.

This was getting interesting, but I didn't love how they weren't including me in the conversation. But it didn't matter because Finn killed every iota of attraction I'd been feeling toward him by sputtering, "He's almost as young as Charles!" I slowed down and dropped back.

Alex looked outraged. "What the fuck? He is not!" He finally turned to address me. "How old are you, Drake? Twenty-seven, twenty-eight?"

I couldn't decide whether to be flattered at how mature I'd come across or appalled at the toll all the stress was taking on my skin. "I'll be twenty-three in a couple of months." I over-rode Alex's gasp. "And, for the record, not that you consulted me, I'm not interested in dating, fucking, or otherwise spending time with either of y'all."

I wasn't proud of my temper. It came from my dad after all. But being the youngest of the Derrys meant Dirk and I had been minors for most of Melodious Moon's run. We hadn't had any say in the band's direction or contracts. Of course my father had convinced my older siblings in the band to give him complete control even after they were adults. At any rate, I was done having decisions made for me, not to mention being talked about as if I weren't present.

Finn stopped walking. "Drake, I'm—"

I held up a finger. "I promised Charles I'd play guitar with him, so once we're done here, you'll give me his phone number and I'll arrange it with him directly."

Behind me, Alex whispered, "So hot."

I flipped him the bird. "Shut up, Alex. Now show me this gap."

TEXT CONVERSATION
TUESDAY, 10:13 A.M

WESLEY:

Did you make it to Vermont okay?

DRAKE:

I'm here. I'm trying to fix some security
issues with the fairground before Poppy
arrives.

WESLEY:

I'm sure Zeke is glad to have your help.

DRAKE:

He's an interesting guy

CHAPTER 4

FINN

Tuesday, eight days before the festival

I fought the urge to run away from Drake, mortified by how rude Alex and I had been to talk about him as if he weren't present. As if Drake were something for Alex and me to negotiate between us without his input.

Alex demonstrated how we got in and out of the fairgrounds. I cringed as Drake narrowed his eyes at the obvious path we'd worn in the grass outside the fence. Anyone who saw it would be able to tell there was a way in.

He glanced up and down the length of the fairground fencing. "Well, I guess I'll be spending my morning inspecting the entire perimeter." His shoulders sagged as he made a note in his phone.

"Sorry," I muttered.

He glared at me. "It's damn lucky I found out. Now give me Charles' phone number and go away."

Alex grinned at me from behind Drake's shoulder. Asshole. I opened my contacts. "Uh, I could text it to you. You might need my number in case...." I couldn't think of a reason. Alex turned around, his shoulders shaking. I'd kill him later.

Drake rolled his eyes. "Will it make you leave faster?" He told me his number so quickly I had to ask him to repeat it.

I texted Charles' contact info to him, then I put my phone away. "I'm sorry about earlier. We shouldn't have been arguing over you like that."

Drake drew himself up to his full height. Damn, the way he carried himself was impressive for his age. "You're right. You shouldn't have." He went back inside the fairgrounds without saying goodbye.

Grinning, Alex grabbed my bicep and dragged me toward the parking lot. When we were several yards away from where Drake had left us, he whistled softly. "Damn, bro. I'm sorry I didn't notice sooner."

I jerked my arm away from him. "Notice what?"

He chuckled. "The chemistry between the two of you. It's like fire." He mimed an explosion with his hands.

I shook my head. "No way. He's too young."

He snorted. "Maybe in years. But he's no naïve kid, that's for sure. Why not give it a try?"

"You heard him. He's not interested." I hesitated next to my SUV. "Plus, Charles isn't settled in yet. I don't think it'd be good for him to see me dating, especially with someone who's only here temporarily."

Alex's expression told me I was a dumbass. "No one's talking about dating." He pointed toward the fairgrounds. "He's a young guy in his prime. Pick a night when Charles has guitar lessons or whatever, and see if Drake wants to get naked."

I frowned. "He's pretty pissed at me."

Alex threw me a cocky grin as he got in his car. "Well, they say hate sex is the best sex. He'll be up for it, guaranteed."

CHARLES:

Meeting Drake after school to play guitar.
Not sure when I'll be home.

ME:

Have fun

It was only then that I realized Charles *would* have fun with
Drake. More fun than he ever had with me around. Drake was
less than ten years older than Charles, but an adult and a
fucking rock star to boot. My mid-thirties, boring ass couldn't
compete.

I'd done my best to spend time with Charles one-on-one,
but he became monosyllabic when we went out to dinner. He
hated going on nature walks. Movies were good, but they
didn't help us create an emotional connection. And I
couldn't play the goddamned guitar like Charles' father
could.

Like Drake could.

Would Charles even want to come home after an evening
with Drake?

Alex interrupted my thought spiral to invite me to the pub
with him and some of our other friends. Hoping their
company would get me out of my head, I headed over as soon
as I was done with work, merely throwing a jacket over my
scrubs. They were mostly clean.

The guys all greeted me with smiles and hugs. At least
some people valued my company and wanted to spend time
with me. Sam and Jason tried to draw me into their argument
about whether, if your D&D character was a merchant as well
as a thief, you could have two languages instead of just one.
But I couldn't focus on the conversation, because I kept imagining how thrilled Charles must be to be playing music with
Drake. And I couldn't drink my beer because my stomach was
in knots.

After about forty-five minutes, Alex leaned over. "What's up with you?"

I shook my head. "I'm fine."

He gave me a *don't try to bullshit me* look.

I sighed and spoke in a low voice so the others couldn't hear. Jason and Sam were debating the rules for darts, with Mickey egging them on, so they were well occupied. "Drake invited Charles to play guitar with him tonight."

"Yeah? He said he was going to. I'm sure Charles is excited." He studied my face. "But you're not? Why?"

I twisted my beer bottle back and forth on the table. "It's stupid, I know, but I keep thinking about how Drake is so much more cool and exciting than I am, and Charles will be disappointed he has to come home to such a boring guardian."

Alex flicked me on the ear, and I flinched. "Stop that!"

"Let's think back to a time in the very distant past, when dinosaurs roamed the Earth and you and I were in high school."

I glared at him. "Yes?"

"Did we think our parents were cool and exciting?"

I made a face. "No."

He spread his hands out. "No teenager thinks their parents are cool and exciting. But, Finn, that's not what kids need from a parent." I grimaced at him, and he amended, "Or parental figure."

I pondered this. "Because kids need their parents to be boring and practical, so they have a stable home life."

"Exactly. So they know they're safe."

I rubbed my jaw. "That makes sense."

He patted himself on the chest. "You can always rely on me for the best advice."

I cocked my head. "Always? What about—" I grinned when he held up a hand.

"Stop bringing up Ms. Hayworth's garden gnomes!"

I leaned over and gave him a hug. "Thanks, Alex. I'm going to head out so Charles has a boring and safe person to come home to after his wild night jamming with a rock star."

I made my excuses to the others and left. It only took minutes to get home, and Charles wasn't back yet. I paced the living room, debating whether texting him at 8:30 p.m. to see if he needed a ride would be too helicopter of me. The sound of the key in the door barely gave me enough time to drop onto the couch and feign relaxation.

"Hey." I looked casually up from my phone, as if I'd been scrolling social media instead of stewing over texting him. "Did you have a good time?"

He gave me the biggest smile I'd seen since his parents died. "Drake is so cool!" He propped his guitar case against the wall and—voluntarily!—came to sit down on the other end of the couch. "He has, like, a ton of instruments and equipment. He let me play three of his guitars to see what the differences were. He said I was good!"

I smiled. "That's fantastic. And he would know." Holy shit, Charles was talking to me!

He nodded enthusiastically. "He knows all these famous people. He knows *Poppy*, and he said he'd introduce me to her when she comes next week for the festival!" He wiggled around in his seat as if he couldn't sit still.

"Great!" I cast around for something to keep the conversation going. "So you played together?"

"Yeah! He showed me some fingering techniques, and we played a couple of songs together. He's so much better than me, but he said it just takes practice. He said we can do it again later in the week, so at my lesson tomorrow I'm gonna ask Mr. Griffin what songs we should try."

I wished Alex were here so we could giggle like twelve-year-olds at *fingering techniques*, but I pretended to be an adult instead.

"That's a great idea. Did you talk about Uncle Zeke's suggestion for you to perform in the amateur contest at the festival?"

Charles' smile dropped. Shit. "Drake said I didn't have to do it if I didn't want to." He picked at a stray thread on his jeans.

I studied him. "Are you considering it?"

He gave a one-shoulder shrug. "Maybe. Drake said he'd help me prepare. The theme is songs from the '90s and 2000s, and I could sing one of Mom or Dad's favorites."

I wished I were closer so I could put my arm around his shoulders, not that he'd let me. "I think they'd be proud of you if you wanted to do it, but they'd also understand if you didn't."

He nodded, still not looking at me. Fuck, what was I supposed to say now? I spun my phone in my hands. "Um, when I have to make a big decision I'm not sure about, like when I was trying to figure out where to go to vet school, I imagine myself in each situation to see how it might make me feel. So you could picture what it would be like to play and sing on the stage in front of the crowd. And you could picture what it would be like if you were in the audience watching other people performing, but you wouldn't be playing a song yourself."

He blinked at me. "That's a pretty good idea."

I laughed. "I have a few here and there. You have to watch out for them."

He grinned. "You wanna split the rest of the maple butter bars from Uncle Zeke's?"

I thought my heart would burst from happiness as I followed him to the kitchen.

"What's up with the zombie act?" Nova looked pointedly at the coffee maker I'd just refilled after draining the last of the pot into my cup.

I groaned. "Charles is thinking about entering the amateur competition at the music festival. He stayed up late trying out a bunch of songs, and I didn't have the heart to tell him to stop. If he signs up, he won't even have two weeks to practice." I grimaced. "Which probably makes me a pretty shitty parental figure, since he was dragging ass this morning same as me."

Nova snorted. "He's sixteen. He'll stay up late even if you tell him not to. Did he decide on a song?"

I tilted my head. "I think so? Or at least he narrowed it down to two. One of them is 'Can You Feel the Love Tonight', which actually sounds pretty good. I think the other one is that Santana song 'Smooth'?" I made a face. "At least, it had a long guitar intro. He never got to the lyrics. Maybe he needs to practice it some more."

Nova grinned. "You'll have a front row seat to every rehearsal."

Fuck. "Thanks a lot."

The bell over the front door rang, and she dashed out of the break room to check the client in.

I found the energy to make it through the day. My last appointment left at 4:30 p.m., and afterward I worked on paperwork for a while, hoping to leave at a decent time. Right as I was finishing up, Nova called me on the intercom. "Hey, the SPCA is on line one." So much for leaving early. The rescue group functioned as Animal Control for Maplewood and the surrounding towns.

"Got it, thanks." I picked up the call. "This is Dr. Hunnicutt."

"Hey, Finn, it's Rita at the SPCA."

I relaxed. Rita didn't usually call with emergencies. "Hey, what's up?"

She sighed. "We found a hoarding situation. Do you happen to know of anyone who wants some chickens, or who could temporarily house any?"

"Oh, crap. How many are we talking?" There were a few people who had hobby farms I could contact.

"We have about forty we haven't placed yet."

I stopped myself from cursing, though I was sure Rita had heard worse. "Wow. That's a lot."

"Yeah, and we have multiple feelers out, but if you could help us place even a few, it would be appreciated."

"Yeah, sure. I—" An image of Dolores' large pen at Zeke's place filled my mind. There was plenty of room for a chicken coop, especially on the side away from where Dolores had dug her burrow. And Zeke had run with Charles' notion that Dolores was lonely. Tortoises were solitary by nature, but chickens wouldn't bother her. "You know what? I may have somewhere a few of them could go. I need to see how quickly we could get a coop there though."

"We have plenty of chicken wire we can provide to keep them contained for a few days. The weather's supposed to be nice this week, so they'd just need food and water."

"Let me get back to you."

"Thanks, Finn. You're a lifesaver."

After hanging up with Rita, I pulled out my cell and dialed Zeke.

"Finn! Drake tells me your boy plays the guitar real good."

"Yeah, he does. Hey, Zeke, were you serious about adding another animal to Dolores' pen?"

He paused. "Welp, your young'un seemed convinced she was lonely, so it wouldn't hurt none. You got a stray or somethin'?"

"Not me, but the SPCA is trying to place a bunch of

chickens. Dolores probably wouldn't be territorial with birds. We can order a coop for them, but in the meantime the SPCA would provide some chicken wire, and we could put together something temporary."

"*Hmmm*. It'd be nice to have fresh eggs around here. How many do you think we have room for?"

I suppressed my aggravation. Contrary to popular belief, veterinarians were not walking encyclopedias about every non-human species on the planet. I ran a quick google search on my computer. "I wouldn't do more than six. And you don't need a rooster. The hens will lay eggs without one."

"Good. I don't need no noisy fucker wakin' me up at dawn. Where should I send Drake with the van?"

I smiled evilly, picturing Drake wrestling chickens into Zeke's rattletrap vehicle. "Let me find out and get back to you."

"You'll come help, right? Bring Charles."

"He's got a guitar lesson this evening, but I'll be there." I wouldn't miss it. Alex's voice rang through my brain. *Hate sex is the best sex.*

Maybe, if I played my cards right, I could find out for myself.

TEXT CONVERSATION
WEDNESDAY, 6:51 P.M

ZEKE:

While you get the chickens settled in, I'm going to Burlington to pick up a coop. I'll stay the night with a buddy.

ZEKE:

Make sure you take Finn to dinner to thank him for his help.

ZEKE.

Don't forget to feed Dolores and Mabel. See you in the morning.

ZEKE:

Tomorrow's the committee meeting for the music festival. Library community room at 6pm. I'll meet you there. Don't be late.

CHAPTER 5

DRAKE

Wednesday, seven days before the festival

I stuffed my phone in my pocket and opened the door to exit Zeke's ancient panel van. Why he kept this thing, I hadn't asked. I'd been too tired to interrupt his tales of driving the van while he followed this or that band on tour.

Finn pulled into the parking space next to me, so I gritted my teeth and got out. I'd spent most of the day overseeing the repairs to the fencing around the festival grounds, and all I wanted was to pass out on the very comfortable couch in my cabin.

Instead I had a vanload of angry chickens, and my helper was the attractive but annoying veterinarian I couldn't seem to get rid of. Charles was at his guitar lesson tonight, so we didn't have him as a buffer.

Still, Finn hadn't had to help me, so I feigned a positive demeanor. I'd gotten so much practice growing up, it was second nature. I gave him a smile as he walked over to me. "Zeke went to Burlington to pick up a coop. He'll be back in the morning."

He nodded. "Do you already have a plan for a temporary shelter?"

"No." I looked over at the pen. The ground was patches of dirt and grass, with some shrubs and a small shade tree. "It should definitely go over here, away from Dolores' hidey hole."

"Agreed." We walked over to survey the area. He pointed. "If we made a circle of chicken wire and attached it to the fence in that corner, then put a blanket or something over the top, it'd work well enough until morning." He pulled out his phone. "I'll text Nova and see if there are old blankets or sheets around here."

"Sounds good." I trudged back to the van and opened the back, where we'd stored the roll of chicken wire, wire cutters, and the small bag of feed the SPCA had provided us. The chickens were stuffed into a dog crate, which we could put on one end of the temporary enclosure.

I dropped off the chicken wire with Finn inside Dolores' pen, then I went to the kitchen to get some food for her. I didn't want her to get freaked out by her new neighbors, and a snack might help. I also filled a bowl of water for the chickens.

When I came back, Dolores was already nudging Finn's leg, looking for a treat. "Here. I brought some food to distract her."

"Thanks." I didn't miss the way he checked out my ass as I climbed over the fence.

I set the water bowl down near where the pen would go, then I got Dolores' attention before dropping the food, some carrots and spinach, near her burrow. She abandoned Finn and headed over as fast as her legs could go.

When I climbed back over the fence to go to the van, I deliberately positioned myself so Finn could admire my assets if he so chose. He would've seen me looking, though, so I didn't watch.

I got the crate of chickens out of the van. They squawked and flapped their wings, but at least they didn't peck my hands.

Finn set down the wire he was bending to take the crate from me. Our fingers brushed, and he jerked the crate away. He cleared his throat. "Nova told me where to find some spare blankets."

"Great." I climbed back over the fence—he was turned the other way so didn't see—and started wrapping the edges of the chicken wire around the bars of the crate. In a few minutes we had an area for the chickens to walk around in, separated from Dolores. Finn went into the house to get a blanket while I put the water bowl in the enclosure and spread chicken feed over the ground.

Dolores poked her nose at the wire a couple of times, but she didn't seem bothered by the chickens, who were clucking nervously and fluffing their feathers as best they could in the crowded crate.

Once Finn came back with the blanket, I opened the door to the crate. None of the chickens rushed out, probably because we were still hovering over them. We secured the blanket by tucking the edges into the holes in the chicken wire.

"I think it'll hold til morning." Maybe. As long as the chickens and Dolores left it alone.

Finn brushed his hands off on his jeans. "The chickens are tired after the stress of being moved. It'll be fine."

One by one the chickens left the crate to explore their new enclosure. We'd acquired six altogether. Two were ordinary-looking brown hens. We had one huge one that was mostly black with orange windowpane spots, kind of like a Monarch butterfly. There were two white ones, but one of those had weird floaty feathers that made her look more like a Muppet than a chicken. The last was black and white with a mane of long feathers cascading down her neck. All of them seemed to settle down as they checked out the area and realized there was food and water.

I pulled off my straw cowboy hat and ran my fingers through my hair. "I'm starving. Can I offer you dinner as a thank-you for helping with all this?"

When Finn didn't respond, I glanced over at him. He was staring at my hair. Shit. I ran my hand through it again. "What's the matter? Do I have feathers in my hair?"

He seemed startled, and he shook his head. "Sorry. I haven't seen you without a hat on except at the vet clinic, and I wasn't really paying attention then. Your hair's gorgeous."

I felt my face flush. "Uh, thanks. Family trait. All of the sibs are blond, though my sister Mona dyes hers." I fiddled with the brim of my hat. He was still staring at my head, so it seemed almost rude to put my hat back on right then. Which was... weird. I didn't even like him. Though he'd been a big help today, and he hadn't irritated me again. And he'd stared at my ass a couple of times. Maybe I should give him another chance. "Uh, so, dinner?"

Finn moved closer. "I was thinking...." Now his eyes were trained on mine. The heat in them was unmistakable, and my arousal stirred. Well, shit. Finn had pissed me off twice now, but that was then. I could forgive and forget. Especially since getting laid seemed to be on the table.

"Yes?" I raised an eyebrow while I cocked a hip and put my hat on top of the blanket covering the chicken enclosure.

He smiled and gave me a slow, appreciative look. My dick started to test the elasticity of my jeans. I checked out his scrub pants, and Finn was having a similar issue.

He pushed his hair out of his eyes. "I was thinking we should get cleaned up first. Before we go to dinner. You've got a shower in your cabin, right?"

When had he moved closer? He lifted his hand and tucked

a lock of my hair behind my ear, trailing his fingers over the outer edge and lobe before his hand landed on my shoulder.

I licked my lips. "Yeah, I've got a shower." My voice came out raspy. "It's large enough for two."

His smile deepened. "Can I kiss you?"

"You'd better." I lifted my face to meet him halfway.

Look, I've kissed a lot of guys. Sex, especially when you're a touring musician, is easy to come by. (Pun intended.) So I know how rare it is to have chemistry with someone, to feel that *zing* when you touch each other. Touching Finn, kissing him, was more than a zing. It was a fucking electrical shock.

I gave a low, throaty groan and moved closer, running my hands down his back. He pressed his hand between my shoulder blades to bring our chests together. Damn, we needed to be naked. I jerked my head back, breaking the kiss. We panted as we stared into each other's eyes. "We should move this inside. I want your skin. Plus, Zeke has cameras."

His grin reappeared as he took half a step back. "No argument here." We put the remaining chicken wire and the bag of feed in Zeke's shed. Finn picked up my hat and we headed to my cabin.

I didn't run, but I did walk very, very quickly. Finn chuckled, but I didn't hear any complaints. Once I'd shut the door behind us, I ripped my hat out of Finn's hand and tossed it toward the kitchen counter. Then I whipped my t-shirt over my head.

Finn sucked in a breath but wasted no time in removing his scrub top as well.

"Shower's that way." I pointed, though Finn had likely been in these cabins at some point. I waited until we got into the bedroom to remove my boots. They weren't loose enough to toe them off, so I had to sit on the edge of the bed.

Finn wasn't hampered by restrictive clothing. He kicked off his clogs then loosened the drawstring on his scrub pants.

One yank later and they were on the floor, his underwear with them.

"Oh, now that's what I'm talking about." I licked my lips. For such a lanky guy, Finn had a thick beast of a cock. I couldn't wait to get my mouth around that bad boy.

He put his hands on his hips, his fingers framing his erection. "Get a move on. You're still half-dressed."

Oh, right. I tossed my boots to the side and, standing, pushed my jeans and underwear to the ground.

"Fuck, yes." Finn headed my way, his gaze avidly on my cock, but I held up a hand.

"Shower. I feel like I'm still covered in chicken feathers, and it's not sexy."

He made a face. "Same, now that you mention it."

"We can throw your clothes in the washing machine later." Okay, enough practicalities. I led the way into the bathroom, putting a little extra *oomph* in my walk for Finn's benefit.

He crowded in behind me, shutting the door as I started the shower so the water could warm up. I didn't have a chance to turn around—as soon as the water went on, Finn pulled me back against his body. His cock was hot between my ass cheeks.

"Fuck." I reached back to grab his thighs, then I leaned my head back against his shoulder.

He took advantage of the exposed skin and kissed my neck. "I haven't been able to take my eyes off you since you brought Charles to the clinic." He thumbed my nipples, then ran his hands down my chest but avoided touching my dick.

I clutched his wrists, trying to make his hands go where I wanted them to.

He chuckled and pulled out of my grip. "I haven't washed my hands since I touched the chickens, so the fun stuff will have to wait."

"Oh, shit." I jerked away from him and held my own hands out to the side.

Finn laughed. "It's fine. We're only dirty. The chickens, amazingly enough, didn't show any signs of mites or lice. Plus I brought some powder to put in their coop once it's set up just in case."

Grimacing, I went over to the sink and scrubbed my hands with soap. There was soap in the shower, but still.

Chuckling, Finn washed his hands at the sink as well. "I'll try to remember you're squeamish about animal dirt."

I started to put my hands on my hips but held them up instead. "Excuse you, I have a pet rabbit, and at home I spend a lot of time at an animal rescue ranch. Sue me for wanting to be clean." I pointed at him. "Aren't vets supposed to be like doctors, always washing their hands and trying not to transfer germs and stuff?"

His eyebrows shot up, and he stabbed a finger in the direction of the shower. "We're about to be covered in water and soap!"

I threw up my hands. "Well, get on with it!"

His ass jiggled enticingly as he stomped into the shower enclosure. I was gratified to see his erection was still just as stiff as mine.

I closed the glass door behind us, and Finn pulled me under the spray, his mouth hard and insistent. Hell yes. I was a few inches shorter than him, and he obligingly spread his legs apart so we could rock our dicks against each other. Fuck, that was good. I moaned into his mouth.

I reached over to the built-in shelf and fumbled for my shower gel. The smell of citrus and mint filled the air. I didn't bother pretending to wash either of us; I went straight for our dicks.

"Yes!" Finn clutched my ass as I squeezed my hands

around our erections. It didn't take very long before he tore his mouth from mine. "Coming!"

I wasn't far behind, crumpling into Finn's body as I shuddered my release. His arms came up to support me, and I panted into his neck.

After a moment I felt him reach for the shower gel, and he washed me thoroughly. I stood there with my eyes closed and let him run his hands all over my body. He soaped me up, then he shampooed my hair. I'd never let anyone take care of me like that before, not that anyone had tried.

After he rinsed me off, I opened my eyes and smiled. "Thank you. My turn." I could see he was about to object, so I snatched the shampoo off the shelf. "Stand still."

He snorted but leaned his head down so I could wash his hair. Since I was feeling lazy, I used the shampoo on the rest of his body instead of switching to the shower gel. I enjoyed tracing his skin with my hands. He was ticklish in places, but other spots, such as his nipples, made him moan and thrust his hips. He was half-hard again by the time I finished with him.

I was way too tired for any more sex tonight, but I appreciated the compliment. We got out of the shower and dried off, and I gave Finn some boxer briefs and a t-shirt to wear while I put his scrubs in the washing machine. I could've given him a pair of sweats to wear home, but I'd only offer if he told me he wanted to leave.

I dearly wanted to lie on the bed and go to sleep, but I needed food, and Finn probably did as well. "There's a bunch of frozen stuff in the freezer. Wanna split a pizza?"

"Sure."

I set Finn to filling glasses of water while I preheated the oven and examined our pizza options. "Pepperoni or cheese?"

He shrugged. "Either is fine with me."

I pursed my lips. "I'll make both, then we can give the leftovers to Mabel for her dinner."

Finn scrunched up his face. "Forest monsters eat pizza?"

I raised an eyebrow at him. "She eats chicken casserole. And sewer turtles eat pizza, so why not?"

I'd opened a bottle of cabernet last night, so we finished it off with our meal. I was grateful as hell when Finn announced that he'd accompany me to drop off Mabel's dinner. Though that did force me to produce a pair of sweatpants for him to wear.

He didn't hesitate to wear his orthopedic shoes to tromp through the woods. I put on a clean pair of jeans and my boots again. He didn't appear bothered by the chilly air, but I wore a hoodie.

The woods seemed quieter tonight, and I found myself keeping my voice low. "It's this way." I didn't want to take the time to stop by Zeke's for a flashlight, so we used our phones to light our path.

The moon, almost full, shone through the leaves when there was a break in the trees. Occasionally we could hear insects or other creatures, but mostly all we heard was our feet in the grass and leaves. It might've been this quiet on my past treks to take Mabel her dinner, but I'd had Zeke with me, yammering about how the festival operated or which people on the festival committee were pains in his ass and which got things done.

Tonight, though, the silence was unnerving.

I looked back at Finn, who was following me. "Have you been out here at night when one of the festivals is happening?"

He shook his head. "Other than visiting Zeke or attending a festival, I haven't been out this way at night at all."

We were less than a mile from the fence between Zeke's compound and the festival grounds. "I bet it's loud. I wonder if Mabel would even come over here to eat then." I snorted at myself. "If she exists." Though I had seen something moving through the trees before Charles had run onto the highway. Something big.

"I asked my friend Nate about her. He's a forestry technician, and he's never seen any evidence of her. But Charles swears he saw her, and Alex has always maintained he saw her when we were kids. Both of those sightings were behind my parents' house, so I don't know."

A loud crack, like a branch breaking, came from our right. My hair stood on end. I cleared my throat. "Dinner's coming, Mabel!"

Finn didn't stay over. I should've expected him to need to be home for Charles. Besides, it was just sex. A hookup. No reason to be dwelling on how good his hands had felt on me or how he'd kissed me like it meant something.

I wouldn't turn him down if the same opportunity presented itself again, though.

Tonight was the festival committee meeting, but before that I wanted to go into town for lunch and do a little exploring. I'd spent the majority of my days at Zeke's compound or the festival grounds next door, and I was going a little stir crazy.

I'd tried to let myself sleep in, since Zeke wouldn't be banging around outside at dawn to wake me up. But guilt made me roll out of bed at 7:30 a.m. to give Dolores and the chickens their breakfast.

I threw on the sweats Finn had worn last night along with my hoodie, putting my feet in my boots sans socks. I just needed to get some veggies out of Zeke's fridge for the tortoise and spread some feed for the chickens. Then I could get a shower and make coffee. Maybe I'd spend some time working on the song I'd been trying to write.

I dragged myself out the door and around the cabin to head to Dolores' pen. Well, Dolores and the chickens' pen now.

But the blanket we'd used to cover our temporary coop was on the ground. And the chickens were... everywhere.

One of the brown ones was sleeping on the hood of my car. Two of the others were sitting on the fence around the enclosure, and two more were pecking at the grass near Dolores' burrow. The sixth chicken, the big white one, was standing on Dolores' back as she ambled toward me, no doubt wanting her breakfast.

"Fuck." Maybe they'd get back in their enclosure when I put their feed down. I pulled my phone out of my pocket and panned the camera over the entire scene. Then I opened my texting app.

ME:

> Looks like all our hard work was for nothing. [video]

I didn't bother sending it to Zeke. If he cared, he could check the security cameras.

"Okay, hang on, Dolores, and I'll get you some food." I found the energy to jog up the steps to the porch and then hurry inside to Zeke's kitchen. At least Mabel didn't need breakfast. Or she was used to getting it somewhere else.

Back outside, I put the food down for Dolores. Her chicken rider eyed me warily but didn't move.

I was glad I'd put the feed in Zeke's shed. The birds would've eaten it all if they'd been able to get to the bag.

I scattered the feed on the ground inside the area Finn and I had fenced with chicken wire. All six of them flapped their way over, happily pecking at the ground. Without the blanket, though, they were vulnerable to predators or they could get lost in the woods. I groaned as I gave up on my plans for an outing to town, at least until Zeke returned with the coop.

My phone chimed.

FINN:

Well, shit. I've got appointments all day or I'd come help you.

ME:

No worries. I'll just babysit them til Zeke gets back.

With the chickens occupied, I dashed back to my cabin to start the coffee maker and take a quick shower. Once I was dressed, I found a travel mug in the cabinet, and I took my coffee and my guitar outside.

Zeke's porch had a good view of the enclosure, so I settled on the porch swing, determined to make some progress on the song I'd been having trouble with. I was writing it for Poppy, but at this rate I doubted I'd have it done in time to play for her when she was here next week.

Two badly worded stanzas later, I was beyond grateful to hear the driveway gate open and Zeke's truck come through. He parked next to my SUV, and I hopped up to help him with the coop he had in the truck bed.

He got out and surveyed the chickens. "Huh. Those're some weird-lookin' birds. I hope their eggs taste okay."

I scrunched up my face. "I don't think it matters what the chickens look like."

He shrugged. "Help me get this thing out of the truck. Once we get it set up, I gotta go back to Burlington. My friend's in a bad way."

I gaped at him in horror. "Like sick? In the hospital? You should be with them instead of here."

He waved this off. "Nah. It's only an hour drive, and they'll be fine in a day or two."

"O-kaaay?" I followed him back to his pickup and we unloaded the coop. It was nice and sturdy, about five feet tall and four feet deep, with more than enough room inside for six chickens. A large, fully enclosed wire run attached to the front. The coop and run could be moved to give the chickens access to fresh grass or whatever over time.

"Right." Zeke dusted his hands off on the seat of his jeans. The chickens were in their new coop, and Dolores was back in her burrow. "Wait here. I need to get you my festival notebook for the committee meeting tonight."

"Wait, *what*?"

But he was already in the house, the screen door slamming behind him. In less than a minute he was back, carrying a large binder stuffed with papers. He handed it to me.

"Uh, you won't be at the meeting?"

"Naw, but you'll be fine. Everythin' you need's in there." He punched the cover of the binder with his forefinger.

"You don't have it electronically?" The binder must've been four inches wide, and there wasn't any room for more pages.

Zeke snorted. "I get a headache lookin' at the little screen. It's all there."

"But isn't this the last meeting before the festival? How am I supposed to know what needs to be done?" My voice was getting higher as panic set in.

Zeke clapped me between the shoulder blades with his big hand. "You can do it. Festival's been going on for almost thirty years. Runs like clockwork. Most of the issues don't show up til the day before it starts."

And then that fucker got in his truck and drove away.

MAPLEWOOD MATTERS BLOG, THURSDAY 8:19 P.M

The new rock star in town is reported to have had dinner at Red's tonight. Will he remain faithful, or will he also grace Sparky's with his presence?

We wait with bated breath to find out.

CHAPTER 6

DRAKE

Thursday, six days before the festival

I skipped lunch to read through the Binder of Doom. After ten minutes I opened my laptop and started a spreadsheet with tabs for each of the sections Zeke had marked in the binder. Almost everything did seem to be under control, but there were some key points he'd noted where he was still waiting on information. Luckily he'd put the name of the committee member responsible, heavily underscored, next to each question.

At 3:00 p.m. my stomach growled and I shut the binder. I'd been through the whole thing twice, and I felt fairly confident with my notes. I'd bring the laptop and the binder to the meeting, so I'd have everything for reference.

I had three more hours until the meeting was supposed to start. What did I know about running a meeting? I was a musician, for fuck's sake.

However, I knew exactly who *did* know how to run a meeting. My eldest brother Steve. He was the non-musical one of the family, and our father had *not* been happy about that.

But despite dear old Dad kicking Steve out of the family, he'd become CEO of his first startup before he'd been thirty. And now he and his business partner were working on a new project. He'd led thousands of meetings. I unlocked my phone.

ME:

Can you please call me sometime in the next 3 hours?

I didn't have to wait even thirty seconds.

"What's wrong?" His tone was urgent.

"Nothing." Sometimes I enjoyed being a little shit to him. I blamed it on us being separated for all of Dirk's and my teenage years. I had a lot of brattiness built up that Steve was destined to experience.

He sighed into the phone. "Why did you need to talk within the next three hours?"

"Oh!" I made sure my voice conveyed that I'd forgotten all about my text to him. "Right. That. I just need some advice."

I heard him say something to someone else, probably his business partner Cal, and then it sounded like he was walking. "Okay, shoot. What's going on?"

I gave a long, aggrieved sigh. "I have to run a meeting with a bunch of local movers and shakers, and I don't know how."

There was a pause. "What kind of meeting?"

I explained about the festival committee and Zeke abandoning me for his sick friend.

"So you have to go through all the outstanding action items, find out their statuses, and maybe make decisions on them?"

"Yeah, pretty much."

He chuckled. "Drake, do you remember the one and only Melodious Moon concert I attended?"

"Yeah?" It'd been our final concert as a family band.

"You were the person who made sure the stage was set up correctly. You were the one who gave the venue manager a piece of your mind when the sound system wasn't set up right. Dirk told me that when y'all were on tour, you were the main interface with the concert arenas, since Dad fucked off all the time. You've also been interacting with movers and shakers since you were a little kid. There's nothing about running this meeting you can't do."

Well, shit. "I hadn't thought of it that way."

"It's doing exactly what you've done before, but in a different setting."

"I get it. Thanks, Steve."

"Let me know how it goes, but you'll do great. How's Vermont?"

I chuckled. "This trip was positioned as helping out Wesley's old buddy, but 'helping' has turned into 'doing'. Still, I'm enjoying it." I told him about the chickens. "How are Gamora and Mantis?"

"Hah. They love our new backyard. I don't think they'll want to go back to the condo life. I'll send you a picture."

I looked wistfully out the window of the cabin at the grass and trees. Part of why I was trying to do songwriting full-time was so I could live somewhere like this. While I enjoyed performing, I hated touring. And I couldn't do it without Dirk. I'd never last on the road by myself.

We chatted for a few more minutes, and I felt better after talking to Steve. He was right. I could run this meeting with my eyes closed.

It was almost 4:00 p.m., and I was starving. I put on the most business-like outfit I'd brought—black jeans and a dark gray button-down shirt. I topped it with my black bowler, then I packed up my laptop and Zeke's binder, and I was on my way.

On the way into town I kept an eye out for somewhere to get food. As I hit Maple Street, the main drag, I saw Red's Restaurant, whose building looked like it had originally been a railroad car. I vaguely remembered someone warning me about two diners, but I couldn't remember the details and I was hungry enough to take a chance.

As soon as I walked in, a thirty-something brown-haired guy in a red uniform shirt waved from behind the counter and told me to sit anywhere. I picked a booth near the far end where I could people-watch. There were only five or six other customers, since I'd beat the dinner rush. I set my hat on the seat beside me. These days I didn't get recognized very often, but that would change when Dirk's new movie came out. I might have to dye my hair or—shudder—wear a baseball cap.

The same red-shirted guy came over and handed me a laminated menu. "Hey, there. I'm Mickey. Today our special is a bacon cheddar burger. Let me know if you have any questions on the menu. What can I get you to drink?"

"Uh, just some iced tea, please. Wait, it's not sweet is it?"

He looked at me like I had two heads. "No, but there are sweeteners on the table there." He pointed.

I shook my head and smiled apologetically at him. "Sorry. I've been living in Texas the last five years, and it's a crapshoot as to whether they serve regular iced tea or if they're going to spring sweet tea on you without any warning."

Mickey grimaced. "Dude, you need to move up here. You're safe from sweet tea in Vermont."

I smiled. "That's a relief."

He glanced around the diner, then leaned in and lowered his voice. "Hey, are you Drake?"

I raised my eyebrows. "I am."

He grinned. "Cool. I thought so from Alex's description."
My eyebrows went higher. "Thanks for helping Charlie—

sorry, Charles—on Monday. Everyone was real worried when he went missing."

"I was happy to. He's a great kid."

He nodded, then stepped back. "I'll bring your tea right out. Have a look at the menu while you wait."

Well, it wasn't unexpected that people would be talking since I was new in town, but I was oddly relieved it'd been Alex who'd gossiped with Mickey about me rather than Finn.

I decided on the special cheeseburger, and Mickey wrote my order on a little notepad like they'd probably done back when this diner was first built. It fit with the black and white tiled floor and the chipped Formica tabletop.

My chest felt a little empty, being in an unfamiliar town without Dirk. We'd always been on tour together—with the family band or without. And the few occasions we'd made time for a vacation, we'd done that with each other too.

I pulled out my phone and opened my texting app.

ME:

> I know you're probably filming, so no need to reply right away, but remind me to tell you about the chickens I'm now temporarily in charge of. Gamora and Mantis would be pissed if they knew.

He replied almost instantly.

DIRK:

> So you're a chicken tender?

ME:

> Fuck off

Mickey brought my food, and it smelled delicious. "Thanks, man."

"Sure. Save room for some maple custard pie for after. It's

our specialty." He spun on his heel and headed back to the kitchen.

I set my phone down to concentrate on feeding my belly. The text notification chimed, and even though it was almost definitely Dirk again, my brain immediately speculated that it could be Finn. Shit, this was bad. I couldn't obsess over the hot veterinarian. I was only here for two weeks. And we didn't even like each other.

Though I had a hard time remembering why at the moment.

But it wasn't Finn or Dirk who'd texted.

> **CHARLES:**
>
> Hey, Drake! Mr. Griffin, my guitar teacher, says I should do the amateur competition at the music festival. I'm debating between Can You Feel the Love Tonight (my mom's favorite song) and Smooth (my dad's favorite). What do you think?

I frowned. One of those songs was well within Charles' current capabilities, but I didn't think he was up to playing Santana yet. Still, I should give him a chance. Maybe the music teacher had worked with him on it.

> **ME:**
>
> Those are both great songs. And they're actually close enough in key that you could do a mashup if we have time to work it out. But you'd have to have both of them down cold first. I've got a meeting at the library until around 8pm. If it's okay with Finn, I could stop by after and you can play them for me.

Because that's what Charles needed. I wasn't offering to go to their house for any other reason.

CHARLES:

Finn says that's fine. Park in the vet clinic
lot and take the path behind the building.
You can't miss the house.

I tried to picture what was behind the vet clinic, but my mind kept sending me pictures of a path through more creepy woods. Hopefully Mabel didn't hang out in that part of town on her way to get dinner at Zeke's place.

I texted back that I'd be there, then I finished my excellent meal. I'd planned to park downtown and walk around before the meeting, but I was enjoying just sitting and doing nothing for a change. I let Mickey talk me into trying the maple custard pie, which was as good as advertised. I was glad I liked the taste of maple, because I had a feeling I'd be seeing it on a lot of menus around here.

At 5:20 p.m. I reluctantly left the diner and walked down the block to a coffee shop called Special Blend. I greeted the teenager behind the counter. "Hi, I need some cookies or something plus coffee for a meeting. We'll have seven people."

"Sure! We can do disposable carafes. Do you want regular or decaf?"

"Uh, I guess both?" I shrugged at her. "This is the first time I'll be at this meeting, so I have no idea what they want."

She nodded and busied herself filling the carafes while I studied the pastries. When she stood at the ready with an open white box and a pair of tongs raised in the air, I pointed. "How about six maple tarts, six of those oatmeal cookies, and six almond scones?"

She hesitated. "Are you sure about the scones? Caspian, the owner makes them, and—"

I held up a hand. "Sold. They look delicious." Maybe there'd be leftovers. I'd be ready for some dessert by then. Or I could take them to Charles and Finn's house.

She shrugged and put the scones in the box with the tarts and the cookies.

My little errand hadn't taken too long, so I'd have plenty of time to get set up before the committee members arrived.

Aside from me and Zeke, there were six people on the committee for the Maplewood Music Festival. Roy Griffin, Charles' guitar teacher and the owner of the Harmonic Circus music store, was a longtime friend of Zeke's. He was also the emcee for the amateur music competition on the last day of the festival.

Bo Boyd was the representative from the city of Maplewood, and Adrian Gates, who was one of the owners of The Striped Maple pub, was in charge of recruiting vendors. Graham MacDougall, owner of an advertising agency, was responsible for marketing. The remaining two committee members, Jonah Washington and Frances Kaminski, together headed up logistics and ticketing.

Everyone's responsibilities were clearly laid out in Zeke's binder, but his notes—not to mention his instructions to me this week—made it clear Zeke took quite a bit of responsibility on himself instead of delegating.

I'd found photos of all the committee members online, so I hoped to recognize them when they arrived.

When I got to the library, I followed the signs to the community room. It was a big open room with several tables and chairs scattered around. Even better, it had a projection screen you could pull down from the ceiling and a projector that, despite its apparent age, had a USB port. And I had a USB adapter for my MacBook.

I pulled two tables together so we could all sit in a square with one end facing the projection screen.

I'd just gotten my spreadsheet to display when the first attendee arrived.

He walked into the room but pulled up short. "Oh, am I in the wrong meeting?"

I grinned. "You're not. This is the music festival committee meeting. Zeke couldn't make it. I'm Drake Derry. You're Roy, right?" He was probably sixty or so years old, with mostly gray hair pulled back in a ponytail. He was wearing a faded blue cardigan over a Nirvana concert tee.

He blinked at me. "Yes? Wait, Drake Derry? You're performing on Thursday and one of the judges for the amateur competition."

"That's me. I also got roped into running this meeting. It's a long story."

"Um, wow. Okay. It's nice to meet you."

Next up was Bo Boyd. He looked to be about Finn and Alex's age. I wondered if they'd gone to school together. He blinked in wonder at the screen, and after he introduced himself he practically leapt on the coffee.

The others trickled in, most expressing confusion either at Zeke's absence—apparently this was the first committee meeting he'd missed since the festival was founded—or at the spreadsheet projected on the screen. I wasn't surprised to find out Zeke usually just paged through his binder as he led the meeting.

They were all also very excited about the coffee and treats, but there were lots of whispers over the scones. They ended up breaking one apart and sharing it, and then only Bo took a second one. Whatever. I was sure Finn and Charles would eat the rest.

Once everyone adapted to me and the snacks, the meeting went smoothly. I'd expected at least one objector or complainer, but everyone was very supportive and seemed willing to compromise to make things happen. What kind of bureaucratic utopia had I landed in?

We finished the last tab on my spreadsheet with plenty of

time for me to get to Finn and Charlie's house. I looked around the room. "Anything I missed?"

Shaking heads all around. Graham toasted me with his coffee cup. "This was great. Thanks for putting it all together on the spreadsheet. It makes it really easy to be sure everything's checked off the list."

"Yeah, can you come back next year?" Adrian joked. "We love Zeke, but he's not very organized. We cross our fingers that he remembers to put updates in his binder. No way he'd make a spreadsheet for us."

"*Oooh*, what if the spreadsheet was online, and it was updated in real time?" Frances said dreamily as they all stared at the screen.

There was a chorus of more *Ooohs* around the table.

Roy raised a hand. "Let's take a vote. All in favor of Drake running the music festival committee next year, say aye."

Everyone loudly said aye and raised their coffee cups.

I smiled and shook my head at them as I unplugged my laptop from the projector. "Y'all are terrible. I'll see you at the festival opening on Wednesday."

"Will you be playing 'Santa's Secret Stocking' during your set on Thursday?"

I glared at Jonah. "No. And the next person who asks is banned from the festival."

Everyone laughed. As much as I appreciated the royalties that song brought in—and let's face it, "Santa's Secret Stocking" was the major source of income for me and my siblings who'd been members of Melodious Moon—if I never had to hear it or sing it again, I'd die happy.

Everyone cleaned up their trash and helped me put the tables back where I found them. When I got to my car, I texted Charles I was on my way. I received a thumbs up in reply.

I parked at the vet clinic and spent three whole minutes giving myself a pep talk about acting cool and collected around Finn. "It was only a hookup. You've run into your hookups before. Okay, not really. But still. It was casual, and there's no need to be weird."

Right. I could do this.

The stone path behind the vet clinic was only about a hundred feet long. There were trees on either side, but they weren't overgrown and there were lights. The house itself was painted brick red with white trim. The front porch ran the width of the house with benches on either side of the front door.

Finn answered my knock. I'd thought I'd been prepared to see him, but I hadn't counted on him being fucking shirtless.

"Oh!" I took a tiny step back as I drank in the sight of his bare skin. "Um, hi." I dragged my eyes up to his, and he laughed.

"Sorry, I spilled some of my dinner on myself. I was about to get a clean shirt." His face turned a little ruddy, which gave me a significant amount of my confidence back.

I shrugged and winked. "Don't do it on my account."

"Oh, my *god*! Are you two *flirting*?" Charles materialized behind Finn. I couldn't decide if his expression was horrified or just shocked.

"Charles!" Finn glared at him.

I chuckled to break the tension. "Sorry, Charles. We'll try to keep that away from your vulnerable ears in the future."

His eyes bulged. "There'll be a *future*? Future flirting? Wait. Are you guys *dating*?"

Oops. I shot a desperate look at Finn.

He heaved a huge sigh and gestured for me to enter the house. "Nobody's dating, Charles. Drake was making a joke." He didn't glance my way, but he called over his shoulder. "Drake, I had Charles bring his guitar out to the living room so you'll be more comfortable. There's only one chair in his bedroom. I'll be in my study so I don't *accidentally hear anything.*" I could feel his eye roll in my soul. "Do you need some water or iced tea?"

"No, thanks. Uh, I brought some leftover scones from my meeting."

He waved a hand. "I just ate. Charles, they're all yours."

"Score!" Charles shouted.

Still without looking at me again, Finn vanished around a corner.

TEXT CONVERSATION, THURSDAY, 8:03 P.M

DRAKE:

I killed it at the meeting!

STEVE:

Of course you did. Congratulations!

DRAKE:

They were so happy I knew how to use a computer, they held a vote and it was unanimous in favor of me running the festival next year, lol

STEVE:

Would you want to?

DRAKE:

I don't think it's really an option

STEVE:

Too bad

CHAPTER 7

FINN

Thursday, six days before the festival

I hurried into my bedroom to grab a t-shirt. Fuck, I hadn't planned to be half-naked when Drake got here. Even though, if I were being honest, his reaction was pretty flattering.

Too bad Charles never went to bed at a decent hour. I couldn't sneak Drake into my bedroom for a quickie without him noticing. I flushed again at the memory of Charles over-hearing Drake flirting with me.

We were not dating. It was laughable to think someone as interesting—and young—as Drake would consider going out with a much older small-town vet whose only hobbies were running and playing Dungeons and Dragons. And I wasn't in the market right now, anyway, what with Charles and all.

I didn't plan on staying single until he went off to college or anything, but I felt awkward looking for my forever person when Charles had lost his parents so recently. Maybe in six months or so, when he was more settled and secure in his new home.

Drake would be long gone by then.

But nothing was preventing us, while he was here, from having a no-strings repeat of last night.

Fully dressed, I left my bedroom and crossed the hall to my study. I couldn't see them from this part of the hallway, but I could clearly hear Charles telling Drake about his friend Kirk not wanting to perform in the amateur competition.

I went into the study and shut the door firmly and loudly, so Charles wouldn't feel self-conscious. Though why he was comfortable playing in front of Drake, a famous musician, and not me, I didn't understand.

But, I reasoned, as Charles' guardian it was my responsibility to make sure he was safe with an adult guest in our home. A weak-as-fuck argument, and if Alex or my twin sister Addy ever found out, they'd kick my ass. Still, it was enough to assuage my conscience, and I cracked the door so I could hear what was happening in the living room. I silenced my phone and parked my desk chair next to the door in case Charles or Drake came this way and I had to shut it quickly.

"No," Drake was saying. "Snacks are for after you sing, not before. Come on and show me what you've got."

"Yeah, before we get to the songs, um, I wanted to say I'm sorry I got weird at the door when you and Finn were, uh, flirting."

"No worries, bro. I wasn't thinking."

"I was surprised is all. I didn't mean to come across like I thought it was gross or something. If, uh, you and Finn wanted to go out or whatever, that's cool."

My jaw dropped open. Charles was okay with me dating? Or at least dating Drake? Not that I was in the market for a long-distance boyfriend. And not that Drake and I would ever make it to the boyfriend stage.

I told my brain to shut up as I held my breath waiting for Drake's response.

"Oh, uh, thanks for saying that. I—Finn and I haven't talked about it, and I'm only here for a couple of weeks, so...."

"Yeah, I get it. I just wanted you to know. Finn used to go on dates before—before I moved here. I heard him telling my mom stories a couple of times. But he hasn't gone out with anyone since I got here. I feel like I'm cramping his style or something. Him suddenly having a kid is probably a turnoff for other guys."

Oh, fuck. I needed to talk to Charles. My attempt to give him a stable home life was making him think he was in the way? Shit.

Drake had paused, but then he said, "What? I really don't think Finn sees you as some sort of... obstacle to his dating."

"Yeah? So why hasn't he been going out?"

"Uh...." Drake stumbled over his words, probably because he knew damn well I *had* been 'going out'. "Maybe he wanted you to feel like you were his priority, not the randos he met at a bar or whatever. You should really talk to Finn about this."

"Yeah." Charles' tone left no doubt he wouldn't be bringing it up to me. I guessed that meant I had to be the parental stand-in and force the conversation.

"Okay, let's get back to the songs. You said these were your parents' favorites? I'm sorry. It sounds like they're no longer... with us?"

Shit. I probably should've briefed Drake on Charlie's situation.

There was a pause, then Charles said, "They died in February. Car crash."

"Oh, shit. Charles, I'm so sorry. That must've been devastating for you."

"Yeah." He plucked at a guitar string. "I didn't want to move here, but I guess I'm lucky I had Finn."

Probably the closest I'd get to a declaration of love from Charles this year.

"Definitely."

"Dad and I were taking guitar lessons together." He chuckled. "He was terrible at it. But he kept trying."

"All you need to be a musician is a love of music. Natural talent is nice and everything, but hard work can get you there too."

There was a pause. "I like that. Um, are your parents still around?"

Drake made an odd sound. Kind of like a laugh and a sigh. "My mom died when Dirk—he's my twin—and I were little. My dad.... Well, five years ago we discovered my dad had embezzled most of the money our band had made, and he fled the country."

I barely stifled a gasp.

"Holy shit!" Charles said it for me. "That's horrible! At least I know my parents loved me."

"You should hold on to that. But let's talk about your songs. I like the idea of picking one to honor your parents, but I gotta say, 'Smooth' is pretty challenging for someone just starting out."

"Yeah, I'm not as confident on that one."

"Okay, well, let me hear you play 'Can You Feel the Love Tonight' first. Then we'll get to the other one."

Even though I'd heard him play it before, I was impressed at how well Charles played the Elton John song. He'd obviously been practicing. And who knew where he'd gotten his ability to sing, because neither his mother nor I could carry a tune.

But his playing and singing fell apart when he started "Smooth". I grimaced. I would've shut the door and given him his privacy, but I wanted to hear how Drake handled giving his feedback.

Charles stumbled to a stop about halfway through the song. "It's crap, isn't it?"

Drake laughed. He *laughed*! I stood up from my chair, ready to throw him out of my house. But then he said, "I wouldn't have put it like that. But it's a sign of a good musician when you recognize you're attempting something you're not quite ready for."

I sat back down.

"Not sure I'll ever be ready for it."

"That's not true. You absolutely nailed it for a couple of bars in the middle." He hummed part of the chorus. "With practice you can absolutely own this song. Unfortunately, we have, what, ten days until the competition? I think you're better off sticking with the one you know you can play well right now."

"Yeah, makes sense. Thanks, Drake."

"Anytime. You wanna run through it a couple more times, or are you done for the night?"

I eased the door shut, making sure the latch didn't make any noise as it engaged. I pushed my chair back behind my desk and opened my laptop. Might as well get some work done.

But only a couple of minutes later, Charles knocked on the door. "Can I come in?"

"Of course."

He opened the door and glanced over his shoulder before slipping inside. He was holding a scone in one hand, no napkin. I made a mental note to assign him to do the vacuuming this weekend.

I raised my eyebrows. "What's up? Where's Drake?"

"Bathroom. So, he said he has to go home and feed Mabel because Zeke's out of town. It's really dark, and I don't like the thought of him walking through the woods by himself." He looked at me with pleading eyes.

Was he matchmaking? I stared him down as he took a huge bite of the scone. As expected, crumbs flew everywhere.

I sighed, but before I could chastise him, Charles' eyes went wide, and his face scrunched up. He held up a finger and ran out of the room. I got up to follow him to the kitchen, where he was spitting into the sink. He'd dropped the scone into the disposal.

"What's the matter?"

He turned on the tap and stuck his mouth under the stream. After he'd swallowed a few mouthfuls, he straightened up and wiped his mouth on the sleeve of his hoodie. He made a face and pointed at the bakery box. "Salt. There's salt on the outside, like a pretzel or something."

I raised my eyebrows. "I bet he went to Special Blend. Caspian likes to experiment." I opened the bakery box and picked up one of the scones. I broke off a small piece and put it in my mouth. The salt combined with the almonds made the whole thing seem a little dry, but if you melted some butter on it, *hmmm*. "I'll try them with my coffee in the morning."

Charles looked at me like I had a screw loose. "They're all yours." He went to the cabinet and got a glass for more water. "About what I was saying. Drake shouldn't be alone in those spooky woods. There's no one to hear him if he needs help." He gazed at me earnestly. Definitely matchmaking.

I... didn't hate the idea. Oh, there was no way Drake and I would end up actually *dating*, dating. But hooking up? Hell, yes, count me in.

I decided to mess with Charles. I cocked my head and put on an *a-ha* expression. "You want to go with him to make sure he's okay?"

His mouth dropped open in horror. "Fuck no! Not me! I wanted *you* to go with him." He craned his head to look into the living room. "Shit." He called out, "Drake, we're in the kitchen!"

Drake came down the hall. He wasn't wearing his hat, and

I remembered being naked in the shower, running my fingers through that silky blond hair.

I side-eyed Charles before saying, "Hey, Charles says you need to go feed Mabel. It's almost ten o'clock. Why don't I come with you?"

He stopped dead at the threshold to the kitchen, blinking hard as he jerked his head back. "What? Why? There's no reason you should leave your house this late just to—" He blinked one more time, then shut his mouth. "Um, but now that you mention it, those woods are really fu—uh, creepy."

I laughed. "You can curse around Charles. He's sixteen. It's not like he hasn't heard it before."

Drake smiled and gave an apologetic shrug. "Sorry."

Charles sucked in a breath. "*Oh.* Hey, Drake, do you play D&D?"

I gaped at him. What the hell was he doing now?

"Sure. There's a campaign I drop into when I'm home."

Charles turned to me. "You should invite Drake to your game tomorrow night." He smiled at Drake like it was a done deal. "Finn and all his nerdy friends play at least once a month. They're having it here tomorrow. I'm spending the night at Kirk's house. His friend Tommy's coming too."

I frowned at him. "Since when?" I held up a hand. "Not that I'm not happy you're making friends, and I'm not trying to say you can't go, but this is the first I'm hearing about it."

He waved a hand casually in the air. "Kirk texted me earlier. So, Drake's in for D&D. I can text Alex to let him know if you're too busy. You should get on the road. It's only going to get darker out there. I'm exhausted. Long day. I'll be in bed asleep way before you get back. Thanks for the help, Drake. I really appreciate it." He squeezed past Drake and patted him on the shoulder as he went by. Then he was gone.

I put my hands on my cheeks. "What just happened?"

Drake chuckled. "Earlier he apologized for his reaction

when we were teasing each other at the door. He essentially gave me permission to date you. By the way, he thinks he's, quote, 'cramping your style' and guys don't want to date you because you have him now."

I rubbed my forehead. "He's right that I haven't been going out with anyone, but it's because I wanted to give him time to settle in here. I'll talk to him. But now he's manufacturing ways for us to be alone together?"

He grinned. "Apparently." He lifted one shoulder. "Seems rude to let his efforts go to waste. You wanna come feed the scary forest monster with me?"

"You know what? I really do."

"Okay, spill." Alex poked me in the bicep as we covered the last leg of our morning run around the park downtown.

"What?"

"You *know* what. You've been smiling all morning. You never smile this much."

I rolled my eyes. "So sorry my happiness is bothering you."

That didn't work, but I hadn't expected it to. "You got laid, didn't you?"

I shrugged. "Just a hookup."

"Sure. Does your hookup have anything to do with Charles texting me about Drake coming to D&D tonight?"

I groaned. "I need to talk to him. He's matchmaking, and I don't want him to get invested in something that's never going to happen." I glanced at Alex. "He also told Drake last night he thinks the reason I haven't been seeing anyone is because no one wants to date me now that he's living with me."

"Oh, fuck."

"Yeah. I was trying to make sure he felt secure and that he

was my priority, but Noelle apparently told him some of the dating stories I used to entertain her with when we talked. So he was expecting me to be going out all the time or something."

"And he wants you to date Drake? Any particular reason he picked the guy who's only in town until the end of the music festival?"

I was glad my face was already red from running. "Last night he witnessed me and Drake, uh, bantering."

He hooted. "Bantering? You mean flirting. I need to get Charles to tell me exactly what you guys said." I shoved him and put on a burst of speed to beat him to the sidewalk at the end of the park path. He laughed as he caught up when I slowed to a walk. "You're allowed to flirt with hot musicians, Finn, even though you're officially a parent now. You can date, even have a—*gasp*—boyfriend!" Despite Alex's teasing tone, I could hear the wistfulness in his voice.

"It'll happen for you, you know."

He shook his head and looked away. "Nah. There's no unicorn for me, especially since I insist on living in this weird little town. I'll just have to live vicariously through you." He turned to me and grinned evilly. "Which is why I've decided to help Charles in his mission."

"What? Wait, how?" I tried grabbing for him, but he danced out of my reach, still with that fucking smirk on his face.

"Drake might not be Mr. Right, but he's the only victim on the horizon with any potential."

"Victim!"

He tapped his chin in mock thought. "We'll start tonight at D&D. Charles said he'll be staying at a friend's house, so it's perfect."

I tried to stare him down, but he wasn't paying attention. "Perfect how?"

My phone rang. I pointed at Alex as I fished it out of my fanny pack. "You will not do anything. I can manage my love life, or hookup life, just fine on my own." I looked at my phone, then raised my eyebrows as I answered. "Drake? What's up?" Was it wrong to hope for a booty call? But he knew I had to work this morning.

"Hey, uh. One of the chickens. You know the big black and orange one?"

"Yeah. Is something wrong with her?"

"I'm not sure. She won't let me inside the coop to clean it. And she's trapped three of the other hens in there with her. The other two got out to eat breakfast. She's sitting in the doorway to the coop where it connects to the screened-in run. But when I try to open the other door at the back, she comes at me with her beak and claws."

I stifled a laugh. "Are you okay? Did she hurt you?" Alex, who'd been listening avidly ever since I'd said Drake's name, pointed toward his car and mouthed, *Do we need to go over there?*

"I'm fine. I just want to make sure she and the others are okay."

I was pretty sure the hen was merely being protective of her eggs, but I was fully willing to jump on the excuse to see Drake again. Last night after we'd fed Mabel, we'd spent a glorious hour with our dicks in each other's mouths before I'd dragged myself home. I couldn't wait to be alone with him tonight after D&D.

"*Hmmm.* I don't have any appointments until later this morning. Alex and I were just finishing our run, so we'll stop by on our way home." Alex smirked as he looked between me and the vet clinic half a block away.

"Thanks, Finn." The relief in his voice was palpable.

"Sure. See you soon."

Alex walked faster. "I guess we've got a stop to make *on our way home*."

"Shut up. I didn't want to make him feel guilty."

Alex volunteered to drive. Once I was in the car, I texted Nova to let her know I'd be in a little late.

"Now tell me what's wrong with the chicken?"

I sighed. "Probably she's just broody—trying to keep Drake away from her eggs. But he wouldn't know how to get past her, and she's big enough she's blocking some of the other hens from going outside to eat."

He grinned. "I am so going to record this."

I groaned.

"What? You can put it on your socials. After I edit it, it'll go viral in a hot minute."

"Why are we friends again?"

A few minutes later we pulled into the driveway for Zeke's compound. As he'd promised, Drake had added me and Alex to the access app, and with a touch to Alex's phone screen, the gate opened.

We parked next to Zeke's place, and I could see Drake sitting on one of the large rocks inside Dolores' pen. He was wearing his straw cowboy hat, a denim jacket over a white t-shirt, cut-off jeans shorts, and cowboy boots. I had a hard time tearing my eyes away from his bare legs.

"Hey, thanks for coming!" he called out when we emerged from Alex's car.

Alex waved at him. "No problem. This is much more entertaining than taking pictures of the mayor's press conference that I have to go to later."

I glanced down at Alex's hands. He hadn't brought his camera, but he did have his phone.

Sighing, I walked over to Dolores' pen. Drake's eyes took in my running outfit, and his gaze lingered on the front of my compression tights. Fuck. I'd better keep this visit professional, or I'd never hear the end of it from Alex.

I climbed over the fence and approached the coop. Two of the birds were in the screened-in area, pecking at the ground. The large Cochin hen, as Drake had said, was standing in the opening of the coop at the top of the ramp that led down to the ground. The coop itself was about four feet long and five feet high, including its legs. The opening to the run was only a little over a foot square, so the hen easily blocked the others from entering or exiting. At the rear of the coop was a larger door, but she could easily rush the short distance to it before it was fully open.

"She's not interested in eating?"

"No. I tried some bread, which the other two ate, and their regular food. She won't budge. Unless I open the back door, of course."

"Okay. So probably she's laid some eggs in there." I turned to look at Drake as I spoke. Just being polite, not anything to do with his long legs, bared to the morning sun.

He frowned. "You said they don't need roosters to lay eggs, but the SPCA did say there'd been some roosters in with the hens. Would she be acting this way because she'd laid actual chicks?"

"No. Hens can't tell the difference. But if she's reacting like this to these eggs, fertilized or not, she'll react this way to any future eggs. She needs to be separated from the other hens, or you'll be dealing with this behavior every morning. Ordinarily I'd leave her in there and move the other chickens, but if she's trapped other hens in with her, it's a problem."

"Plus I don't have anywhere else to put five chickens." He stared toward the coop.

"Let's see if we can get the other hens out of there for now, and you can get a smaller coop just for this one."

Drake gave me an *oh, hell no* look. "I hope they teach chicken whispering at vet school."

"Cute." I put my hands on my hips, glancing around for something to block the hen's attack. My eye caught on Drake. Was he staring at my groin again? I considered shifting my position, but I didn't. "Hey, Alex, could you bring me one of the cushions off the chairs on the porch, please?"

"On it." He trotted up the steps to grab one. Then he sailed it through the air at me like a Frisbee. "I've got to record this!" He pulled out his phone again.

Ignoring him, I took the cushion, a solid red square—no flowery upholstery for Zeke—and went around the back of the coop to the larger door. The coop itself was about five feet tall, and the door was around three feet wide by two feet tall. I eyed Alex, who was hovering behind me, phone lifted high. "You'd better watch out, or you'll be a target too."

He winked. "You're my human shield."

Drake stood off to the side with a concerned expression on his face. Damn, those legs were something else.

Chicken first, legs later. I took a breath and leaned over to unlatch the coop door, pulling it wide in the same movement. I thrust the cushion through the opening just in time to prevent the chicken from gouging my face with her claws. She flapped and squawked, grabbing and pecking at the cushion. I pushed her toward the other end of the coop, leaning my upper body inside. The three chickens who'd been roosting on the beams took the opportunity to make their escape into the outdoor enclosure.

Mission accomplished.

Except now that the doorframe wasn't helping to block her access to me, the chicken had more room to dodge around the cushion. I took a quick look around the coop as I tried to keep the cushion between me and her. Yep, there were five eggs in one of the nesting boxes.

"Drake, I'm about to try to grab the eggs, but I need something to put them in. Can you find a bowl?"

"Here you go." He shoved his cowboy hat through the door next to my hips.

"Great. Hold it right there for a minute so I can put the eggs in." The chicken flew up, and I barely got the cushion high enough to block her outstretched talons. "Shit. Going for the eggs!" I reached out with my free hand and, angling the cushion to shield myself, I grabbed two of them as gently as I could. Drake leaned farther in to get the hat closer to the nesting box, and I twisted my body to give him room. I dropped the eggs in the hat, and then I grabbed two more. I needed to be careful placing them with the others, but the chicken noticed what I was doing and launched a rapid-fire offensive that I could barely hold back. "Shit! I don't want to drop them on the others!"

"Hand them to me." Drake pushed his shoulders through the coop door, squeezing in alongside my waist, so he could put his other hand out to take the eggs.

"Pull back!" I managed to grab the last egg, then Drake and I backed out of the doorway. I blocked the opening with the cushion until Alex could slam the door shut.

The door rattled as the hen hurled herself at it. I exhaled in relief as I placed the last egg in Drake's hat. "She definitely needs a coop of her own."

"Fuck, yes." Drake looked me over. "Are you hurt?"

"I don't think so. Oh, there." I had one nasty scratch on my forearm. I turned the cushion over to see the side the chicken had attacked.

"Holy fuck!" Drake took a step back to make room for Alex to get a close-up with his phone.

The cushion was, well, a lost cause. The fabric was torn in multiple places, with stuffing peeking out.

"Shit, that could've been you!"

I smiled at Drake. "I've faced down worse, I promise." He chewed his bottom lip as he examined the cushion. It was adorable. I mentally slapped myself. "Are the eggs okay?"

He tilted his hat toward me so I could see. "They look fine to me."

"Good. Now you have two options. Option one is you put the eggs in the kitchen and have them for breakfast."

"Okay?"

"Option two is, before you do that, we find out if they're fertilized or not."

He frowned down at the eggs. "You can tell?"

I nodded. "It's easy. But what's your stance on baby chicks?"

He met my eyes and grinned. "Zeke'll love them."

I laughed. "Good point."

As if she knew we were talking about her, the Cochin hen hurled herself down the ramp into the outdoor run, squawking all the way.

"Shit, let's get inside." Trying not to ogle Drake's ass—and failing—I followed him over the fence and up the steps to the porch. I put the cushion back on the chair, destroyed side down. "You can barely tell anything happened."

Drake snorted. "Until someone shows Zeke the video Alex is making." He pointed behind me where, yes, Alex still had his phone aimed at us.

I rolled my eyes and went inside. Drake set his hat down on the kitchen table. My arm had stopped bleeding, so I decided to check the eggs before dealing with my wound.

I picked up the hat. "I'm going to the bathroom to see if the eggs are viable."

Drake and Alex both stared at me with their heads cocked to the side, identical expressions of confusion on their faces.

I heaved a sigh and held up my phone. "I need a dark room."

Drake and Alex looked at each other with raised eyebrows, then simultaneously looked back at me.

I gestured between them with my phone. "This is seriously disturbing. Stop it. You can come with me if you're that curious."

Drake laughed, and Alex, who was still filming, grinned. "Lead the way."

It was a tight fit in the half-bath off Zeke's living room, but we managed it. I handed the hatful of eggs to Drake, then I asked Alex—who was closest—to shut the door and turn off the light.

He flipped the switch. "I didn't have bathroom threesome on my to-do list for this morning, but I'm here for it."

"Shut up." I turned on my phone's flashlight, then I picked up one of the eggs. Touching the narrowest end of the egg to the lens where the light emitted from the phone, I showed the other two the glowing orb. "See the veins? This egg will hatch a chick."

They both *Ooohed*, and Alex got a close-up for his video. The other four eggs were also fertilized.

Alex opened the door, and we returned to the kitchen.

I put Drake's hat on the kitchen table again. "Does Zeke have a heating pad or something, do you know? They just need to be warm until we relocate their mom.

"I'll text Zeke about the heating pad." He eyed my arm. "And to see if he's got a first aid kit."

I went over to the sink to wash my arm. The bowl we'd used for Mabel's dinner last night was sitting on the counter. "Do you go get this every morning?"

He looked at me like I was crazy. "I don't want to be late with her next meal and have her find an empty bowl."

Yeah, okay. A rampaging cryptid—or bear, or whatever was eating the food—wasn't anything I wanted to deal with either.

The scratch wasn't deep. It had oozed some blood initially, but that had stopped by the time we got to the kitchen. Zeke texted back, so Drake went to get the antibiotic cream along with the heating pad. "He says there's a picnic basket in the pantry we can use for the eggs."

"Thanks. That'll work great."

After cleaning the dust off the picnic basket, we put the heating pad in the bottom with a towel over it. Then we wrapped the eggs in the towel and set it on top of the heating pad. Alex, who'd been filming us off and on this entire time, got a close-up before we shut the lid of the basket. Then he sat at Zeke's kitchen table and started messing with his phone.

Following Drake over to the sink, I gestured toward Dolores' pen. "I've got to work all day, so I can't help you with a new coop."

He waved this off. "I'll figure it out. Is there a farm supply store around here? Zeke went into Burlington to get that big coop, but we don't need anything fancy."

"Yeah, just on the east side of town. Once you get it set up, put the eggs in the new coop and shove the hen in there with them. She'll do the rest."

"Great. I can't wait to try to move her." I snickered, and he pretended to hit me in the arm. "Hey, I've been meaning to ask. Why don't you have any pets? Isn't it like a rule that vets have a ton of animals?"

I rubbed my jaw. "My dog, Maisie, got cancer last year." He made a consoling noise. "Yeah, it was bad, but at least she went quickly. I was starting to think about getting another dog when Charles came to live with me." I smiled. "He's been badgering me for a pet. If a stray or abandoned animal doesn't come our way in the next couple of months, I'll get him one for his birthday in August."

He nodded, his eyes on his hat as he rinsed out the inside.

"Um, can I ask...? Charles is obviously related to you, but how?"

I crossed my arms. "He's my biological son." Drake whipped his head around to stare at me with wide eyes. I shrugged. "It was the summer before our freshman year in college. Noelle had been accepted to the University of Washington, and I was going to Cornell. When she got pregnant, she wanted to keep the baby, but she still wanted to move to Seattle. I signed away my parental rights, but we kept in touch, and as soon as I opened my practice I started donating to Charles' college fund."

Drake raised his eyebrows. "Wow. A lot of guys would've walked away and not looked back."

"No. Signing away my rights was the best decision for Charles and Noelle. It wasn't because I didn't care. Noelle married Jin when Charles was two years old. He was a great guy." I stopped talking to swallow down the wave of grief. "Jin adopted Charles, but their wills stated that I was to be his guardian if something happened to both of them. They brought Charles to visit Noelle's parents in Maplewood at least once a year, so he knew who I was and how we were related. But losing his parents has been rough on him."

Drake nodded. "I bet. But what about you? It has to have been rough on you too."

I frowned. "What do you mean? Having Charles live with me? It's been an adjustment, but we're doing okay."

He set the hat on the counter to dry and wiped his hands off on a dish towel. "I meant you lost your friends. Have you let yourself grieve for them?" Then he held up his hands, looking contrite. "Tell me to mind my own business, sorry." He bit his lower lip.

I shook my head. "That's... I think only Alex has asked me that." I glanced over at the kitchen table, where the man in question had stopped pretending not to listen. I glared at him, and he held up his phone with the time displayed. "Shit!" I started walking toward the door. "Sorry, I've got to get to work. I'll see you this evening!"

Alex followed as I jogged down the porch steps. "You won't be *that* late."

"I will by the time I get changed. I'll call Nova from the car."

When I got hold of her, she told me not to worry. "Al can take vitals and patient history. You've got time." I collapsed back in the seat in relief. Al was our most senior vet tech, and he was worth his weight in gold.

After a few minutes, Alex cleared his throat. "So," he started in a way-too-casual tone. "That was a pretty deep conversation to have with someone who's just a hookup."

Fuck.

TEXT CONVERSATION FRIDAY, 8:49 A.M

ZEKE:

The fire chief left me a voicemail –
something about the EMTs who'll be on
standby during the festival. Go by the
station today and see what he wants. It's on
Clover kind of kitty-corner to the park.

ZEKE:

I heard you went to Red's Restaurant
yesterday. Make sure you go to Sparky's
today. You're too famous to have favorites.

DRAKE:

What?

CHAPTER 8

DRAKE

Friday, five days before the festival

I rolled my eyes as I pocketed my phone. Well, if I had to go to the fire station, I might as well walk around downtown and check out this other diner.

But first, the feed store for another coop. Thank fuck Zeke had left his credit card for me to use. This was getting ridiculous.

Since my cowboy hat was still damp, I had to wear the fedora. I disliked wearing it with my cowboy boots, but the good people of Maplewood would just have to deal with today's Indiana Jones-meets-Texas-twink aesthetic.

I got a long blink from the employee at the feed store, but he helped me readily enough. He even had a coop that let you slide out the nesting boxes from outside, which would prevent future bloodshed. It didn't come with its own run, but he showed me one that could be attached. Perfect. And since this coop was a lot smaller than the first one, I could put it together all by myself. Getting the chicken in it, well, that might be another story.

As much as I would've liked to have Finn help me again—

preferably wearing those running tights, *hnggh*—he wouldn't have time between the end of his workday and getting ready to have everyone over for D&D. Maybe I could bribe Charles to come over after school. He'd seemed excited about the scones last night. I could stop by Special Blend and pick up some cookies when I was in town. I'd need something to bring to D&D anyway.

I'd never been in a fire station before, but one of the big doors was open, showing off a large red fire truck. A ruddy-faced burly guy, probably in his forties, was hosing it down. He shut the water off when he saw me. "Can I help you?"

"Hey, I'm looking for the fire chief. Do you know where I can find him?" I wished Zeke would've told me the guy's fucking name.

He set the hose down. "I'm the fire chief. Patrick Brennan." He wiped his hand on the back of his pants and held it out to me.

I shook it. "Hi, I'm Drake Derry. Zeke Knight asked me to come by because you'd left him a voicemail about the EMTs at the music festival. He's out of town and I'm helping with the festival in the meantime."

"You are? Huh. I've been here for over ten years, and I've never seen Zeke delegate anything."

I grinned. "It's not so much delegation as ordering around."

He laughed. "Come on in to my office and I'll show you the coverage we have. We're down a person right now, which is why I'm doing the grunt work today." He hiked a thumb at the truck. We walked toward the back of the building, and Chief Brennan paused to stick his head in a doorway. "Eric, finish cleaning the truck. I've got a meeting."

I heard a faint, "Yes, Chief." We went down a short hallway. The office was sparsely furnished but spacious. The only decorations were some certificates and commendations on one wall, and photos of firefighters or of the chief with people who looked like politicians on another.

He pulled out a map of the festival grounds, and he'd marked the EMT station on it. Then he handed me a schedule for the EMTs. "Like I said, we're down a person, so while there'll be at least one EMT on site at all times, last year we were able to have two. But you can still call 911 and we'll come."

"Got it. Hopefully we won't have any major problems." I'd been to enough music festivals to know there'd always be people with minor scrapes or twisted ankles, but true emergencies were rare. I fingered the paper. "Is there any way you can email this to me?"

Chief Brennan blinked at me in surprise. "Sorry, Zeke never checks his email. But sure, if you give me yours, I'll be happy to."

Crap, no wonder Zeke had made me come down here in person. He was expecting to get a piece of paper.

I thanked the chief and left the station. Sparky's Diner wasn't far away, only a few doors down from the vet clinic, so I decided to walk and enjoy the day. Sparky's also appeared to have started life as a railroad car, but it had been expanded in the back. The inside, other than being blue, was similar to Red's, but everything seemed to be in better repair. I even saw a modern POS system at the counter.

"Hey, welcome to Sparky's! I'm Ian." An older guy came out from behind the counter. "Just one today?"

"Yes, thanks."

"Great. You can sit at the counter, or we have a booth open."

"Booth, please."

He led me to a booth next to a window. The table beside it was filled with five older women, but they weren't your run-of-the-mill grandmother types. They were way too fashionable, for one. I hadn't seen anyone else in Maplewood who wore a beret and Prada eyeglasses. One of them was wearing pearls around her neck and a pleated skirt, and another one was wearing skinny jeans and rhinestoned high-tops.

All five of them stared at me as I sat down and put my fedora on the seat next to me. Ian handed me a menu. "Don't miss the Mabel Meatloaf—it's our specialty. Can I get you anything to drink?"

After verifying that they didn't serve the sweet version, I ordered an iced tea. Ian left me to look over the menu and went off to get it.

I ignored the whispers, which, as they got louder, seemed mostly made up of "*You* ask him!"

Ian came back with my tea, and I decided to take a chance and order the Mabel Meatloaf. When in Maplewood.

After he left, I turned to my audience. "Hello, ladies. Can I help you with something?"

One of the shorter ones, who had white hair and blue eyes very similar to my own, perked up. "We wanted to know if you're Drake Derry."

"I am, yes."

She grinned and straightened in her chair. "We—" she circled her finger to indicate the five of them. "—are the Rock-togenarians."

I waited, but she seemed to be done speaking. "Um, okay?" Was it a club or something?

They could tell I wasn't getting it. The one in a tailored pantsuit with her white hair in a chin-length bob put her hand on the first woman's arm. "We're a band. I'm Agnes. This is Rae." She indicated the one who spoke first. "These are Lydia, Eleanor, and Celia. We'll be performing at the amateur competition next Sunday."

"Oh! I see. What kind of music do you play?" A feeling of dread formed in my belly. Would I have to pretend to enjoy an enthusiastic rendition of some sixties hit like "Please Mr. Post-man" sung in off-key quavery voices?

She smiled and spread out her hands. "Whatever we're in the mood for. Rae here is our punk aficionado, but the rest of us like to branch out a little. And we've picked a more mainstream song for the competition of course."

"Oh, of course." They had to be pulling my leg. "I like punk. Who are your influences, Rae?"

She smiled. "The Stooges were my first introduction to the punk scene. Or what would become it, I suppose, at that time. Iggy Pop was everything I wanted to be. But then it was the Sex Pistols, Black Flag, Rancid. I love them all."

Holy shit. "Wow. I'm looking forward to seeing you perform at the festival."

One of the other ladies, Lydia, I thought, leaned forward. "We hear you're friendly with that lovely Dr. Hunnicutt."

"Uh. Sure?" Play it cool, play it cool.

"He's a wonderful man. Attractive and dependable."

Rae scoffed. "Drake's more likely to be interested in what our Finn's got beneath those scrubs he wears."

Thankfully, I didn't have to answer. Ian brought them their check, and all five of them looked at their watches. "We have to go, but it was lovely to meet you, Drake. Perhaps I'll see you at the compound. Zeke and I are friendly." Agnes stood and walked out like a model on a runway.

I stared after them. She didn't mean.... Nope, not thinking about it.

I was just finishing my maple cream pie—which to be honest I didn't care for as much as the maple custard pie at Red's—when my phone chimed with a text from Alex. We'd exchanged numbers when I'd added him to the access app for the gate to the compound.

A second text came through before I could even click on the first message.

ALEX:

I finished the video of Finn's heroic egg
rescue! This version is just for you and Finn.
I gave Nova a heavily edited version for the
vet clinic's socials. Don't worry, I took out
all the parts where you two are eye-fucking
each other. [link]

ALEX:

Also, I named all your chickens. Here's a
gallery of their photos and names
underneath. I printed it out and laminated it
for you. I'll give it to you tonight. You can
thank me later. [photo]

Deciding to delay watching the video, I opened the photo
of the chickens. He'd taken video stills of each of them and
labeled them with names. I laughed so loud Ian looked over
with a raised eyebrow. "Sorry!" I called.

The chickens had all been named after characters from
The Lord of the Rings. The big hen who'd caused so much
trouble today was called Aragornette. Her photo was a close-
up of her angry face. The other hens were Legolass, Gandal-
fina, Samantha, Mary, and Froda.

I hoped Zeke liked *The Lord of the Rings*, because I was so
putting that laminated photo on the side of the coop.

I took a deep breath, minimized the volume on my phone,
and clicked on the link to the video. The faint strains of what I
thought was the theme song from an old western movie
played. I didn't know what Alex had done to the video, but
he'd made Finn appear to be a hero riding in to save the damsel
in distress—me, that is—from the evil chicken. And multiple
times he'd zoomed in on Finn ogling my legs and ass and me
ogling Finn's running tights from the front and back. At least
it was mutual.

The music switched to Led Zeppelin's "Immigrant Song"
as Finn brandished his trusty chair cushion and fended off the

marauder. Alex had made the chicken—Aragornette, I supposed I should say—appear almost deadly.

The chicken was vanquished, and the eggs were saved. The music changed again as Alex lingered on a closeup of Finn's injured arm. *The Lord of the Rings* main theme started out soft and came to a crescendo as Finn held up a glowing egg. Alex had managed to catch the veins of the chick inside.

Ian kept glancing over as I laughed. I saved the video to my phone to watch again later. Especially the parts where Finn was checking me out. There was no denying he and I had chemistry, probably more than I'd ever had with anyone else. It was too bad we only had a little over a week left together.

Which was fucking depressing. I hadn't even been in Maplewood a week yet, but I'd miss this place. And Finn, Charles, and Alex. Maybe not Zeke, though, I thought with a snort.

But that was something to deal with when the time came. For now I had D&D to look forward to, and then a whole night alone with Finn.

I watched the video all the way through twice before replying.

ME:

> Thanks for the chicken headshots. I love the names. And thanks for the video. It's hilarious. Though you could've done me a solid and zoomed in on Finn's junk.

ALEX:

> Not for love or money. You'll have to get that kind of shot on your own.

I hoped Finn's other friends were as fun as Alex. Still chuckling, I paid my bill and walked outside into the spring sunshine. Vermont's humidity was a thousand times better than what you got hit in the face with in Texas.

I crossed the street to get to Harmonic Circus, the music shop owned by Roy Griffin, where Charles took guitar lessons. I didn't need to buy anything, but who didn't love a music shop? Plus it was always a good idea to butter up your colleagues.

Which I guessed Roy was now. *For* now. Whatever.

The door to the shop was sky blue, and when I opened it the bell made more of a clunk than a ringing sound. Roy was on the phone, sitting on a stool behind a glass counter. I waved at him and looked around. One of Jake Lord's early hits was playing over the sound system, and I reminded myself to send a strongly worded text message to Wesley—a.k.a. Jake Lord himself. He'd severely undersold the amount of work I'd be doing to "help out" his good buddy Zeke.

But right then I made a beeline for the racks of sheet music that ran almost the entire length of the store. I couldn't wait to look through it. Roy also had the usual high school band instruments, plus drums, guitars, and keyboards. A staircase led to the second floor, which I'd definitely check out after I did the polite thing and chatted with Roy once he was off the phone.

He eventually hung up and joined me in my deep dive into the sheet music. I'd already tucked several songs under my arm. Yes, I knew I could find the same thing electronically, but this was one area of my life where I loved the paper.

"I've got several Melodious Moon songs." He pointed to my left.

"Yeah, I think I've got those memorized."

He snorted. "I was hoping you'd sign them for me."

"Oh. Of course." This led to him herding me upstairs to also sign the vinyl records. He even had the album Dirk and I had made after Melodious Moon imploded.

"Charles said you were helping him prepare for the amateur contest."

"I am." I frowned. "You don't think it's a conflict of interest since I'm a judge, do you?"

He laughed. "Son, there'll be a whole panel of judges. You can't swing the vote all by yourself. As long as you don't try to compete, you're fine."

I smiled. "I think I can restrain myself."

After I stowed my new sheet music in the SUV, I headed over to Special Blend to get some treats to take to D&D, plus a second box for Charles in case I could bribe him to help me with the chicken.

There was a new clerk behind the counter today, a slimly-built guy with black hair and dark eyes. Damn, this town had some eye candy.

"Welcome to Special Blend! I'm Caspian, the owner. How can I help you?"

"Hi. Nice to meet you. I'm Drake. So, I need something to bribe a teenager, and then I need to take snacks to a party."

He laughed. "I've got you covered. How about some cookies for both? I made the snickerdoodles myself." He pointed to a display of chocolate chip cookies and snicker-doodles.

"Perfect. Let's do two boxes of a dozen each, half and half of both kinds."

When I got back to the car, I took a photo of the cookies and texted it to Charles.

ME:

Is this a sufficient bribe to get you to help me with something mildly dangerous at Zeke's compound? [photo]

Based on what time it was, he had to be in class, but it only took him a minute to reply.

CHARLES:

Depends who made them. And does Finn know about this dangerous task?

I cringed.

ME:

The owner of the bakery made the snickerdoodles, I'm not sure who made the chocolate chip. And no, Finn doesn't know. But it's not life-threatening, I promise. I'll come pick you up and bring you back in time to go to your friend's house.

CHARLES:

Can Kirk come too? He wants to meet you. Pick us up at my house at 3:30. And you can keep the snickerdoodles. We'll take the chocolate chip.

CHARLES:

Finn said you have chickens now. They'll eat the snickerdoodles.

CHARLES:

Probably.

ME:

Kirk can come, but what's wrong with the snickerdoodles?

I picked one up. It looked good. It smelled a little smoky under the sweet, but not bad or anything. I took a bite. I chewed twice before I searched desperately around my SUV for a bottle of water. Fuck. The cooler was inside my cabin.

I swallowed, putting the rest of the cookie back in the box. I stuck my tongue out and panted. Shit, that was spicy. Probably chipotle or ancho chili powder mixed with the sugar and cinnamon. If I'd had a shot of tequila, it would've been amazing, but at the moment it was just painful.

Never mind. I'll give them to Zeke.

I killed the time before I had to pick up Charles and Kirk by taking the coop back to the compound and getting it mostly set up. Aragornette gave me the evil eye the entire time I worked, so I was doubly glad I'd arranged for backup to get her in her new home.

There was enough room in poor Dolores' pen to put Aragornette's coop next to the other one, but I made a note in my phone to tell Zeke he needed to move the fence to give her the space back. The pen could easily expand into the grassy area next to the house.

Charles and Kirk were waiting in the vet clinic parking lot. Kirk was a cute redhead with curly hair and freckles. They hopped in my SUV, and Kirk gushed, "Wow, it's so cool to meet you! I can't wait to see you perform at the festival!"

I smiled. "Thanks. Would you two like some backstage passes? I know the guy in charge."

Kirk raised his fists in the air. "Bro! That'd be awesome!"

Charles looked at him. "I wish you were doing the amateur competition with me."

He shook his head. "No way. I promised Mr. Griffin I'd be on the Harmonic Circus float for the Pride parade. That's soon enough. I'm not ready yet."

Charles rolled his eyes. "You're ready now."

I nudged him. "Being ready isn't only about having the talent and skills. You have to be ready here too." I tapped my temple. "If Kirk decided he'll be ready at a later date, you're not helping by pressuring him to perform now."

He made a face. "Shit, I'm sorry, Kirk. I'm just obsessing

over being up on that stage by myself. I wasn't thinking about it from your perspective."

Kirk reached over the seat and cuffed him on the shoulder. "It's all good. But thanks, Drake. That's exactly how my brain is looking at things."

"You're welcome. And, Charles, if it would help you, after we deal with the chicken, we can walk down to the amphitheater, and you can stand on the stage to get a feel for it."

In the back seat, Kirk whisper-shouted, "*Yes!*"

Charles lit up. "Please. I'd like to do that. But what does *deal with the chicken* mean? You said what we'd be doing was slightly dangerous. And there's a *chicken* involved?"

"Um, yeah. We need to move one of the chickens to a separate coop because she was too protective of her eggs. Finn got them out this morning but she's been giving me a death glare all day, so I wanted some backup."

I could feel him staring at me, but I kept my eyes on the road. "Describe *too protective of her eggs*, please."

I darted a glance at him. "I think Alex sent Nova the video to post on the vet clinic's socials."

"On it!" Kirk wasted no time getting his phone out. Then he leaned forward between the seats and held the phone so he and Charles could both see it. The music started, and Kirk enthused, "*The Magnificent 7*! Nice!"

They laughed and swore through the video. This version was much shorter than the one Alex had sent me. It ended as I turned onto the driveway for Zeke's compound.

Charles stared at me some more. "And you want us to do exactly *what* to that chicken?"

I held up a hand. "Let's assess the situation, and you don't have to get near the chicken if you don't want to. All I need to do is move her to her new coop. It's all set up. We just have to put her eggs in there and then transfer her over."

"Uh huh."

We got out of the car, and the boys headed for the coop. Kirk exclaimed over Dolores while I went inside to fetch the eggs.

A peek through the large access door at the back of the big coop showed Aragornette was roosting inside with a couple of the other chickens. The rest were outside pecking at the ground.

Charles helped me open the new coop and get the eggs settled in one of the nesting boxes while Kirk filled a bowl with water. Then I scattered some feed in the outdoor runs of both coops. I was hoping Aragornette would come outside. The big coop's run was large enough for me to go inside and throw a blanket over her.

She didn't come out.

I put my hands on my hips. "Any ideas, guys?"

Charles held up his phone. "What if we *want* her to attack you?" I blinked at him, and he smirked. "You were going to throw a blanket over her when she was in the run. What if you opened the door to the coop and held the blanket in front of you? She might attack the blanket and you could wrap her up."

I didn't have any better ideas.

First I got some gloves out of Zeke's shed, then I grabbed another old blanket from the stack he'd said we could use on Tuesday. It was more like a quilt, so I was hoping it'd be thick enough so Aragornette's claws wouldn't penetrate.

All too soon I stood in front of the rear door to the big coop. Charles was in charge of opening and closing the door. Kirk, Alex would be delighted to find out, had his phone pointed at me to record today's adventure. I wondered what music I'd get for a soundtrack.

Steeling myself, I held up the blanket and nodded at Charles. He swung the door open, and I shoved the blanket through, holding it high so Aragornette couldn't fly over it and attack my head.

Nothing happened. I cautiously lowered a corner of the blanket. Aragornette was still sitting on the bar across the upper part of the coop. She stared at me curiously but didn't move. I dropped the blanket and reached a gloved hand toward her. I could just reach her.

She didn't react when I petted her back. I carefully put one hand under her and kept the other on top. She let me pick her up with only some mild clucking and flapping. "Charles, once you close this door, go stand by the door to the other coop and be ready."

"Got it."

In an almost disappointingly dramaless experience, I carried Aragornette the few steps to the new coop and put her inside, right on top of the eggs in their nesting box. Then I backed out and Charles shut the door.

"Well, fuck. That was easy." I shook out the blanket.

Kirk put his phone in his pocket. "I was hoping for more scary chicken video footage."

Charles shuddered. "I for one am glad you didn't get any."

We all climbed out of Dolores' pen. "Y'all wanna go see the amphitheater? We can take one of my guitars." I checked my watch. "I need to feed Dolores and Mabel when we get back, so I don't have to worry about it after D&D. Then I'll take you home." I started walking to my cabin.

Charles rolled his eyes but didn't call me on my insinuation that I'd be coming home tonight.

Kirk gasped. "Charles told me you feed Mabel every night. Can we come with you?"

"Sure. Wait here." I went inside and grabbed my acoustic guitar. The electric would've made a better experience for the boys, but I didn't want to deal with the amp.

Kirk seemed to have the most energy, so I made him carry

the guitar case as we trekked through Zeke's compound and then the festival grounds. The amphitheater was at the farthest point from Zeke's property.

Eventually the boys and I were standing on the stage, gazing out at the empty rows of seats and the grassy hill beyond.

"Wow, this is big! I've only ever played on the little stage in the town park." Kirk shoved his hands in his pockets and looked around uneasily. It was the first time he'd shown any sort of lack of confidence.

I took the guitar out of the case and handed it to Charles. "Play your song and try to imagine all the seats full and people sitting and standing on the grass."

Tentatively he strummed the first chord, turning his head this way and that to hear how the sound carried. I grinned. "Go on."

He played more assertively, even singing the first few lines of the song. Then he stopped and told Kirk, "You have to try this."

Kirk took the guitar and competently played the intro to 'Sweet Child O' Mine'. He didn't sing though, and he stopped after the first stanza. He shook his head. "I don't think I'm meant for big stages like this." He gave the guitar back to Charles, who put it in the case.

"But you're playing on the float in the Pride parade next month." How was that different?

Kirk nodded. "It'll be easier. I'll only be able to see the people right in front of me. Not as many as this." He gestured out at the seats.

I thought Kirk might be underestimating the size of a Pride festival crowd, but I didn't want to worry him, so I kept my mouth shut.

When we got back to the compound, I had the boys feed Dolores while I defrosted a container of beef stroganoff I'd found in Zeke's freezer. I threw it in Mabel's bowl with some slightly wilted vegetables from the fridge. If Zeke didn't come home soon, I'd need to go to the grocery store.

Charles seemed less than enthusiastic at helping to feed Mabel, but he wouldn't hear of staying behind. Probably worried he'd appear lame in front of his friend, though Kirk didn't strike me as the type to care about anyone's machismo.

Kirk asked to hold the bowl of food as we walked. When we were among the trees, he looked around before asking, "Have you seen Mabel?"

I shook my head. "Something's eating the food, but it could just as easily be a bear or raccoons."

Kirk bounced on his toes. "I bet it's Mabel. Have you heard *The Cryptid Corner* podcast?"

"Uh, no?"

"The host is, like, *from* here. It's like Mabel inspired him to investigate cryptids all over the world."

"Huh. Sounds interesting." Not. I didn't need some podcast fueling my nightmares.

Ten minutes later we were back at the compound. I stopped at my cabin and grabbed my backpack and the box of chocolate chip cookies—since I'd separated out the snickerdoodles—from the coffee shop.

Charles' eyes lit up when he saw the bakery box. "Are those the chocolate chip?"

"You can have one each. The rest are for the D&D group."

"Okay. What'd you do with the snickerdoodles?" I'd told them about the extra hot spice Caspian had added.

"They're in the cabin. I don't know when Zeke'll be back, but I can put them in the freezer for him. Or do you think Mabel would like them?"

Charles turned around to exchange a look with Kirk. They both shook their heads. "Better not risk it."

Good point.

TEXT CONVERSATION FRIDAY, 5:20 P.M

DRAKE:

Why didn't you tell me the scones I brought over were weird?

FINN:

Because they were a gift, and I didn't want to make you feel bad? Plus, I dunked them in my coffee this morning and they were pretty good.

FINN:

Did Charles complain about them?

DRAKE:

No, I guessed, since he didn't want to try the cookies I bought for D&D tonight. Probably a good thing, because the snickerdoodles were spicy

FINN:

He's not into experimenting with food, sorry. It was still thoughtful of you

DRAKE:

Well, the cookies Caspian didn't make were more to his liking. I'm at your house, FYI. Charles and Kirk are about to leave. You don't mind if I look through all of your drawers and cabinets, do you?

CHAPTER 9
DRAKE

Friday, five days before the festival

Charles let me and Kirk into the house. The boys ran to his room to get his stuff for the sleepover, so I dropped the box of cookies off on the kitchen counter and put my backpack on the couch in the living room. I didn't want to be presumptuous and put it in Finn's bedroom. It wasn't even 5:30 p.m., and he didn't get off work until after 6:00. Then we had an hour before the D&D attendees arrived.

I wondered if Finn would be up for a blow job if we had time. This friends with benefits thing was pretty convenient, I had to admit. Neither Dirk nor I had ever had a steady partner —too much touring and traveling made it difficult to see the same person regularly. And it wasn't as if I'd met anyone who seemed worth making the effort for.

But Finn was absolutely worth the effort—not that it took much—to see him while I was in Maplewood. I liked him, and he turned me on something fierce.

Charles and Kirk came out of the bedroom. I held up a hand to stop them from leaving. "Charles, can I borrow your guitar? I've got a little time to kill, and I should work on the song I'm writing."

His face brightened. "Sure! Let me get it for you—you don't want to go in my room. It's a mess." He handed Kirk his backpack and hurried back into the bedroom, returning almost immediately with his guitar.

"Thanks, I appreciate it."

"Anytime." He handed it to me. "It's probably not as nice as you're used to."

I shook my head at him. "Your dad gave this to you. That makes it a lot more valuable than my Gibson. I'll be careful with it."

He smiled. "Thanks. Just put it inside my door when you're done."

They left, and I sat down to work on the song that wasn't coming together. I should've probably started something new, but my gut told me I had the beginnings of a great one if I could get the words and melody where they needed to be.

Charles' guitar had a nice, warm sound. It was actually perfect for the song, since the lyrics I had so far were about missing a friend—a stand-in for me missing Dirk.

I figured out a fun riff, but the words still weren't gelling. I was relieved when Finn came home and interrupted my struggles.

"Hey!" He looked tired but glad to see me.

"Hey. Thanks for letting me hang out here until you got home."

He walked over to the couch where I was sitting, and I set the guitar aside and stood up. Did we kiss? What was the protocol with friends with benefits?

Finn seemed to be having a similar conundrum. "Uh." He looked around and pointed at my backpack. "You want to put that in my bedroom? I mean, if you're still planning on staying the night. It's okay either way!" He held his hands up in a placating gesture.

I grabbed one of his hands. "I'm staying."

He smiled in relief, his eyes crinkling adorably. "Good."

Not letting go of his hand, I stepped closer. "How much time do we have before your friends get here?"

He leaned forward until his mouth was almost touching mine. "Not enough."

Someone pounded on the front door milliseconds before opening it, and Finn and I jumped apart. Alex breezed in, hip-checking the door to close it behind himself as he juggled a bunch of stuff in his arms. Finn rushed over to help him.

I mourned our almost-kiss, but I made up for it by admiring his ass in his scrubs. Fuck, did he take that thing to work every day?

I followed Finn to see if I could carry anything, but the two of them had it covered. I waved at Alex. "How's it going?"

He grinned. "Great. I have your chicken photos all printed out."

"Thanks for doing that." I told them how cooperative Aragornette had been when we'd moved her to her new coop.

Alex gave me an amused smile. "I'm glad you weren't injured, but I was kind of looking forward to another video."

Finn noticed the box of cookies, and the two of them cross-examined me about who had baked them before they opened the box.

"I wish someone had warned me about Caspian's tendency to experiment." I complained. "By the way, what's up with the diners? Somebody told Zeke I ate at Red's yesterday, and he ordered me to eat at Sparky's ASAP."

Finn and Alex both nodded solemnly. Alex opened his box and began setting up his DM screen and all the stuff he needed behind it. "They have a long-standing feud." He squinted up at the ceiling. "Something involving a dessert recipe? Can't remember exactly." He shook his head. "Anyway, you either have to declare for one diner exclusively, or you have to make sure you visit each one an equal number of times. Trust me, somebody's always keeping track."

I stared at him. "That's fucked up."

Finn snorted. "Welcome to small-town life." He pulled a bowl from a cabinet and poured a bag of chips into it.

"You need help?" I couldn't cook for shit, but I could put out snacks.

"Sure."

I hurried to put Charlie's guitar back in his room—just inside the door so I didn't have to look—and my backpack on Finn's bed. When I got back to the kitchen, he had me put some cheese on a plate with crackers, which was well within my range of skills.

When there was a knock at the door, I volunteered to let people in since Finn knew what he wanted done with the snacks and Alex was still setting up the table.

The first to arrive was Mickey from Red's diner. "Hey, Drake! Good to see you again." He came bearing a pot of soup and some bread. The other diner wasn't represented, so I guessed not everything had to be equal between them.

The next person was a cutie with brown hair and a short beard. "Hi, I'm Sam. I use they/them pronouns."

"Hi, Sam. I'm Drake, and I use he/him pronouns. Come on in." Sam had brought homemade peanut butter cookies, and they looked delicious.

Before I closed the door behind Sam, a man with a shaved head who was about my height but with a little more meat on him came up the walk. "Hey, you must be Drake. I'm Andre."

We shook hands, and I waved Sam and Andre to the kitchen just as someone else knocked. This turned out to be Jason, a large muscular guy with brown hair and light hazel eyes. Damn, did Finn know anyone who wasn't attractive? Even for what I'd seen of Maplewood so far, this crew was stellar.

Jason was followed quickly by our last player, who turned out to be Bo Boyd from the music festival committee. He, like the rest of them, seemed to have been expecting me. I wished Finn would've given me the rundown on his friends, but it wasn't like we'd had time.

The food was spread out on the island, and after we served ourselves, we all settled around the table. Finn put me between him and Andre, directly across from Alex behind his DM screen.

Alex announced, "We've got a larger than usual group tonight, with Drake visiting and Bo able to join us. So we're doing a one-off quick campaign that we should be able to finish in a couple of hours if everyone pays attention." He glared around the table at us to make sure we'd heard him. "Okay, for Drake's benefit, please go around the table and introduce your characters."

I wasn't surprised to find out Finn was a half-elf cleric who leaned chaotic good. He'd never make it on the dark side. His miniature was carefully painted with no exotic colors.

After I told everyone about my rogue character—chaotic neutral, thank you very much—Finn cleared his throat. "I, uh, didn't have a rogue miniature, but I thought you could use this elf-bard I had from an old campaign." He held out another painstakingly detailed miniature. It was blond and wore a hat.

My mouth dropped open, and I took it from his hand. "Finn! This is amazing! Thank you so much." I leaned over and kissed him on the corner of his mouth. Oh, shit. I froze, staring at him. I was pretty sure the friends with benefits handbook didn't cover public displays of affection.

He gave me a little smile, and started to say, "You're welcome," but Jason interrupted.

"Hold up there. I didn't expect this development."

Finn looked at me questioningly. I guessed I had to decide how to proceed. Nothing for it but to own it. I shrugged nonchalantly, putting on my best rockstar-of-the-world persona. "Finn and I are spending some time together while I'm in town. I didn't mean to distract everyone from the game, though. Andre, what's your character?"

No one brought up me and Finn for the rest of the night. But what they did talk about, when we were taking breaks from the game, were moments from their shared history. They were all around the same age. I was at least ten years younger. Most of these guys had gone to school together. Maybe not all in the same grade, but they'd grown up knowing each other.

Me, I'd had my siblings. Well, after Mom died and Dad had sent Steve to live with Grandfather, I'd at least had most of my siblings. And now Dirk and I had Steve back, and Mona stayed in touch, but Heath and Hunter had gone no contact.

I didn't really have friends my age. I was friendly with Steve's friends in Texas, and I had a relationship of my own with Wesley and his husband, but they were decades older than me. I did text with Poppy every few days, but she didn't have a lot of downtime. I didn't have anyone to hang out with like this. Joke around with, talk about shared experiences with.

A lyric crystalized in my mind. And another. And another. Holy shit, I had the song! I stood up from the table, and everyone looked at me. "I'll be back in a few. Finn, you play for me, okay?" I didn't wait for a reply, just rushed to Charles' room and grabbed his guitar. I caught a glimpse of his room, and it wasn't too messy, just covered in typical teenage clutter. I took the guitar into Finn's bedroom where I could shut the door and not disturb the others.

I sat on the end of the bed and opened the dictation app I used for songwriting. Quickly I spoke the lyrics so I wouldn't forget them. Then I strummed Charles' guitar. The riff I'd come up with earlier melded seamlessly with the new lyrics. Additional words flowed easily. Finally I was in the zone.

TEXT CONVERSATION FRIDAY, 5:33 P.M

ALEX:

I'll be there around 6:30

FINN:

I should be home by then, but if I'm not, Drake's already there.

ALEX:

This is me absolutely NOT bringing up the fact that this is not how people behave with hookups

FINN:

I think we're at the friends with benefits stage, so fuck off

CHAPTER 10
FINN

Friday, five days before the festival

"Did we offend him, or did he just need to take a shit?" Alex glanced toward the hallway where Drake had vanished.

I shrugged. "I don't think he was upset." Though he *had* been quiet for a few minutes before he'd left the room. "I'll go check on him if he doesn't come back soon."

Alex started the game up again, but my attention was split between finding the dragon's egg and worrying about Drake. From the way the others kept glancing toward the hallway where he'd gone, I wasn't the only one. After twenty minutes had gone by, I asked Alex if we could take a break. "I want to check on Drake."

He nodded and everyone else looked relieved. I headed down the hall toward the bedrooms and my study. The door to my room was shut. I reached out to knock when I heard music. Live music. Drake was in my bedroom playing the guitar and singing. He stopped in the middle of a line and tried it again with different phrasing. Then he started over. The song was lovely, and I got a lump in my throat from listening to those few lines.

It finally occurred to me that I was eavesdropping, so I backed quietly down the hall. When I returned to the kitchen, everyone went silent.

Alex gestured impatiently. "Well?"

I smiled. "He's playing the guitar, and it sounds like he's writing a song. From what I heard, it's about friendship." I gestured at everyone. "I think maybe we inspired him."

Everyone grinned and looked at each other. Sam and Jason gave each other half-hugs. I exchanged a smile with Alex. These weren't all of my friends, of course, but they were a large portion of them. We'd all stayed in or gravitated back to Maplewood and each other. I wouldn't be surprised if we were still hanging out together thirty years from now.

We returned to the game, but everyone kept an ear out for Drake. He emerged after a little over an hour had gone by. He came into the kitchen with a regretful smile on his face. "I'm so sorry, y'all. It was incredibly rude of me to disappear like that."

Alex waved this away. "No worries. I had the evil mage hit your character with a freezing spell, and no one's found a way to release you yet."

Drake's smile changed to relief. "Thanks. I've been struggling with a song, and I suddenly had an idea. I had to work on it while it was in my brain."

I pulled out his chair to indicate he should sit. "That's completely understandable. You want a fresh beer?"

Alex held up a hand. "Hold on. I think we deserve to hear this song, since you deprived us of your company for so long."

I expected Drake to decline, or at least to seem reluctant, but to my surprise he lit up.

"Would you mind? I could use some feedback."

"Hell yes! Bring it. Who wants a beer?" Jason stood up and headed for the fridge.

Drake went to go get Charles' guitar, so I got him a new beer and a glass of water in case that was better for singing.

When he returned with the guitar, Drake pulled his chair away from the table so we could all see him more easily. "I'm still working on the title, but as of right now this is called 'Better Than Blood'." He strummed the melody I'd heard earlier and started to sing.

Holy fuck, he was good. I was probably a little biased, but I couldn't understand why Drake wasn't a huge celebrity like Harry Styles.

One lyric in particular stuck with me. "Forged from memories, lost and found. You held me up when blood let me down." I looked around the table at my friends, and I thought, yes. I couldn't say any of my family had let me down, but if they had, these guys—Alex in particular—would've been there for me instead. Drake must have a similar friend group to know that feeling.

He brought the song to a close, and we all clapped and whistled. Drake smiled. "You liked it?"

"Loved it. The message is beautiful." I rubbed my chest.

Andre nodded. "You've got a hit there. When are you going to release it?"

Drake shook his head. "That lifestyle's not for me anymore. I'm done with albums and touring. I'm making a living as a songwriter now."

I could absolutely understand his point. But, wait, did that mean Drake didn't have schedule commitments? Could he stay in Maplewood a little longer?

"*Oooh.*" Sam pursed his lips thoughtfully. "Who should sing the song then? It's kind of got an Ed Sheeran vibe. *Hmmm.*"

Drake chuckled. "I'm sort of obligated to offer all of my songs to Poppy first, unless I've got a really good excuse."

We all blinked at him. Alex found his voice first. "You

know *Poppy*? I mean, she's headlining the music festival. But you *know* her, know her?"

He laughed. "We're friends, yeah. Or, I guess, I'm better friends with her father-in-law, so she became my friend by default." He shrugged like this was no big deal.

We all looked at each other until Jason asked, "Who's her father-in-law? Should we know this?"

Sam gasped. "Wait! I remember. It was like five or so years ago. She's married to Jake Lord's son, right?"

Drake nodded. "Yep. His name is Mac."

"So you're friends with Jake Lord?"

"I am. I met him through my brother Steve, and we all live in the same little town outside of Austin. My brother Dirk lives there too, when he's not filming movies."

I got up to clear the dishes, letting the others pepper Drake with celebrity questions. Poppy and Jake Lord might be more famous, but Drake was just as good a musician. Maybe better.

In my opinion.

We all agreed to finish the campaign another night. It took another thirty or so minutes for everyone to leave. Drake helped me load the dishwasher and take out the trash.

"All done." He shut the back door and went to the sink to wash his hands.

"Thanks. Chores aren't very sexy, but I appreciate the help."

He threw me a wink as he dried his hands. "I don't know. I guess it'd depend on what we were wearing."

I let my body relax, hooking a thumb into the hip pocket of my scrub pants. Oof. Speaking of not sexy. At least I'd taken my fanny pack off. Fuck it. Drake was giving me a good once-over, so the scrubs must not bother him. I'd roll with it. "If I had my way, I'd like to see you in one of your hats and that's it.

Maybe a jock." I tipped my head to the side as I envisioned this. "Definitely a jock."

He prowled over to me. "I could arrange that. Too bad I didn't bring one with me on this trip." He stopped only inches away. "I do have a hat though. So instead of a jock, maybe I could wear your cock." He froze, then his face screwed up in a grimace.

I grabbed at the kitchen island for support as I doubled over in laughter.

He threw his hands in the air. "It sounded much better in my head!"

I straightened, trying to compose myself. "No, it sounded like something a serial killer would say!" I lost it again, my eyes tearing up from my giggles.

Drake huffed. "Too bad you'll never see me naked except for my hat after this."

I sobered, though I couldn't keep my lips from curling up. "Probably for the best. I think I'd laugh every time I looked at your hat. It'd kill the mood."

He raised an eyebrow and lifted his chin. "Are you done? I'd like to get to the fucking part of this evening." Without waiting for a reply, he spun around and walked out of the kitchen.

I wasted no time following, and I rounded the corner of the hallway in time to see him pull his t-shirt over his head. I loved watching the play of his muscles under the smooth skin of his back. He tossed the shirt behind him so I was forced to catch it. I started to make a sarcastic comment, but I caught his scent on the fabric. Some sort of spicy ocean fragrance, with an undercurrent of light sweat. I brought the t-shirt to my face and inhaled deeply.

Of course that was exactly when Drake, his hands on the button of his shorts, looked over his shoulder. I froze in place, and he stopped in his tracks. Then he smiled a slow, sexy smirk as he pulled down his zipper and spread open his fly. "Isn't there somewhere else you'd rather put your face?"

I dropped the t-shirt and stalked toward him. "Take them off. Let me see you."

He eyed me up and down. "Gotta pay to play, Finn. Show me some skin before I show you any more of mine."

I whipped the scrub top over my head and threw it to the floor, thankful it'd been warm today and I hadn't worn a t-shirt underneath. "I've been dreaming about getting you naked all fucking day." I reached out and traced a finger from his jaw, down his throat, to his pec. I rubbed my thumb across his nipple, and he sucked in a breath.

He pulled me closer, and we kissed hard and furious, with no finesse, just devouring each other. I shoved him back against the hallway wall before using my tongue to trace the path my finger had taken. He gripped my hair hard, pulling my face into his chest as I sucked on the nipple I'd toyed with. Drake bucked his hips forward and cried out when I bit down gently.

He grabbed my hair and yanked my head back. His eyes were wild, his lips swollen from our kiss. "Bed, now, or I won't last."

I straightened up to my full height. "Last for what? Was there something you were planning?" I pulled him into my body and shoved my leaking cock, still in my scrub pants, into the vee of his open zipper. The metal dug through the material of my pants and boxers to bite at my skin, but it was just the right side of painful, so I didn't move away. Drake's cock was hot and hard against me.

He stuck his hands down the back of my scrub pants and into my boxers, grabbing my ass cheeks and pulling me forward. I nuzzled into his neck as he breathed out. "I want you in me, and then I want to be inside you."

"Yeah?" It'd been a while since I'd bottomed, but I was

open to it. We'd shared our test results via email earlier today, so we could go without condoms if he was willing. I shivered at the thought. But.... "Not sure I can go two rounds in one night. I'm not twenty-two anymore."

I felt his smile against my cheek as I licked his earlobe. "No worries. There's always tomorrow morning." He lifted one leg and wrapped it around my thigh, pressing harder into my cock.

"Ouch!" I stumbled back, bending forward to get my balls away from the pinch of his zipper. Drake wasn't expecting the move, and he hung off my shoulders as he tried to get his legs under him. I didn't have any leverage, and we went down. Drake slamming to the hallway floor butt-first before I fell on top of him, pushing him flat.

I scrambled off of him. "Are you okay? Did you hit your head? Does anything hurt?"

Drake shook his head as he wiped his hand over his face. I relaxed when I saw he was grinning. "I'm fine. You're the one who said *Ouch*. What happened?"

I grimaced and reached down to gently fondle my junk. No blood, thankfully. "Your zipper pinched my balls."

His eyes went wide. "Oh, shit. I'm so sorry. Are you okay?"

"I'm fine. Don't worry about it."

His expression turned sly. "How can you be sure without a physical examination?"

I laughed. "How indeed. Want to take this to the bed?" I got to my feet and held out a hand to help him up.

He stood, letting the shorts fall to the floor before pulling them up again. "Fucking boots." Holding his shorts up around his thighs, he waddled to the bedroom and sat on the end of the bed. He put his right foot across his knee and grasped the boot, but then he eyed me speculatively. With a cheeky smile he leaned back on his elbows and raised his boot in the air, wiggling it in my direction. "Help, please."

I shook my head at him, but I couldn't stop smiling as I pulled off first one, then the other boot. I tossed them aside and ran my hands up his legs. "These shorts have been driving me crazy since this morning."

"Good. Take them off." He lifted his ass so I could slide the shorts down his long legs. I took my time peeling off his bright blue boxer-briefs to free his straining cock. It smacked against his belly, and he grunted.

Admiring Drake's naked body, with his young, unlined skin, I stood up and toed off my shoes as I pushed my scrubs and boxers to my ankles before stepping out of them.

"Lube?" Drake scooted up the bed toward the pillows. "I'm on PrEP and you saw my test results. I'm good to go without condoms if you are."

Fuck. I gave my cock a firm stroke. "Yeah." My voice was rusty sounding. "Me too. I'll get the lube." I walked over to the nightstand and pulled out the bottle. Drake reached for it, but I held it back. "No, I want to."

One side of his mouth curled up. "Knock yourself out." He made a production of arranging the pillows under his head and hips while I got on the bed. I should probably have pulled the comforter down, but it could be washed.

Drake held his knees to his chest and watched me with glittering eyes as I warmed lube between my hands. His balls were high and tight. I needed to make sure I didn't set him off with my fingers.

I circled his hole, and he relaxed his body, allowing me to slip one finger inside. "Fuck, you feel good." I gripped the lube bottle tighter with my free hand so I wouldn't jerk myself to orgasm before I could get inside him.

He wriggled his hips, trying to move toward me. "More. Hurry. I like a little burn."

I kept my eyes on his as I entered him with two fingers. He moaned, and I wasn't anywhere near his prostate.

"Put in the third. I need your cock."

Not as much as I needed to be inside him. I gritted my teeth as I poured more lube on my hand, my cock hard enough I felt like I'd blow if I even touched it.

He took three fingers easily. "I'm ready. Do it." His face was flushed, and sweat dampened the hair at his temples. He let go of one of his legs to grab my arm. "In me." He practically bared his teeth.

I slid my fingers out of his body and wiped the excess lube on my cock. Drake pulled at my arm, as if he could drag me into his hole.

I grinned, pausing with my cockhead barely touching his entrance. He bucked his hips to get closer, and I dragged a finger down the underside of his cock, enjoying his shout of frustration. "You know, Drake, there's a benefit to getting older. I might not be able to get it up as many times per night as you, but there's something I know I can do that you probably can't."

I pushed in, just a little, just enough for my crown to slide into his hole. God, he felt so good.

Drake moaned, "Yes! More."

I held still, resisting the urge to plunge completely into his writhing body. "Not yet. I haven't finished telling you about my old guy superpower."

He gave me a death stare. "How are you even able to have a conversation right now? Will you fuck me already?"

I pulled at his legs until they were over my shoulders, allowing him to impale himself on my cock and press his ass flush with my body. I managed not to cry out at the feel of his heat surrounding me, but it was close. I feigned a relaxed smile. "That's what I've been trying to tell you, Drake. Being older means I have stamina. I can do this all night without coming. Maybe torment you with tiny little thrusts." I demonstrated by moving my hips only millimeters.

I laughed at his glare. "Or, I could fuck you at the wrong angle, so you'll never quite get to the tipping point of your orgasm." I gave a stronger thrust this time, but I kept the pressure away from his prostate.

He whined and wiggled his hips in a circle, trying to get my cock where he wanted it. Fuck, I didn't have long before I came.

Drake's fingers were still clamped around my bicep, but he used his other hand to grab his dick. "I don't need you to come, asshole." His eyes fell shut as he stroked.

I knocked his hand away and took over, finally giving him the friction he needed, inside and on his cock. It took me three more thrusts to find the right angle, I knew I hit it when Drake shouted, his body bowing up toward me as he came. Long spurts of cum drenched his chest and abs as he clenched around my cock, setting off my own orgasm.

After we'd stopped shuddering, we both relaxed, and I clasped him to my body, ignoring the cum squelching between us. He grimaced as I slid out of him, and his legs fell to either side of me.

I kissed him gently, then I stroked his sweaty hair off of his face. "Am I too heavy?"

"No." He ran his hand over my shoulder. "But you're kind of an asshole in bed."

I laughed. "Don't you think I'm an asshole out of bed too?"

He shrugged, looking down to where he was toying with my chest hair. "You're not too bad." His eyes flashed up to mine. "Sometimes. Unlike just now." He tickled my side, not letting up until, laughing, I pulled him into a kiss.

MAPLEWOOD MATTERS BLOG, SATURDAY 6:18 A.M

Well, well, well. Guess whose car was left in a certain vet clinic parking lot overnight?

And we all know the home of our beloved Dr. Finn Hunnicutt is only a few steps away. This blogger has it on good authority that the younger member of the household was spending the night elsewhere, leaving the doctor free to entertain visitors....

CHAPTER 11

DRAKE

Saturday, four days before the festival

I woke up to pee just past 3:00 a.m. When I got back under the sheet—all we had left after we'd destroyed the comforter—Finn reached out and pulled me against him.

Fuck, was cuddling part of this... whatever the fuck we were doing? My dick liked it at least. I rolled into Finn's body and threw my leg over his hips. I chuckled at his erection. "I guess you're awake."

He didn't respond, just turned and kissed me, rubbing his straining cock against mine. I broke away from his lips to spit into my palm, then I gripped us together as Finn attacked my mouth. He pushed against me until I was on my back, and he braced himself over my body, driving into my fist and sliding exquisitely along my dick. We both came within minutes.

He kissed me once more before rolling off me, onto his back. We lay there panting and trying to cool down. Eventually he got up to get something to clean us off with, and he pulled the sheet up over us again. I was still too warm to cuddle, but it was nice to be next to someone.

"I haven't slept—like sleep slept—with very many guys."

He turned his head on the pillow. "No? Not many long-term partners?"

I shook my head. "None. Only hookups. We traveled so much." I shrugged. "And no one really caught my attention, you know?"

"Yeah."

Our hands brushed under the sheet, and he put his palm against mine and laced our fingers together. I swallowed against the rush of emotion it caused. Just post-sex hormones, I told myself, blinking my prickling eyes.

Finn cleared his throat. "I talked to Charles about my lack of dates since he's been here. And about you and me *dating*." He lifted his free hand to make air quotes.

"Yeah? What'd you tell him?"

He grimaced. "I told him I hadn't been going on any dates since he'd come to live with me because I wanted him to feel secure, that this was his home and he came first. I told him I'd planned to give it six months or so and then talk to him before I went out with anyone."

I snorted. "That you told him about, you mean."

"Well, yeah. Anyway, he said...." He coughed, and I could see his grin in the dark of the room. "He said essentially it was a miracle a sexy, famous younger guy like you was interested in me, and I'd be an idiot not to go after you, because—and I quote—*This is your best chance since you'll be too old to date soon*."

I covered my mouth to stifle my laughter.

He rolled toward me so he could poke my side with his free hand. "Yuk it up, youngster. I can edge you for hours when you're least expecting it."

"Ha ha. I don't have that much of a hair trigger. I can probably edge you just as long." Which was a complete lie. "Anyway, how did Charles seem after your conversation? Does he understand he's not cockblocking you?"

"I think he got it. And I reminded him you were only here temporarily, so he shouldn't get his hopes up about us staying together."

Why did my chest ache when he said that? It was only practical, since we were merely friends with bennies, and I'd be back in Texas in less than two weeks. I squeezed his hand. "You're a good parent."

Finn blew out a breath. "I'm lucky he's almost an adult. He doesn't need a ton of actual parenting, just more guidance or whatever."

"As long as you're making an effort, that's what he'll remember. He's lucky to have you."

He sighed, then nodded. "I agree. I wish I could do more to help him through the grieving process though. I offered to find him a therapist, but he said he didn't need one. I'm worried he's hiding his pain."

I turned so I could put my free hand across his chest. "He probably is. Teenagers aren't known for sharing their feelings with the adults in their lives, even when it's something as huge as losing their parents." I hesitated. "I mentioned this before, but how are you doing with your own grief?"

He gave me a kind of twisted smile as he put his hand over mine on his chest. "I have good days and bad days. I always pictured Noelle and Jin retiring here in Maplewood. Her parents passed away a couple of years ago, but she kept the house she grew up in. It's a rental property now. Charlie— Charles, sorry—can decide what to do with it when he's an adult." He took a deep breath. "Did he tell you why he doesn't want to be called Charlie anymore?"

I shrugged. "No. I figured it was because he's a teenager and wants to sound more grown up."

Finn shook his head. "No. It's because he wants the name Charlie to be special to when his parents were alive."

"Ohhh. I get that."

"I do and I don't. I know it's not up to me, but I'm worried he's kind of... compartmentalizing his life. Making a before and after timeline so he can stuff his emotions into the before part. But that's a therapist-type question, and he refuses to see one. I've been making a point to tell him my memories of his parents, keep them present for him. He does seem to respond positively when I bring them up."

I squeezed his hand. "I'm sure you're helping him. One of the worst things about when my mom passed away was how my dad just sort of... stopped mentioning her. Me and my siblings could only talk about her when he wasn't around, or else he'd shut us down. So keep doing what you're doing."

He turned on his side to face me. "I overheard a little of your conversation with Charles the other night. It sounded like your father... wasn't great."

I couldn't stop a laugh. "That's an understatement."

"Will you tell me? You don't have to."

"I can, but it's a long story for the middle of the night."

He smiled. "Neither of us has to work tomorrow, and Charles probably won't be home until the afternoon. We can sleep in. Tell me." His expression was encouraging, like he really wanted to hear about my poor-little-rich-boy childhood.

"Okay, you asked for it. Um, Dirk and I are the youngest of six siblings. Our dad always wanted to be a famous musician himself, but Mom got pregnant with our oldest brother Steve, and Dad had to get a regular job. So he decided if he couldn't be a rock star, he'd make his kids do it, form a family musical act with him as our manager." I rolled my eyes, though I didn't know if Finn could see me in the dark. "Hence all of our soap opera-style names. Except for Steve. He was named after our grandfather."

"And all of you had musical talent?"

I grimaced. "Ding, ding. You win the prize for asking the right question. Steve can't carry a tune to save his life, and he was more interested in computers than guitars. But the rest of us were fucking musical prodigies, so guess who got shipped off to live with our grandfather a year or so after Mom died?"

Finn gasped. "No! Seriously? Your poor brother."

"Yeah. And once the band started to get noticed, Dad didn't want us distracted by worrying about Steve, so he told us Steve was jealous of us and he and grandfather hated us." I shut my eyes. "We believed him, because why wouldn't we? He was our dad. I never saw my grandfather again."

"Oh, shit. I'm so sorry." He let go of my hands to pull me into a hug. Fuck, when had someone other than Steve or Dirk hugged me? Okay, Poppy was a big hugger, but that was more greetings and goodbyes. This was comfort. I slid my arms around Finn and basked in the feeling of his warm skin under my cheek and chest, and his hands rubbing circles on my back.

"What about your brother? Did you ever see him again?"

I nodded against his chest. "Our grandfather died when Dirk and I were sixteen. Dad was livid when he found out his father had left his entire estate to Steve. He told all of us Steve had poisoned Grandfather's mind against us. We were all brainwashed to think of Steve as this evil person who hated his family, even though he'd never said or done anything to us siblings directly."

Finn's hands flexed on my back. "Your father's a fucking asshole."

"Hah. I haven't even mentioned how he withheld affection or gave us the silent treatment if we did something he didn't like. And he especially hated that all of us were queer. Anyway, the whole time we were making records and going on tour, Dad kept saying he had savings accounts set up for each of us, and we'd get access to them when we turned eighteen. Our older siblings didn't mention it, so Dirk and I never suspected there'd be an issue getting our money."

"Oh, boy."

"Yep. Right after our eighteenth birthday, we sat down with Dad and asked him to go over our accounts. He told us not to worry about the money, and he'd give us larger allowances now that we were adults. Heath, Hunter, and Mona had all agreed." I shook my head at the memory. "Dirk and I wanted to control our own money going forward, but Dad refused. He said the accounts were offshore and only he could access them."

"He embezzled the money."

"Exactly. Well, not according to him. And the law says only the money that came in after each of us turned eighteen was embezzled. Don't get me started. Anyway, Dirk and I were pissed. We started to dissect Dad's behavior, and for the first time we questioned all the crappy shit he'd told us."

"About your brother and your grandfather."

"Right. We went to visit Steve, and he told us how he'd been deliberately iced out of the family by our father. Dirk and I live near him now, at least when we're not traveling. Mona has a good relationship with him too, but Heath and Hunter are weirdly loyal to Dad, even though they know he stole their money."

"Your dad's not in jail?"

I snorted. "As soon as he was served the papers saying we were suing him, he left the country. He's out there somewhere living off our money, but I'll be happy as long as we never hear from him again." I sighed. "So, if you're sleeping with me to get at the piles of cash you think I have lying around, I have some disappointing news for you."

Finn chuckled, his chest lifting up and down. "I'll keep that in mind. So you're making your living as a songwriter these days? You made it sound like you traveled a lot. Is that necessary for being a songwriter?"

"No, thank fuck. But Dirk and I were touring up until a couple of months ago, when he got a part in a movie. He wants to be an actor. I was planning to just work from home, but Wesley—that's Jake Lord to you and everyone else—asked me to come here and help Zeke out."

He toyed with my fingers. "I'm glad you agreed."

"*Mmmm.* Me too."

He frowned. "I've been meaning to ask, is Zeke sick or something? It's none of my business, but in the past he's always seemed to run the music festival with a sort of my-way-or-the-highway method. I'm shocked at how he's hardly been around since you got here."

"He hasn't said anything to me, and Wesley didn't really give me a reason." I kind of wanted to complain about getting the entire festival dumped in my lap with no preparation, but I kept my mouth shut. That was between me and Zeke.

Finn brought my hand up to his lips and kissed the tip of my thumb. "I may not be able to help you with the festival, but I can certainly help you relax in your free time." He eased my thumb into his mouth.

I grinned as I slid my leg over his hips. "I'd love to take you up on that."

"*Ew*! Finn! You can't clean up after yourselves? I don't want to see your... sex clothes all over the house!"

I came awake to Charles marching past the open doorway with one hand over his eyes. With the other hand he threw the shirts Finn and I had left on the floor last night on our way to the bedroom.

Kirk and a teenager I'd never met peered in and waved at us as they followed Charles toward his room. I tugged at the sheet covering me and Finn to make sure we weren't flashing anyone.

Finn groaned in my ear. "Aren't teenagers supposed to sleep until noon?" He was spooned around me, his morning wood pressed against my ass. What a waste of a good boner.

"What time is it?" My phone was in the pocket of my shorts, which were on the floor.

He heaved a sigh before twisting his upper body, presumably to look at the clock on the nightstand. "Not even 10:00 a.m."

"Fuck." I burrowed my head into the pillow. "I suppose we need to get up and find out why they're here." Then I sighed. "I need to go feed the chickens and Dolores anyway. They'll be pissed about how late it is."

"Wait a few more minutes. Maybe they just stopped by to pick up a game or something. I'd prefer not to get arrested for exposing myself to teenagers when I get up to close the door."

But they didn't leave.

I looked over the side of the bed. "I can't reach any of our clothes from here. Why don't we both get up with the sheet held in front of us?"

"Yeah, okay."

Holding the sheet firmly against the front of my body, I sat up. Finn scooted around me until he was also facing the open door. We pulled the sheet off the bed and held it between us and the hallway as we rushed over to shut the door.

When we were safe from accidental eyes, Finn dropped the sheet and rubbed his face. "Want to grab a quick shower?"

"You go first, since you're the one who has to see what the kids are up to." I picked up my shorts to get my phone.

"Lucky me." Finn grumbled under his breath all the way to the bathroom.

I unlocked my phone, which thankfully still had a charge. Zeke had texted.

ZEKE:

> Got home this morning. Took care of
> Dolores and the chickens, so no need to
> rush back. I tried to check on the eggs you
> told me about – figured out right quick why
> you put that one in her own coop. FYI,
> those egg drawers don't open so well when
> the hen is trying to peck you through the
> opening.

ZEKE:

> Thanks for handling everything while I was
> gone. You're doing a great job.

Why did the compliment make me tear up? Fuck, this was the second time in less than twelve hours. What was happening to me?

I took a deep breath. Okay. I was fine. Maybe I just needed to eat something. Heck, now that I didn't have to run back to Zeke's compound, I could take Finn out for brunch. We could spend the day together, if he was free.

Though I was pretty sure that wasn't what friends with benefits usually did.

Of course, friends with benefits also didn't usually cuddle while they talked about grieving processes and awful fathers in the middle of the night.

But this was casual. Finn and I had agreed on that, no matter what Charles was thinking. I'd go back to Texas, and Finn and I would one day remember our fling as a fun, temporary romp.

Except the thought of going back to Texas held zero appeal. I wanted to stay in Maplewood longer. I wanted to stay with Finn longer.

Look who'd gone and gotten emotionally invested.

Fuck. My. Life.

ME:

> Thanks, Zeke. I'm happy to help. I hope
> everything went okay with your trip.

After checking to make sure the shower was still running, I opened my text thread with Dirk.

ME:

> I fucked up. I'm falling for the veterinarian.

His reply was almost instantaneous.

DIRK:

Goddammit, I can't leave you on your own, can I? You want to come visit me after the festival is over? You can't come on set, but I can still help you drown your sorrows.

ME:

> I'm considering hanging around here for
> another week or so

DIRK:

The fuck? Can you call me? I don't have to be on set today.

ME:

> Not right now. Later.

The shower stopped. I grabbed my backpack and took it and my phone to the bathroom. Finn had stepped out of the tub, and he was toweling off his sexy, naked body.

I shut the door behind me so the warm air wouldn't escape. "Good news. Zeke's home and he fed Dolores and the chickens."

He looked up in alarm. "He didn't take the eggs, did he?"

I laughed. "No, I'd told him about them. But he did say he understood why Aragornette has her own coop."

"Good. So we have extra time together." He eyed me up

and down. My cock was immediately interested. Then he groaned. "Fuck. Right. Check on Charles first."

"And I need some food. Can I take you to breakfast? Or brunch, I guess?"

He smiled a slow, sinful smile. "Only if I can take you to bed afterward." He scowled. "Unless Charles and his friends decide to hang out here all day."

"We can always go to the cabin. I don't think Zeke will say anything."

"Perfect." He left the bathroom to get dressed.

I stood there staring at the door he'd shut behind him.

Friends with benefits didn't spend twenty-four hours together at a time.

But I hadn't been the only one suggesting it. Could Finn be interested in me romantically? How would I be able to tell? It's not like I'd ever been involved with anyone before. Dirk wouldn't know either.

But Steve would know. He was married and everything. He'd tell me what to look for, and then I'd know whether Finn thought what we were doing was just casual or if he wanted more.

Whew. I picked up my phone again. I felt so much better having a plan.

TEXT MESSAGE CONVERSATION, SATURDAY 10:12 A.M

DRAKE:

How do you tell if someone has feelings for you?

STEVE:

I have many questions. Can this be a phone call?

DRAKE:

No. I'm supposed to be taking a shower.

STEVE:

Do I need to manufacture an emergency so you can leave?

DRAKE:

No, you jerk. Just answer the question.

STEVE:

I think it depends on the person.

DRAKE:

Like what? How did you know Baz was interested in you?

STEVE:

His tongue down my throat, mostly

DRAKE:

Eww. I meant romantically

STEVE:

He told me.

DRAKE:

Well, fuck. What about Felix?

STEVE:

He and Malcolm hooked up, and they decided to be boyfriends almost the next day.

DRAKE:

That's no help. What about Cal? Didn't you say he started dating somebody a couple of months ago?

STEVE:

Yeah but they hated each other at first

DRAKE:

Perfect.

CHAPTER 12
FINN

Saturday, four days before the festival

I knocked on Charles' door. I heard whispering, then a burst of laughter. Great.

Still, after I was allowed to enter, it was good to see him smiling, even if it was more of a smirk. "Yes?" When had he learned to raise one eyebrow like that?

"I just wanted to check on you guys, since I didn't expect you home til later." I leaned around the doorframe and waved at Kirk and Tommy. They waved back with smirks of their own. Charles' computer was off, and his guitar was in its case. Clutter in the form of clothes and game cases were scattered around as usual, but none of the boys were holding anything. Charles' leather jacket was on the bed, so maybe they were about to leave?

"We're good." He didn't seem stressed out at least. What the hell had they been doing? *Talking?* If that was the case, why couldn't they do it at Kirk's house?

"Okay. Um, if you're going to hang out here, I'm taking Drake to breakfast."

He made a show of looking at his watch. "Don't you mean lunch?"

I rolled my eyes. "It's only a little after 10:00 a.m."

"You should take him to Sparky's. They have the best waffles." Kirk rubbed his stomach.

Tommy shook his head. "I like Red's better for breakfast. Their French toast is to die for."

They both gazed at Charles expectantly, as if he'd cast the deciding vote. He shrugged. "I haven't been to breakfast at either place."

You know those moments when time slows down, and you understand in your gut that your plans for the day—your plans involving naked time with Drake—are a lost cause? I had one of those moments when all three faces turned accusing looks in my direction.

Well, shit. "You're all welcome to join us. Let me go see when Drake'll be ready to leave, and you three decide where we're going."

I left them to debate diner options and retreated to my room. The shower was running. Would it be rude to go into the bathroom and talk to Drake right then? When he was wet and soapy, and....

And there were three teenagers in the house.

Sighing, I sat on my bed and scrolled through social media to pass the time until Drake emerged. Alex's video—the public version—had been a big hit on the clinic's feed. The other version, well, I was saving it for after Drake went home to Texas and I was alone again.

But, after last night when he'd said he could do his songwriting from anywhere, I was determined to do everything I could to get him to stay in Maplewood longer.

When he came out of the bathroom, Drake was wearing a pair of cherry red boxer briefs and nothing else. He grinned and walked over to me with an exaggerated undulation in his hips. Fuck.

I held up a hand. "The boys are going to breakfast with us."

He stopped moving, and his eyebrows flew up. "Is everything okay? Why did they stop by?"

I shook my head. "I have no idea. They didn't say, and I'm trying not to be all up in Charles' business. But they didn't look upset or anything."

"Good. Okay, let me get dressed and we can go."

The boys chose Red's diner, which I was grateful for, since Mickey had been at my house last night. I'd have felt awkward going to his archenemy's place of business mere hours later, even though I was friends with both families. That fucking feud was a pain in the ass.

After Bethany, who was a year ahead of the boys in school, brought coffee and we ordered, Drake looked around the table. "So, I think I deserve to know what was so important y'all felt it necessary to tromp through Finn's house so early." He lifted his mug and took a sip, all the while alternating his gaze between the three boys.

Charles broke first, bumping shoulders with Tommy. "Tommy here didn't believe I'd actually seen Mabel on Monday. I wanted to show him how badly my dad's jacket got scratched up from me running through the woods and falling on the road."

I had to stick my face in my coffee cup to give myself a reason to close my eyes. Just imagining what could've happened if there'd been more cars around when Charles fell, or if Drake hadn't been able to stop in time.... Fuck.

"You were pretty scared. I believed you'd seen something freaky."

The boys began to debate the existence of not only Mabel, but other "cryptids" they'd heard about on a podcast.

I looked at Drake. "Thanks for solving the mystery of what prompted their visit this morning."

He toasted me with his coffee cup and winked. "You can reward me later."

"Oh, can I?" I smirked. "How so?"

He leaned in. "You can come out to the compound and... help me clean the chicken coops." He wiggled his eyebrows.

I laughed. "Count me in. I wouldn't want you to... clean the chicken coops by yourself."

Charles whipped his head around and gasped. His eyes flicked between me and Drake, and his face drained of color.

I frowned. "What's wrong?"

He shook his head, his lips pressed together. I couldn't ask again because Bethany came to the table with an enormous tray to drop off our food. She passed out the plates and told us to enjoy our meal, then she was gone.

Everyone dug into their food except Charles. He poked at his eggs with his fork, but he didn't eat.

He'd been fine just before Drake and I had started flirting with each other. Was that what was bothering him?

Kirk asked Charles something about his guitar lessons, but Charles acted like he didn't hear him. We all waited a moment, and then Drake asked Kirk how long he'd been taking his own lessons.

I let Drake carry the conversation, eating about half my food while Charles stared at his plate, stewing over whatever was bothering him. When he still hadn't eaten anything, I knew I had to say something. Fucking hell, Noelle, I was not cut out for this.

I nudged him with my elbow and spoke in a low tone. "Tell me what's wrong."

When he turned his head to face me, I gaped at the tears welling in his eyes. "Charles! What's the matter?" On my other side, Drake paused what he was saying for a second but then continued on in a slightly louder tone. Fuck, he was probably better parent material than I was.

Charles swiped the back of his hand over his cheeks. "Sorry. I know I told you I was okay with you dating. But I didn't expect...." He tried to stifle a sob, and my heart sank. He wasn't ready for me to date after all.

I put my arm around his shoulders. "Hey, remember what I said. You come first. If you need me to focus on you for a while, I can do that." Drake paused again, then resolutely kept talking. He was telling the boys about his brother who was making a video game or something. Fuck, this was a disaster.

Charles shook his head. "It's not that. I just...." He threw up his hands and slid out of my hold to shove his chair back and stand up. "I gotta get some air." He took off toward the restaurant entrance.

Drake looked stricken, and Kirk and Tommy seemed to not know what to do.

I stood up. "Stay here. Finish your breakfasts. I'll catch up with you later, Drake."

He nodded, frowning. "I'll take care of the bill. I hope he's okay."

"He will be."

I wove through the tables to the front of the restaurant. I'd had a faint hope that Charles would be standing out front waiting for me to find him, but I wasn't that lucky.

I looked down the sidewalk in either direction, but he wasn't visible. Okay, to the left was a residential area Charles wouldn't be very familiar with, but to the right was home and the park. Right it was.

I walked as fast as I could without running. I was so focused on scanning the distance for Charles' blue hoodie, I nearly snapped at a couple of clients who tried to stop me to chat. I'd had to shout an apology over my shoulder as I strode past them.

I hesitated at the corner of Maple and Morgan. Would he go to the park or go home? It probably depended on whether he wanted me to find him right away or not.

Well, if he was home he'd stay there for the few minutes it would take me to search the park. I stepped off the curb to cross Maple, then I started to cross Morgan, jumping back with a yell when an oncoming car honked at me. Shit, I did not need to get run over. Charles had lost enough parents already.

After looking both ways for traffic this time, I crossed safely to the park. The main path had a good sightline to most of the area.

I nearly collapsed in relief when I saw the mop of brown hair, so like my own, on the south side of the park. He was sitting on the ground next to a tree with his head on his knees and his arms wrapped around his legs. I was lucky I'd noticed him, as he'd taken his hoodie off and was using it like a pillow on top of his knees.

Okay, what now? I could leave him be for a little while, but I didn't want him to think I didn't care enough to come after him. Shit. I'd have to wing it. Again.

I walked over, not trying to hide the sound of my footsteps in the spring grass. Charles' shoulders hunched further. He knew it was me.

I sat down a couple of feet away. In his space but not crowding him. I didn't speak, mostly because I wasn't sure of what to say. It was a little chilly in the shade, but Charles could put on his hoodie if he was cold. I leaned back on my hands and tilted my head up to look at the leaves overhead, trying to get my muscles to relax and my heart rate to slow down.

"Sorry I freaked out." He hadn't moved much, just turned

his head sideways in my direction. His eyes were red and his cheeks were blotchy.

I smiled and shook my head. "You didn't do anything wrong. In fact, if something was upsetting you, getting out of there was the best thing you could've done."

"I guess." He closed his eyes. "Drake probably thinks I hate him or something."

I kept my voice as relaxed as I could. "I doubt that. Do you wanna talk about what made you upset?"

He pressed his face into his hoodie again. "You'll think it's stupid." His voice was muffled but I could hear him.

"Hey." I scooted closer and put my arm around his shoulders. "You had an honest reaction. Nothing about that is stupid."

He shook his head and dropped his knees to the ground but remained hunched over, pressing the hoodie to his face as he sobbed.

Fuck. I put my other arm around him and pulled him into my chest. I hadn't seen him cry like this since his parents' funeral. Which didn't mean he hadn't *been* crying, of course.

When his tears slowed and he lifted his head, I offered him the end of one of his hoodie's sleeves, as it was still fairly dry. He chuckled and wiped his face. "Sorry."

"It's okay." I braced myself. "Did you change your mind about being okay with me and Drake dating?"

He looked at me with a shocked expression. "What? No!"

I exhaled with relief. "Okay. What made you so upset then?"

"What Drake was saying, how he was teasing you. It reminded me of how Mom and Dad were. They'd always say things that sounded like innuendos, but they'd be talking about doing chores or something else boring."

Right. Drake had invited me to help him clean the chicken coops. "I can see how that would've triggered a memory."

He turned his head away. "I miss them so much." He pressed his fist to his lips, and his body jerked with silent sobs.

"Let it out, Charlie. Sorry, Charles." Shit. Like he needed more reminders of his parents. And, yep, he was crying harder now. Fuck.

"I don't—" He sucked in a breath before letting out another sob. "I don't *like* being called Charles. I want to be Charlie again."

"Okay. You can be called whatever you decide. I like Charlie better too." Noelle had chosen the name Charles to honor one of her grandfathers. It wasn't like I'd had any say, but I'd been relieved when she'd used the nickname Charlie right away.

He nodded and his crying slowed. "I thought keeping the name for Mom and Dad would make it more special, but every time someone calls me Charles, it just reminds me that they're gone."

I squeezed him to my chest. "I'm sorry this is so hard, Charlie. I wish I could do something to help. I love you."

He went still. "Are you mad you got stuck with me?"

I frowned down at the top of his head. "No! Never. I wish I could've moved my job so you wouldn't have had to leave Seattle and your whole life there, but I'd have been upset if you'd ended up with someone else as your guardian."

He nodded. "Me too."

My heart felt like it would expand right out of my chest, and I couldn't stop a smile. I pressed a kiss to the top of his head. He only squirmed a little bit.

He was silent for a moment. "I think maybe it was good for me to leave. Here I don't expect to see Mom and Dad around every corner. And the people are nice. I like living with you." He turned his head to sneak a look at me. "Even if you won't get me a pet."

"Hey! I told you, if we don't find a stray by your birthday, you can pick out what you want. Within reason. No chickens."

He chuckled. Back in Seattle their family dog had passed away a few years ago. Noelle and Jin had told Charlie they wanted to travel after he went to college, so they weren't getting another pet.

But I missed having a pet in the house, so I was happy to do this for him.

He sat up and rubbed his face. Then he looked around the park. "Sorry I was being all whiny."

"Charlie. You need to express your emotions, even the uncomfortable ones. I don't expect you to act like everything's good when it's not."

He nodded and fiddled with the string on his hoodie. Should I try again? Fuck it, might as well. "Have you given any more thought about seeing a counselor? We could go together if that would make it easier."

"If I don't like it, can we stop going?"

"Um, well, sometimes the first counselor you try isn't the right fit. So if you don't like the first one, how about you promise to try one more before we call it quits?"

"Okay."

"Great." Thank fuck. "You ready to head home? You've got to be starving."

He winced. "What time is it? I feel bad for leaving the guys."

"Drake said he'd get their breakfasts. I'm sure they'd like to hear from you though, to make sure you're okay." And I needed to text Drake. But what would I say? "Um, about Drake...."

Charlie sat up and turned to face me. "I don't want you to stop seeing him, Finn. I like him. I just...." He spread out his hands. "I can't guarantee I won't have a freak-out again if you guys get, you know, romantic and shit." He must've seen my expression because he pointed a finger at me. "No. I don't want you to act all different or weird when I'm around. I'll get used to it, okay?"

"Okay, but it's not like anything Drake and I have can go anywhere. He lives in Texas."

Charlie rolled his eyes as he stood up. "For now."

MAPLEWOOD MATTERS BLOG, SATURDAY 1:26 P.M

Onlookers were ecstatic to report what appeared at first to be a heartwarming scene, a family meal at Red's with our beloved veterinarian and a certain much younger musician, along with Charles and his friends. Were we witnessing the beginning of a long-term romance?

Sadly, a conflict of unknown origin occurred, resulting in the vet following Charles out of the diner and not returning. According to eyewitnesses, the young musician appeared disheartened as he paid the bill. However, it was observed that he left a large tip, so at least Bethany had a good morning.

CHAPTER 13

DRAKE

Saturday, four days before the festival starts

Around 3:00 p.m. I finished cleaning the chicken coops. Okay, I didn't do a great job on Aragornette's coop, but she was still in *Hulk Smash* mode. I needed to look up how long eggs needed to incubate before they hatched.

Zeke had offered to help me with the chore, but I needed the distraction. Plus, Zeke wasn't a spring chicken—hahaha—and he didn't need to be doing so much physical labor. I'd made a note in my phone to ask Nova about finding someone to come by and clean the coops after I went back to Texas.

I kept checking my phone for word from Finn, but there was nothing. Kirk and Tommy hadn't had any idea what had caused Charles to be so upset, and they'd looked as worried as I was. Probably for different reasons though.

Because if there'd been any thought left in my mind that what was between me and Finn was just friends with benefits, well, now I knew the truth. I was gone for him. Emotionally invested. Crushing at a minimum, but I knew it was more.

Fuck. My. Life.

Because, like Finn had said at the diner, Charles came first. I knew it. I agreed with it.

But I'd thought Charles approved of me dating Finn. He'd said so. He'd arranged to be out of the house last night so Finn and I could be alone.

If he'd changed his mind, well, that meant what Finn and I had was over. And I was devastated. Far more upset than I'd be if this was merely a convenient, casual hookup situation.

I dwelled on that depressing realization all through showering and changing clothes. Every moment while I ran a load of laundry and cleaned up the cabin.

Finally I sat down with my guitar. Might as well see if I could make some money off my heartache.

Before I could get started, my phone chimed with a text. I leapt for it, hoping it was Finn.

But it wasn't.

CAL:

Steve said you wanted to talk to me. I have some time for the next hour or so if you want to call.

Well, shit.

ME:

I think it's a moot point now, so never mind

CAL:

Now I'm even more intrigued. Steve wouldn't say what you wanted to talk about. Why don't you call me anyway? Maybe I can help

Ugh. My gut said not to call Cal and rehash my tale of woe. But if I didn't, he'd tell Steve, and then I'd have to endure Steve asking me what happened.

So I set my guitar aside, flopped back onto the couch cushions, and called.

"Hey. Tell Uncle Cal what's going on."

I grimaced. "Please never refer to yourself as *Uncle Cal* ever again."

He chuckled. "Fine. Where are you, anyway?"

"Vermont." I told him how Wesley had asked me to help Zeke out.

"Okay. What was it you wanted to talk to me about? Even if it's no longer necessary."

I blew out a breath. "I met this guy."

"Ohhh."

"Yeah. We didn't get along at first, but... there was some mutual attraction. We decided to have a friends with bennies arrangement, but I started thinking it might be more. I was asking Steve how he knew Baz was attracted to him, but they didn't really have any sort of getting-to-know-you period before they started dating."

"Got it. You picked me because Greg and I weren't big fans of each other before we got together."

"Exactly. But, like I said, it doesn't matter." I explained Charles's outburst and what Finn had said about putting Charles first. "Which I fully support, by the way. It just sucks for me, because I'm pretty heavily into Finn."

"But he hasn't said he's ending things?"

"No. I don't think he's ghosting me, though I could be wrong."

"Yeah, it's a little early to make that assumption. He's probably hanging out with the kid."

"Right."

"Okay, well, while you wait, I can tell you how I knew Greg was attracted to me."

I sat up. "Tell me."

"From the moment we met, there was this sort of

magnetic pull between us. I know that sounds kind of woo-woo, but it's the best way I have to explain it. But also he would *look* at me, you know? Like he couldn't *not* look at me. And he gets anxious in crowds, but if I was next to him, or, even better, physically touching him, he'd relax."

"Huh."

"Does that help?"

"I think so." I didn't know about any magnetic pull, but I'd certainly caught Finn staring at me from time to time.

"You're a smart guy, Drake. If Finn wasn't into you, you'd be able to tell."

I sighed. "Yeah. I know. I guess I was just looking for validation."

"Nothing wrong with that. What are you going to do to take your mind off things?"

I fiddled with one of my guitar pegs. "Write a song about my feelings."

He laughed. "I wish I had that sort of outlet. But also consider going somewhere with people. Get out of the house. Not only will it distract you, it'll show Finn you're not moping around waiting for him to make the next move. Surely there's a bar or pub or something there."

"That's a good idea, thanks."

"Do you like the place outside of your relationship drama?"

I grinned. "I kind of do. It's super weird. Get this, every night I have to go into the woods to serve dinner to this weird forest creature who may or may not exist."

"What? What forest creature?" His tone was oddly sharp and urgent.

"Her name is Mabel. According to the locals, she's tall and covered in leaves."

"But you've never seen her?"

"Not me." I told Cal about Charles' run-in with Mabel.

"Huh."

"What's with all the questions? Are you into cryptids or something?"

"Oh. Um, you know I'm a geek at heart. Cryptids are cool. Even Greg thinks so."

"Got it."

We chatted for a few minutes longer. Cal promised me a copy of the game he and Steve were developing as soon as it was ready, and I told him I'd send him a copy of my "song of woe", as he put it, as soon as somebody recorded it.

I did feel better once we hung up. And Cal had made a good point about going out and being seen in public tonight. I didn't have to stay out long, but I did want to be visible so Finn wouldn't think I was at home pining for him or anything.

Even though that was exactly what I'd been doing.

I dragged the guitar onto my lap and thought about Finn, about my interactions with him, and how he'd made me feel. The words came before the melody, which didn't always happen. But I got them into my phone's dictation app in less than twenty minutes, and I was pretty damn happy with the results. Turned out I *could* make money from my heartache.

The melody, however, wasn't as cooperative. In the past I would've just asked Dirk for feedback, but nowadays I was songwriting solo. I decided to let the melody percolate in my brain overnight and, per Cal's suggestion, go out. Maplewood had a pub, The Striped Maple, and a bar with food called The Forbidden Maple. I decided The Forbidden Maple sounded more exotic, so I'd try that.

Since I'd be indoors most of the evening, I regretfully left my hats at the cabin. When I went to get in my SUV, I was surprised to see Agnes, one of the Rocktogenarians I'd met at Sparky's yesterday, sitting on the porch with Zeke. The two of them were drinking something that looked like an Arnold

Palmer. However, based on how much they were laughing, I was betting they'd added an additional alcoholic ingredient to the tea and lemonade.

Zeke agreed to feed Mabel, and Agnes seemed excited to go with him to drop off the food. Excellent.

It was still fairly early, so I had no trouble finding a parking spot outside the restaurant. The Forbidden Maple had a kind of speakeasy vibe. I didn't have any trouble getting a table, and the prime rib with garlic mashed potatoes was excellent. I finished my dinner right as the place was starting to get completely full.

My phone chimed. It was Finn. All I could see on the preview was, "Charlie's okay. He got emotional because our flirting reminded him of his...."

Well, I could guess the rest. My formerly delicious dinner sat heavily in my stomach. Did I want to read the remainder of it now? Alex, Mickey, Jason, and Sam were walking toward a back room with some big blond guy. I could go hang out with them. I looked down at my phone. I'd never be able to relax with that fucking text hanging over my head. At least if I got confirmation that Finn and I were done, I could drown my sorrows without any additional stress.

Sighing, I opened the text thread.

FINN:

Charlie's okay. He got emotional because our flirting reminded him of his parents. We talked it out and he agreed to go to therapy if I went with him. He's good with us seeing each other. I'm sorry it took me so long to get in touch. I had to feed Charlie, then my phone died and while I was charging it I fell asleep, and a bunch of other bullshit reasons that are completely my fault. Please forgive me. I hope you'll still let me help you clean your chicken coop. [winky face emoji]

I sagged in my chair. Thank fuck. As today had proved, I was not ready to let Finn go yet.

On the other hand, apology aside, where did he get off not contacting me for—I checked my watch—over seven hours after what happened earlier? That must've been some nap he'd had. We'd been pretty active on and off all night, but still.

A little payback was in order. He could put some effort in.

ME:

Glad to hear Charlie's okay, and that he's okay with us. I'm out having drinks if you want to join me.

FINN:

Yes, please. Where are you?

With an evil smile, I shut my phone off. This restaurant was about equal distance from Finn's house as The Striped Maple, but in a different direction. I'd see how long it took him to track me down.

Was it petty? Yes. Was it fair? No. Did I enjoy it? Yes.

Sometimes I let myself act my age. Brattiness for the win.

The server brought my check, so after I paid, I took the rest of my beer and wandered to the back room to see what the guys were up to.

They were all standing around a bar-height table. Sam was the first to spot me. "Hey, Drake! How are you?"

"Great. You mind if I join y'all?"

Everyone seemed glad to have me. Jason introduced me to his boyfriend Bellamy, who had blond hair and blue eyes a little bit darker than mine. I shook his hand. "Damn, man, too bad I already have a ton of brothers, because you'd fit right in."

He grinned, and I immediately clocked how his expression changed from slightly wary to relaxed. This guy was some sort of celebrity, or I'd eat my hat. Not really, though, because I liked my hats too much.

I wound my way over to Alex. "Hey."

"Hey. I was getting ready to text you. I heard Charles had some sort of outburst at Red's today, but Finn hasn't returned my texts. What happened?"

I grimaced. "I'm still not sure exactly, but something I said triggered him. Finn told me Charles was fine, but he only got around to texting me a few minutes ago, so I don't have any details."

Alex blinked. "But gossip said that happened before noon."

I raised my eyebrows. "Which is why I'd appreciate it if you didn't respond if Finn texts you asking if you've seen me tonight. I told him I was out having a drink, and he could join me. But I didn't say where I was."

His face broke into a wicked smile. "Payback's a bitch. I've got you."

"Thanks. I'm sure he'll find me eventually, but he can work for it." I drained the rest of my beer. "I'll be right back." I lifted my empty bottle and he nodded.

The bar was getting more crowded, and I had to slide between two guys to get to a spot where a bartender might see me.

"Well, hello. I don't think we've met. Are you new in town?"

Shit, it was yet *another* attractive man. Maplewood was awesome. This one was around six feet tall, with black hair and brown eyes surrounded by the thickest lashes I'd seen on a guy. He gave me a flirty once-over.

"Hi. Yeah, I'm visiting." I looked down the bar, but the bartenders were both occupied with other patrons.

"Welcome, then. I'm Cooper."

"Oh, who's this?" Another guy shoved Cooper aside. "Hi, I'm Denver." He was tall, with extremely close-shaved hair, blond eyebrows, and blue eyes. "You don't want to know this loser." He gently elbowed Cooper in the stomach, and Cooper pretended to be in pain.

"Y'all are cute." Somehow they'd maneuvered themselves between me and the bar, dammit. "Excuse me, I need to get by you so I can order."

"Not so fast." Cooper pulled himself up to his full height but he couldn't match Denver. "I didn't get your name."

I bit back a curse. This was the universe punishing me for sending Finn on a wild goose chase through the Maplewood bars. "I'm Drake. Can I get by, please?"

Denver sucked in a breath. "Drake Derry? The musician? You're dating Finn, right?"

I gave him my father's deadliest glare. "Something like that."

He held up his hands. "Hey, sorry, didn't mean to step on any toes." But he did move back a little, so I slid by him to take my place at the bar again.

"Hang on." Cooper sidled up next to me. "Are you and Finn like *together*? Or is it something where you're open to other people?"

"We're together, Cooper. Get lost." Huh. It hadn't taken Finn long at all to track me down. I was a little disappointed, to be perfectly honest.

Still, a not-so-small part of me thrilled at Finn angrily staring down Cooper, though the guy didn't seem to find him threatening. In fact, he patted Finn on the shoulder. "It never hurts to ask the question, Doc. Have a good night!" He threw me a wink as he melted into the crowd.

Finn aimed his frown at me. I smiled sunnily back. "Hi! You want a beer?" I turned back to the bar, which I'd kept hold of with one hand. No one was going to get my spot again, no way.

Finn didn't respond, so I looked back at him with an enquiring eyebrow lifted.

"Fine. Thank you."

I nodded and turned around again, smirking and chortling to myself.

"I can see you in the mirror, you know." Finn's mouth was next to my ear, and I shivered. "I guessed you were making me search for you on purpose."

I met his eyes in the mirror behind the shelves of bottles. I blew a kiss toward his reflection right as the bartender stepped in front of me.

The guy pretended to catch the kiss and held it to his heart. "Whoa! What'd I do to deserve that?" He was cute, with warm brown eyes and his hair shaved close to his head.

I laughed. "Just in the right place at the right time." Behind me, Finn put his arm around my shoulder.

The bartender's eyes twinkled. "Must be my lucky night. What can I get you?"

We ordered, and I busied myself with pulling out my wallet while the bartender grabbed our beers. Finn kept his hand on my shoulder as if he didn't want me to get away again. I bit my lip to keep from smiling, though I wasn't very successful. I was loving this show of possessive behavior.

As long as he eased off later, of course.

When we had our drinks, Finn used the hand on my shoulder to steer me out of the crowd. *Hmmm*. Okay, this was getting to be too much. I decided to allow it for now, but only because he was slightly taller than me. When we reached a more sparsely populated area, I twisted around to face him and, as a side effect, knock his hand off. "Alex is over there with Sam, Jason, and Mickey. Oh, and Jason's boyfriend."

He glanced over at them, then back to me. "Can we talk for a minute first?"

I nodded and he gestured toward an open space next to the wall. He didn't put his hand on me again, so he must've gotten the message.

I positioned myself so I could lean against the wall. Finn stood in front of me, fiddling with the label on his beer. "First, Charlie was upset because when we were flirting at the table it was very similar to how his parents used to flirt with each other."

I grimaced. "Poor kid."

"He said he doesn't want us to act any differently around him, but he can't guarantee he won't get sad again. I did get him to agree to see a grief counselor, but he wants me to go with him."

"Great. I'm a big believer in therapy." I smiled.

He smiled back but then his expression darkened. "I'm sorry I didn't contact you this afternoon. I meant to, but I didn't, and that's my fault entirely."

I hesitated, trying to decide how to respond. He seemed earnest, but I needed him to understand how serious this was. "Finn, did you understand that what Charles was saying at the diner made me think we were over?"

He winced. "It didn't seem quite so definitive to me."

I brought out my father's glare again. "Even if it wasn't *definitive*, you still knew it sounded bad."

He nodded, looking sad and pathetic. "I'm sorry. Again. The conversation with Charlie—and he wants to go back to being Charlie now, FYI—was intense. I was exhausted afterward, and I didn't prioritize letting you know everything was okay."

I turned my head so I could blink back tears. When I had myself under control I turned back to him. He'd noticed, based on his horrified expression. "Look, I know we're not officially together or anything. But I'd been starting to—never mind. My point is, you not contacting me all day was stressful and hurtful. I get that Charles—Charlie—comes first. But you can't tell me you didn't have two minutes where you could've told him you needed to send me a quick text?" My voice was getting louder, and I clamped my mouth shut, turning away again. Alex was staring at us from the back room with a concerned expression.

Finn's whole body drooped. "You're right. I need to do better. I *will* do better. I promise." He gave me puppy dog eyes exactly like Charlie's. "I'm sorry I hurt you. And I hope I haven't damaged your opinion of me too badly, because I'd really like to continue seeing you. Maybe even...." He furrowed his brows and looked down at his beer again. I waited, resisting the urge to ask him to finish his sentence. We weren't done with the other conversation, but this was leading somewhere important. He met my eyes again. "Maybe we could date for real? I know you don't live here, and I'm a lot older than you, but I—"

I stepped forward, put my hand on the back of his neck, and kissed him. "Yes. I'd like that."

He smiled. "Does that mean I'm forgiven for today? It won't happen again, I promise."

"You're forgiven. But, Finn, remember how I told you about my dad withholding his attention to punish us?"

He winced. "Shit."

"Yeah, it's pretty fucking triggering for me." I held up a hand. "I'm not asking you to smother me or anything, but I need to know I matter, okay? If something's going on, I need you to check in."

"I understand. And I will." He pulled me into a hug. I liked the feel of him against me. Holy shit, he was my boyfriend. Wait, or were we just dating? Dammit.

I pulled back. "Um, one more thing. Are we, like, boyfriends?" I made a face. "Because apparently I'm twelve years old."

He laughed and leaned in to kiss me. "I'm good with boyfriends."

TEXT CONVERSATION, SATURDAY 9:43 P.M

DRAKE:

So I seem to have acquired a boyfriend

STEVE:

Congrats! When do Baz and I get to meet him?

DIRK:

Hang on, what happened to "oh, we're just casual, it's just fucking"?

DRAKE:

Shit changes. You need to keep up

STEVE:

At least send us a picture

DRAKE:

Hang on. I'll get Alex to take one

DIRK:

Who's Alex? And, before you answer, are they or anyone there open to hooking up when I come visit you?

DRAKE:

[photo]

DRAKE:

You're visiting? I thought you were tied up with filming for the next two months?

DIRK:

I am. And you'll be living the small-town life by then. I hope that place has some decent bars

CHAPTER 14

FINN

Sunday, three days before the festival

I stretched, enjoying the cool sheets and the warmth of Drake's naked body cuddled against mine. He was curled up with his back against my side and his head on my left arm. I couldn't feel my hand, but I wasn't about to move.

I was still processing everything that'd happened yesterday. Charlie's meltdown, his agreeing to go to therapy, me having to grovel to Drake, Drake deliberately trying to piss me off. And us agreeing to be boyfriends. Which was a silly word, but I didn't feel like *partner* was any better. Boyfriend would do.

We'd celebrated our relationship with the guys at the pub, and then we'd come home and celebrated in a different way. But very quietly. Charlie had connected with Kirk and Tommy later in the day, and they'd ended up staying over here last night. I'd stuck my head in Charlie's room when we'd gotten home, but I still needed to tell him Drake and I had formalized our dating status.

I smiled down at his still form. He didn't move much in his sleep. Once he found a position he liked, he was out for the entire night.

My phone buzzed on the nightstand. Crap. I couldn't quite reach it, so I had to drag my arm from under Drake's neck so I could sit up.

"Huh?"

"Sorry. I was trying to get to the phone before it woke you."

He snorted and flopped onto his front. "What time is it?"

I looked at my phone. My mom had texted. Crap. "Um, it's 9:15."

"Who's texting you this early? Is it a pet emergency?"

"No, thankfully." I was on call this weekend, but it was rare we had an issue that couldn't wait. Mostly just pet parents wanting to know whether they should panic because their dog ate something it shouldn't have.

I opened Mom's text one-handed, as my left arm was still out of commission. "My mom wants to know what happened with Charlie at the diner."

He grunted. "Small-town gossip moves fast."

"You have no idea. There's a fucking blog."

He lifted his head. "You're shitting me."

"Nope. I'll show it to you sometime."

I texted Mom that everything was fine and I'd call her later. Then I tossed the phone onto the mattress next to my pillow and leaned over to kiss Drake. "Good morning, boyfriend."

He wrinkled his nose. "It's maybe not something we want to use to address each other, okay?"

I laughed. "Fine, but most of the common endearments are out for me."

"Yeah? Why's that?" He combed his fingers through my hair.

"Because people use those for pet names. And I mean names for their actual pets. I can't call you sweetheart or darling when they make me think of Sweetheart Francis, who's a cat, and Darling Khalil, who's an elderly pug."

He chuckled. "Baby?"

"Too many to count. My favorite is Baby Finkelstein, who's an African Gray parrot."

"Honey? No, never mind. I don't even have to ask."

My stomach growled. "How about we shower and take the boys for another shot at breakfast? We can go to Sparky's this time."

"Sounds good to me."

We showered together. We were almost dead silent, but we still managed to get each other off with a spectacular frotting session. When we were dressed, I knocked on Charlie's door.

"Hey, guys? You want to go to breakfast?"

There was some grumbling and whispering, then Charlie called out, "Give us fifteen minutes!"

"Take your time. My bathroom's free if more than one of you want to shower."

"'Kay, thanks."

To be on the safe side, I sped back to my bedroom and did a quick job of hiding the lube and tugging the bedspread over the rumpled sheets.

Charlie trudged in, his eyes mostly closed and the hems of his pajama pants dragging on the floor. He carried his jeans, a t-shirt, and of course his phone.

"It's all yours. Oh, and, Charlie."

He blinked at me. "Yeah?"

"I, uh, wanted to let you know. I asked Drake to be my boyfriend."

His face broke into a grin. "Great!" Then he put on a wary expression. "He said yes, didn't he?"

"Fuck off."

Laughing, he went into the bathroom.

I found Drake in the kitchen messing with the coffee maker. "I hope there's enough for me."

He pointed at two empty mugs on the counter. "As soon as mine is poured, you can have yours."

My phone buzzed. I ignored it. Probably my mom acknowledging my text from earlier. Then it buzzed again. And again.

"What now?" I pulled the phone from my pocket. I had several texts, so I opened the messaging app. I sucked in a breath. "That little shit. I'm going to kill him."

"What? What's wrong?" Drake paused with the coffee pot poised, ready to pour.

I waved my phone at him. "I told Charlie we were boyfriends now, and he's already texted Mom, Dad, and Addy. They're pestering me for information."

He grinned. "Sounds like he's feeling comfortable enough with you to yank your chain." He poured the coffee, adding creamer and sugar to mine, just like I made it myself.

I paused my retort and thought about what he'd said. "Holy shit, I think you're right. He hasn't teased me or anything since he came to live here. Not til the other night when we were flirting in the doorway. Holy shit." I got a little choked up, and Drake came over to give me a hug.

When I'd recovered, I pushed back enough to look at him. "You won't feel quite so kind toward Charlie when you find out my mom is demanding you come to Sunday dinner this evening."

He froze. "Uh."

"It's up to you. If you're not ready, that's fine, but don't be surprised if Mom ambushes you while you're minding your own business either in town or at Zeke's compound."

His eyes went wide. "She'd do that?"

I nodded grimly. "Without a doubt."

"Right. Okay, then let's get it over with today. At least you'll be with me."

I wrapped my arms around him. "You'll survive, I promise."

When Charlie came into the kitchen with Kirk and Tommy a little later, I pointed at him. "You're on my shit list, mister, and for punishment you're only allowed to order oatmeal for breakfast."

Kirk and Tommy goggled at me, but Charlie laughed. "It was worth it." He turned to Drake. "Are you coming to Sunday dinner at Janet and Brad's?"

Drake smiled serenely. "I wouldn't miss it."

We pulled up to Mom and Dad's house right as Addy was getting out of her car. For once her jeans appeared free of paint stains. She had a bottle of wine in one hand, and she tucked it under her arm as she strode over to wait for us.

Charlie bounced out of the car as soon as I put it in Park. He threw his arms around Addy, and she hugged him tight but gave me a stunned expression over his shoulder. I put my hands out to indicate I didn't know.

"That's my twin sister Addy. She's engaged to a woman named Hannah, but Hannah's in Burlington this weekend."

Drake nodded, then he took a deep breath and got out of the car. He hadn't worn a hat tonight, and it was a little odd seeing him outdoors without one. He had on black jeans and a blue button-down. Even with his stylish haircut, you'd never know he was essentially a rock star.

I got out more slowly, watching as he approached Addy. Once Charlie released her, Drake held out his hand. "Hi, I'm Drake. It's nice to meet you."

After greeting him, Addy took his hand and used it to pull him in for a hug. "Nice to meet you too, Drake." She stepped back but didn't let go of him. "Let's head inside and you can meet Mom and Dad properly. They said they met you when you dropped off Charlie Monday night, but this is different now you and Finn are together. They're a little overeager about it, but I promise they'll calm down eventually." She kept his hand in hers and started up the walkway toward the front door.

Drake glanced back at me with a pleading expression, and Charlie laughed. "We'd better make sure he survives Hurricane Janet."

"Agreed." We hurried to catch up.

Janet opened the door before Addy reached it. "Oh, Drake! I was so happy when Charlie told us about you and Finn!" She ignored Addy in favor of pulling Drake into a hug.

Charlie didn't try to stifle his laugh.

"Don't hog the boy—er, young man—Janet. Let me greet him too." Dad hovered behind Mom.

She slowly released Drake. He attempted to hold out his hand to Dad, but he got another hug instead.

Mom gave Addy and me perfunctory hugs, though she did whisper, "He's so cute, Finn!" into my ear. Then she put her arms around Charlie. "Honey, I know you're still hurting, but we're here for you. You know that, right?"

He mumbled something in response.

I put a hand on each of their backs. "Can we please go inside so I can make sure Drake isn't uncomfortable?"

Janet turned a shocked face to me as she released Charlie. "Finn Hunnicutt, we would never make anyone uncomfortable!"

Charlie sprinted for the door.

"Not intentionally, Mom." I put my arm around her shoulders and steered her inside.

Dinner was relatively stress-free. My parents behaved themselves reasonably well, although Mom kept bringing up the fact that Drake was a twin like I was.

After the fourth time she mentioned twins, I cleared my throat. "Drake, did I tell you Addy's an artist?"

He looked at her with what appeared to be genuine interest. "Really? What kind of medium?"

"I paint. Local landscapes mostly."

"No way. Can I see some of your work?" He looked around the dining room, but Mom had decorated in here with vintage botanical prints.

Addy gave him heart eyes. "Mom and Dad have one I did over their sofa in the den. I'll show you after dinner."

"I'd love that."

"She's got an online gallery too." I reached for my phone.

"After dinner, Finnegan." Mom stared me down until I put my hand back on the table.

Charlie sniggered.

Drake coughed. "Um, my brother Dirk is more of an art connoisseur than I am, so I'm not sure I can give your work the appreciation it deserves, but I'd still like to see it. In fact, I've been meaning to find a piece to bring home for Dirk, and it'd be amazing to give him something of yours."

I put my hand across the back of Drake's chair, my heart feeling full at his thoughtfulness. Addy smiled like he was her new favorite person. "As long as it's something he'd actually like. My stuff isn't for everyone."

"Drake, can I ask a question?"

He turned to Charlie. "Sure."

"Um, I'm not trying to be rude, but your and your brother's names are... kind of different."

"Charlie!"

Drake raised a hand toward Mom. "It's okay. And honestly I agree with you. My oldest brother got named after my paternal grandfather, but Dad talked Mom into giving the rest of us names to make us stand out. He had plans for us all to be famous, even before we were born."

Charlie wrinkled his nose. "That sucks. What if you didn't want to be famous?"

Drake gave him a wry smile. "My father wasn't concerned with what we wanted. Anyway, our first names are merely part of it. My oldest brother is the only one who didn't have his last name changed after our mom passed away."

Mom and Dad made shocked noises, and Drake nodded. "Turns out the name Derryberry isn't as marketable as plain old Derry. So Steve is Steven Derryberry, and two years younger than him are my twin brothers Heath and Hunter Derry. Then after them is Desdemona, who goes by Mona. Dirk and I are the youngest. We had our names legally changed back to Derryberry a few years ago, but we're stuck with Derry professionally."

My family must've done some googling, because no one asked anything about Drake's father.

After dinner Addy dragged Drake into the den to look at her painting. It was one of my favorites, a gorgeous fall day with a crisp blue sky and trees with leaves just turning.

"That's beautiful." Drake pulled out his phone. "Can you show me your gallery?"

They sat on the couch and started tapping at Drake's phone, so I snuck out to see what the others were up to. Dad and Charlie were on the back deck doing something that involved pointing at the trees, so I went into the kitchen to help Mom with the dishes.

When she saw me, she immediately put me at the sink. "You get the worst of it off, I'll load the dishwasher." Mom didn't like anyone else's method of arranging the dishes in the dishwasher. I only had to wait about thirty seconds before she gave her review.

"I like Drake."

"Yeah? I figured you'd think he's too young for me."

She shook her head. "That one might be young in years, but he's old in experiences." She moved a bowl to put a plate behind it. "I don't know him well, of course, but he seems like he could use some people around him." She shot me a look. "People like we have here, who would care for him and make him feel like he has his own place in the world."

I frowned, but my heart practically jumped out of my chest and latched on to her words. "I'm working up to asking him to stay longer after the music festival."

She straightened up and faced me. "You know I'm talking about permanently."

"One step at a time, Mom."

TEXT CONVERSATION, SUNDAY 9:46 P.M

ADDY:

How do we get Drake to move to
Maplewood?

FINN:

We've been seeing each other less than
a week

ADDY:

Never mind. I found out someone else has
it under control

FINN:

What? Who?

FINN:

Addy! Tell me

FINN:

Addy!

CHAPTER 15

DRAKE

Monday, two days before the festival

> ZEKE:
>
> I hope you're awake because we have an appointment at city hall to go over the festival permits in 30 minutes

> ME:
>
> You're buying breakfast afterward

> ZEKE:
>
> It'll be lunchtime by then

I didn't stop moving at all on Monday. The permit meeting took forever, and after lunch Zeke had me in more meetings. In between, he made me answer his phone because he didn't want to. I quickly learned he'd given out his personal phone number to all the vendors and bands. *All* of them. The only other way people could get hold of him was through the *Contact Us* form on the festival website, which was posted for everyone in the universe to see and use. Zeke got irritated when his inbox started to overflow, so he'd stopped checking it.

> ME:
>
> Hey, I have to go through the 1347 emails in Zeke's festival inbox tonight. Sorry.

> FINN:
>
> Sounds awful. I hope none of them are urgent.

> ME:
>
> I've gone through the oldest five, and so far four of them needed calls back

> FINN:
>
> [May the Force Be with You GIF]

> FINN:
>
> Don't worry about me this week. I'd love to see you but I understand the festival will consume all of your time. At least I'll see you on Thursday for your performance

> ME:
>
> Thanks. I decided to hang out here in Maplewood for a while after the festival's over. We can spend some time together then

> FINN:
>
> That's the best news I've had all day

I deliberately didn't mention how long "a while" would be. And he didn't ask. In truth I didn't have anything requiring my presence in Texas. Well, okay, there was one thing. I opened a different text thread.

> ME:
>
> I want to stay in Maplewood for a while after the festival. Is it okay if Gamora hangs with you longer than planned?

STEVE:

Look at her napping on Baz's chest. We're
good. Take as long as you need. [photo]

ME:

Aww. Y'all are the best. Thanks

And Zeke had better not complain about me occupying
the cabin after the festival. I was earning my keep and then
some.

Sighing, I went back to my laptop to open email number
six of 1347.

Tuesday was another whirlwind. Zeke and I must've walked
the festival grounds fifty times. The vendors were setting up,
and Roscoe, Zeke's friend from back in their roadie days, was
helping out by testing the sound systems in the amphitheater
and the smaller stages.

Tomorrow—and every day of the festival—vendors and
the bands who were playing the first sets that day were
allowed to start setup at 8:00 a.m., so I'd need to be around
to supervise. It'd make for long days, especially Thursday
when I was playing in the evening. I needed to spend some
time figuring out how I was going to manage that along
with my festival duties. I didn't even have a set list put
together.

Each day the gates opened at noon, and the first bands
started their sets at 1:00 p.m. Tomorrow, Failing Midnight was
headlining, then Satyr's Kiss on Thursday, with me opening
for them. Friday was Tenor Jones, and Poppy on Saturday.

Sunday was a shorter day, with the gates only open from
4:00 to 8:00 p.m. for the amateur competition. The vendors

could do their tear-down on Monday if they couldn't finish it Sunday night.

Zeke and I got back to the compound around 9:00 p.m. Tuesday night, and I felt lucky it wasn't later. My feet were sore, and I needed a shower badly. At least only some of the problems I'd had to deal with were the result of Zeke not checking his website messages, so I hadn't felt too salty about dealing with them—and him—all day.

Zeke, for all he was several decades older than me, forged down the path to his house with more energy than I could muster. "Nova came by to feed the animals and Mabel. Get some rest, kid, and don't forget to eat."

He power-walked ahead of me, disappearing around the bend in the path before I took the walkway to my cabin's front door. Which was standing open.

What the fuck?

The lights were on, and music was playing. Taylor Swift.

Tentatively I pushed the door all the way open. "Hello?"

"Hey, it's me!" Finn walked over from the kitchen. "Are you exhausted?"

"Yes? How did you get in?" I shook my head quickly. "Not that I'm not glad to see you." I shut the door behind me.

He wrapped his arms around me and pulled me in tight. "That's better." He released me and gave me a too-brief kiss, but one I could feel him smiling behind. "I missed you last night, so I texted Zeke to see if I could get into your cabin and make you dinner. He gave me access on the app."

Half of my brain wanted to worry about Zeke's lack of concern over security, but the other half was too tired and hungry to care. That was the half I declared the winner. Finn headed back to the kitchen while I detoured to the living room and plugged my tablet into the charger. I'd need it again all day tomorrow.

"I know it's usually a winter dish, but I figured stew would be filling and easy to keep warm no matter how late you had to work."

I sniffed. "Wow. Does that have beer in it? It smells great."

"Yep. It's Hop Doctor Brewery's maple lager. And there's bread. I can heat it up if you don't mind waiting."

"No. Please don't bother. Let's eat now. Or did you wait for me?"

He smiled and kissed me again. "I did. I was going to cave if you'd been much later, but this is fine."

I washed my hands while he dished up the stew. The tiny square table had been set, and glasses of water were ready for each of us. He put the bowls on the table then brought over a couple of smaller plates with thick-sliced brown bread.

"Wow, Finn, this is amazing." I sat down and groaned. "I've been on my feet all day." And my Converse weren't designed for that kind of use.

"Why don't you take a shower after dinner, and then I'll rub your feet for you?"

My mouth fell open. "You will?"

"Sure. I'd be happy to."

"Um, okay. I don't think anyone's ever rubbed my feet before." I thought about it. "No, I'd remember."

He looked pleased. "Then it's a requirement. We'll do it in bed so you can fall asleep if you need to."

I frowned, fiddling with my spoon. "But you came over. Don't you want to... have sex?" I'd been about to say *fuck*, but it didn't seem like the right word for what we did together anymore.

He put his hand on mine where it rested on the table. "That's not why I'm here. I wanted to do something nice for you, since you're dealing with a lot of stressful stuff right now."

I was horrified at the tears welling in my eyes. To hide them, I leaned across the corner of the table and put my arm around his shoulders. "Thank you." I put my forehead against his temple.

"You're welcome."

I sat back, but I still had to wipe my eyes with the back of my wrist. "Sorry. I'm tired and hungry, so my emotions are getting the better of me."

He stroked my cheek with his fingers. "You can let me see your feelings, Drake. I want to see them."

I looked into his hazel eyes and nodded. "Okay."

"Okay. Now eat."

After dinner I started yawning. Finn made me get in the shower anyway, which I was sure I'd appreciate in the morning. When I came out, dressed only in my boxer-briefs, he had the lights in the cabin turned off and the sheets pulled down. He was sitting at the end of the bed, wearing a t-shirt and boxers.

"You can stay the night?" I couldn't keep the eagerness out of my voice.

He smiled. "I got special permission from Charlie. Though he pointed out that he'd be less lonely at home if we had a pet."

I chuckled. "I can see his point. Um, I'm not sure I'll be able to stay awake through a foot rub."

He patted the bed. "It'll help your circulation whether you're awake or not."

Gingerly I sat down then swung my legs onto the bed.

"Lie down with your head on the pillow." Once I was comfortable, he pulled my feet onto his lap. "Close your eyes. I'll put the covers over you when I'm done." He stroked my shins.

"Okay. Thanks for doing all of this, Finn. It means a lot." Fuck, I was getting choked up again.

"Shh. Just relax. I'm happy to do it. This is what boyfriends are for."

I smiled and closed my eyes. Finn picked up my left foot and gently pressed his thumbs into my sole. My eyes flew open. "Holy fuck!"

He laughed and pressed harder, moving his thumbs down toward my heel. "Close your eyes, Drake. Remember how tired you are?"

"Yeah, okay. But for future reference, if I were more awake, my dick would be rock-hard right now."

"I'll keep that in mind."

Wednesday morning I got up depressingly early. When I slid out of bed, Finn sat up. "What time is it?" He rubbed his face.

"It's 6:30 a.m. Go back to sleep."

"Nah. I'm gonna go running with Alex." He got out of bed and stretched.

I tried doing the same and groaned. My feet and legs were still sore. "I think I need some orthopedic shoes like you have." I walked over to the closet and surveyed what I'd brought. My Adidas were probably the best bet, even though that pair had been designed with fashion in mind, not standing and walking.

I got dressed, and when Finn was done in the bathroom I took my turn. He was in the kitchen making coffee and wearing his running tights, which I didn't think I'd ever get tired of looking at. He glanced over at me, then frowned. "I brought stuff to make breakfast too. Do you have time?"

"Finn! You didn't have to." Fuck, I hoped I didn't cry again. I'd had enough of that last night.

He smiled. "I know. Come get your coffee and have a seat."

I pressed a kiss to his cheek as I accepted the cup he handed me. "Best boyfriend ever."

"It's nothing. But what about dinner tonight? Can I bring you something again?"

I blew on my coffee. "Thanks for offering, but I'll probably get something from one of the vendors." If I had time. "I'll be there pretty late, it looks like." I sat up. "Hey, why don't you and Charlie come to the festival? Since you've got access to the compound, you can go through the gate in the fence to get to the festival grounds."

"Yeah? I think Charlie's already going with some friends, but I could come."

I smiled. "Alex will be there taking photos, so you can hang out with him or with me in between listening to the bands."

Finn made eggs and toast, and he heated up some precooked bacon. It was just what I needed, and I felt much more ready to tackle my day when I'd finished eating. "You're amazing." I pushed back my plate.

His cheeks turned a little pink, which was adorable. "I think you're pretty special too." He picked up our plates and stood to take them to the sink. "What's your schedule like tomorrow?"

I grimaced. "More of the same, I imagine."

He shut the dishwasher and put his hands on his hips. "But you're supposed to play tomorrow evening."

I groaned and collapsed dramatically across the table with my arms outstretched. "I don't want to. I'm going to be tired, and I haven't even figured out what I want to play." I huffed into the tabletop. "Because I don't want to play."

Finn came back and sat down at the table. He ran his hand over my hair, which felt really nice. "Can I ask why you're playing in the first place? I thought you were just doing songwriting now."

I rolled my eyes. "Because when I first talked to Zeke about helping with the festival, he essentially told me there was an empty spot in the roster and he was putting me there." I shrugged against the tabletop. "It really didn't occur to me to say no."

Finn moved his hand to rub between my shoulders, and I closed my eyes. Fuck, I could get used to being massaged all the time. "Is there anyone who could take your spot last minute?"

I opened one eye. What if there was someone? What if the band playing the afternoon set would be willing to play longer? What if Satyr's Kiss would be willing to start earlier? Or both? "Maybe? I'll think about it." But already my chest felt lighter, and I felt happier, energized even.

I hauled myself upright and gave Finn a kiss. "Thank you for making me think that through."

He smiled. "Anytime. Just like the foot rubs, it's all part of the boyfriend service."

I'd never had a boyfriend before, but I knew damn well most of them weren't this kind and considerate. How had I been lucky enough to land Finn?

I cocked my head. "You know, so far you're the one who's been doing all the *servicing*. I'll have to think of something to make things more even." I pursed my lips and turned my eyes to the ceiling. "Hmmm. What could I possibly do?"

He laughed and kissed me. "I'll let you know if I have any suggestions. Time to get moving."

TEXT CONVERSATION
WEDNESDAY, 8:07 A.M

ZEKE:

Don't forget to check in with all the vendors before we open. This is when they all freak out about every little thing that isn't perfect.

ZEKE:

Make sure Alex MacDougall has a pass to get backstage to all the shows so he can take photos

ZEKE:

I've had two calls already this morning from the t-shirt vendor. Can you stop by their booth first thing?

ZEKE:

Did you remember to update the website with the new lineup for the amateur contest?

ZEKE:

Where are you? I'm at your cabin

DRAKE:

I'm at the t-shirt booth, checking in as per today's published schedule. Here's a screenshot of the to-do list. Everything's on track. [photo]

CHAPTER 16
DRAKE

Wednesday, the first day of the festival

Opening day was even more grueling than I'd anticipated. Zeke and I split the issues, but they were legion. Most were things a Google drive full of documents and instructions could've solved, but this wasn't technically my rodeo, so I kept my mouth shut.

My shoes were a bigger issue. Any moment I had to myself, where I wasn't being badgered for this or that, I found the nearest available anything to lean against, taking at least some of my weight off my feet. Unfortunately, after the gates opened, there weren't a ton of seats in the festival grounds other than near the food vendor stalls—and they were usually all occupied—or in the audience areas for the stages.

The pain in my feet drove home that me playing a set tomorrow night wasn't feasible. I could've asked the bands scheduled before and after me to each add thirty minutes or so to their sets, but the ticketholders had paid to see three acts. I'd prefer they got what they paid for.

I pulled out my phone.

ME:

I need to bail on playing my set tomorrow night. Any ideas on who might be able to fill in for me at the last minute? (hint, hint)

WESLEY:

Not me.

WESLEY:

Hall of Fame is on sabbatical in Vermont. What about them?

ME:

Are you kidding? If they'd be willing, that'd be unbelievable!

WESLEY:

Let me reach out to Bastian Hall. I'll let you know what he says.

ME:

You're the best

Holy shit, if Wesley could get Hall of Fame to come, our festival would be made. As long as they didn't mind opening for Satyr's Kiss. One could argue that Hall of Fame deserved a headline spot, but I'd see what they said before worrying about it.

The opening day crowd was huge. Zeke had texted me that ticket sales were already higher than last year, but I was having trouble enjoying the festival's success. It was 4:00 p.m. I was hot, and I hadn't had any lunch. And the worst part was my feet, ankles, calves, thighs, hips, and spine were all in various states of pain. After I snapped at a band roadie who just wanted to ask a question about the electrical outlets, I took a mental step back. What good was I doing here, if I was causing people to have a horrible experience at the festival? There was no rule that I couldn't take a fucking break and rest.

I texted Zeke to tell him I was going to the cabin for an

hour. He responded with a thumbs up, but I hadn't waited for it. Finn had put the leftover stew in the fridge, and I knew there was more of that bread. I could take my shoes off and soak my poor feet. Maybe I'd text Finn and ask him what shoes he wore. I didn't even care how ugly they were, I just needed relief.

As soon as I was inside the cabin, I took off my Adidas. Fuck, that was so much better. I hadn't decided what I'd wear for the rest of the day, but it wouldn't be those. Maybe I could get something overnighted from Amazon to wear for the rest of the festival.

In ten minutes I was sitting at the kitchen table, eating stew and the lovely bread, while my feet soaked in a huge bowl of warm water.

My phone chimed with a text. I was relieved it wasn't Zeke with a festival emergency.

POPPY:

Mac and I are coming in on Friday night. Any chance you'll have some free time to hang out and catch up?

ME:

I'll make time. Also, I have two new songs to play for you.

POPPY:

Fuck yeah! I've just started thinking about my next album, so this is perfect timing.

ME:

If you like them

POPPY:

I'll like them. If they're not right for the album you know I'll tell you. But I'll still like them

I put a heart on her last text. I'd finished my lunch, but the thought of walking the dishes to the sink was almost over-whelming.

My text chime went off again, and I was grateful to post-pone my journey.

CHARLES:

Where are you?

ME:

In the cabin. Are you at the festival?

I opened Charlie's contact record to update his name.

CHARLIE:

Not yet. Kirk and I will be at your cabin
in 10

ME:

OK? It's unlocked

No response. Fucking teenagers. I chuckled. As if it'd been that long since I'd been a teenager. I couldn't stop my brain from comparing the age difference between me and Charlie and between me and Finn.

It's not about the years, dammit.

I hobbled to the sink with my dishes, then I went into the bedroom. Might as well see what would work for the remainder of the evening.

Ugh. Not my cowboy boots. They were fairly comfort-able, but they were also snug. My feet were swollen as hell. No way could I get those on. I'd also brought some leather lace-ups, but those had zero support.

Converse it was. Fuck. Except.... I looked around. The left one was in the closet where I'd put them this morning. But the right one wasn't with it.

I walked the room, checking under and around all the furniture. I even searched the living room. No shoe. Fucking hell. Not that I'd been excited about wearing the Converse again, but now I was down to only my Adidas for at least today and tomorrow. Shit, I'd forgotten to check Amazon for what I could get overnighted.

Did they even overnight to small-town Vermont?

I went back to the kitchen to get my phone when Charlie knocked on the door and let himself in. "Hey, Drake!"

"Come on in. Hey, Kirk." They were carrying shopping bags. "What's all that?"

Charlie reached into his bag and pulled out my right Converse.

"Hey! What the hell? I was looking for that!"

He wrinkled his nose. "I hope it wasn't to wear, because, Drake, this thing stinks."

I glared at him. "I wore it for sixteen hours yesterday. Did Finn accidentally take it with him when he left?"

He grinned. Kirk walked around him to put his bag on the kitchen table. "These cabins are sweet. Here, sit down."

I blinked. "Me?"

Charlie rolled his eyes. "Yes, you. Your *boyfriend* bribed us to go shoe shopping for you."

I gaped at him. "He did?" Holy shit, Finn really was campaigning for Boyfriend of the Year, and we'd only been officially dating for a few days.

I watched in wonder as the boys pulled out six—six!—boxes of shoes and several pairs of socks.

Kirk pointed at the chair again, and I sat obediently. "That's a lot of shoes."

Charlie grinned. "Your boo said if we weren't sure about sizes to get you both and return what didn't fit." He held up a box of Hokas. "Try these first. The guy at the store said they're really popular for people who're on their feet all day."

Numbly I took the box from him. "What are y'all getting out of this?"

They looked at each other, grinning. "Finn said he'd take us on a weekend trip in June!"

I opened the box and pulled out a shoe. Already I could feel how much sturdier it was than my Adidas or Converse. "Yeah? Like camping?"

"Wherever we want to go *within reason*." Charlie rolled his eyes at the last part.

"Maybe the beach! Or one of those hotels with an indoor waterpark!" Kirk whipped out his phone and started searching.

I put the other shoe on and stood up. "Oh, my god. I need these." I walked around the room. "Okay, you can take the rest back."

Charlie shook his head. "Nope. Finn said you should keep however many pair fit you, and the shoe guy said it's better for your feet if you change shoes in the middle of the day. Also, don't wear the same shoes two days in a row."

I narrowed my eyes at him. "Does the shoe guy work on commission?"

Kirk laughed. "It's true. We googled it to make sure."

Charlie held out the next box, so I sat down and removed the Hokas. In the end I kept three pairs, one of which were clogs that Finn apparently swore by. They'd felt weird when I put them on, but after five minutes I hadn't wanted to take them off. Hopefully any photos of me wouldn't show my feet. Dirk would laugh his head off, and he was too far away for me to wrestle him.

Charlie put the shoes I wasn't keeping back in the trunk of Kirk's car, and, wearing my new clogs without shame, I took the boys with me through the gate from the compound into the festival grounds. My feet were still sore from earlier, but I'd be able to walk around the rest of the night without limping. When Finn showed up later, he was getting the biggest thank you kiss I could manage in public, and then even more when we were alone.

The boys took off toward the food vendors, and I went searching for Zeke. I found him holding court at one of The Forbidden Maple's tables. He waved me over. "Drake here is the one you need to talk to." I was back to solving problems Zeke could've avoided with a Google Drive.

It only took twenty-five minutes to extricate myself, which I took as a win. The band opening for Failing Moonlight was warming up. I headed in that direction right as my phone chimed.

UNKNOWN NUMBER

Hey, Drake, this is Bastian Hall of Hall of Fame. We're open to playing the festival tomorrow, but we have some questions. Could you call me?

Yes! Ten minutes later we had a Poppy-level band booked to open for Satyr's Kiss, who were not quite that popular yet. I spent a gleeful few minutes exchanging texts with Satyr's Kiss and with Zeke. There were many, many exclamation points.

At last I was able to get back to work, so I started toward the amphitheater again.

"Drake!"

I spun around—briefly marveling at how good my feet felt —to see Alex trotting toward me, his camera in his hand. "Hey! You getting any good shots?"

"Just starting out for the night. There was a thing at City Hall all day, so I couldn't get here until now."

I made a face. "You'll have as long a day as I will."

"Yeah, but this is the fun part of my job, so I don't mind. Hey, let me get a picture of you for the website."

I blinked. "Of me? Why?"

He stared at me incredulously. "Drake, all anyone's been

talking about is how much work you've been doing to make this festival go smoothly. Zeke's always impossible to get hold of if they have issues, but you've made it easy."

My face felt hot. "I've just been handling things as they came up."

He rolled his eyes. "Exactly. Anyway, stand here." He positioned me right in the middle of the walkway, forcing all the festival-goers to walk around me. "The amphitheater frames you nicely in the background. Tilt your hat up a little."

I obligingly adjusted my cowboy hat, then I let him manhandle me, arranging me to his satisfaction. As Alex started clicking his camera, Finn appeared over his shoulder, still wearing his scrubs from work. I grinned. "Hey!" I decided Alex had had enough time to get his shots, so I walked around him to embrace Finn. "Thank you so much for my shoes. I'll pay you back."

He kissed me. "Nope. You'll come on the trip with me, Charlie, and Kirk."

I stepped back and searched his face. "Really?"

"Really." He kissed me again, and I hugged him as tight as I could.

I smiled against his neck. "Is that your fanny pack, or are you just happy to see me?"

He broke away, laughing.

"Are you two done yet?"

"Oops. Sorry, Alex." We turned to face him, but Finn kept his arm around my waist. "I'm assuming you're still working?"

I held up my tablet. "Probably until at least 11:30."

"Damn, that's late. I'll wait for you in the cabin, okay?"

I frowned. "Are you sure? Doesn't Charlie need you at home?"

He shook his head. "I asked Mom and Dad to stay over."

I hugged him again. "Boyfriend of the Year."

His cheeks were a little red when I let go.

Thursday was easier than Wednesday had been, in large part due to my feet not hurting. But also the vendors were settled in, the bands were ready to go on time, and everyone found their respective stages without issue. All in all, it was a fun day.

Zeke had agreed to put up the Hall of Fame guys in a couple of the cabins, so I met them at the compound driveway to get them squared away.

"Thanks so much for doing this at the last minute, y'all. Especially when you're not headlining."

Bastian, a forty-something hottie, grinned. "The band's taking a break, but it doesn't hurt to get some practice in here and there."

"Well, I appreciate it. And Satyr's Kiss is over the moon about you opening for them." They'd be telling this story for decades.

"Sorry you're not playing anymore. Hey, would you want to join us on stage for a song or two? We'd love to have you."

I smiled and shook my head. "Thanks, but I need to focus on running the festival. And I'm not trying to promote myself as an artist, so it'd be a wasted effort on your part. But it's nice of you to offer."

He looked insulted. "Wasted effort? Who the hell have you been hanging out with? Drake, we're doing this gig as a favor. Having you play with us would be fun. Fun is always worth the effort."

Ouch. I rubbed the back of my neck. "Sorry. You're right. Every once in a while my asshole father comes out of my mouth. I still have to pass, but I appreciate the invitation."

Bastian nodded. "Lots of us have had people in our lives who continue to sabotage us even after they're gone. No worries. See you at the show."

I didn't see Finn at the festival Thursday, but he was waiting for me in bed when I got back to the cabin around midnight. I showered, and when I slid under the covers, he cuddled close. Fuck, I didn't want to leave him. Would I ever find anyone else who'd treat me as well as he did?

Plus, I wanted a chance to spoil him for a change. How long could I stay?

Or was the better question, did I really have to leave?

Friday afternoon I told Zeke he was in charge for the next few hours, and I went to the compound to greet Poppy and her husband Mac, along with their entourage of security and band members.

"Drake!" Poppy hopped out of the huge SUV and surrounded me in one of her all-consuming hugs. Something inside me eased. I'd been lonely for people who knew me, I realized.

"It's good to see you. Hey, Mac." I had to nod at him over Poppy's shoulder, as she still hadn't let me go.

He chuckled. "Hey, Drake. Full disclosure, I'm under strict orders from my dad to make sure you're okay up here in the wilds of Vermont. I may need photo evidence."

I rolled my eyes. "Wesley's the one who asked me to come here. But sure, whatever makes him happy."

Poppy eventually released me, only to hold me at arm's length and look me up and down. "I think Vermont agrees with you." She whirled toward Mac. "We should rent a house here next summer."

He smiled at her in that besotted way he had. "Whatever you want, hon."

She beamed and bounced on her toes. "Yes! Then we can hang out more, Drake. I'd love it if we could write some songs together, but we've never had time before."

"Um, sure? I mean, I'd love that, and I'm happy to meet you up here."

She cocked her head. Then her eyes widened. "Oh, right. Yeah, you should meet us up here."

I heard a smacking noise, and I turned to see Del, who'd been Poppy's head of security for ages. He was rubbing his forehead.

"Hey, Del. How are you?"

"I'm good, Drake. Can you add me to the security app for the gate? I need to let the tour bus in."

I got him set up, then Poppy grabbed my arm. "I'm dying to hear your new songs. When do you have time to play them for me?"

"How about now? Zeke's handling the festival stuff for the next couple of hours."

I brought my guitar over to Poppy and Mac's cabin, and once everyone had glasses of water or tea, it was showtime.

"Okay, this first one's fairly final, lyric and melody-wise. The second one, I've got the words where I want them but the melody's giving me trouble."

"Got it." She put her phone on the coffee table to record, so she could listen to the songs later.

"This one's called, 'Better than Blood'." I launched into the song I'd been inspired to write by my relationship with Dirk and by Finn's relationship with his friend group. Poppy, as she typically did when Dirk and I played her something we'd written, spent the entire song leaning forward with elbows on her knees and her eyes closed.

Mac smiled throughout, but he wasn't my primary audience.

When the song ended, Poppy nodded. "That'll be a great concert song. My fans will love it. Hell, I love it."

I grinned. "Good to hear."

"Alright, play me this other one."

I took a deep breath. "I call this one 'Friends with Benefits'." I sang it for her, bumpy melody and all. It was one of the most personal songs I'd ever written, and as I sang, I was incredibly glad Finn and I had gotten over ourselves and moved into actually dating.

During the second verse, Poppy sat up and opened her eyes. She didn't smile, she didn't frown, but she also didn't take her gaze off me for the rest of the song.

I brought it to a close, and she shook her head, pressing her lips together. "Drake."

I frowned. "You hate it?"

She shook her head harder and then she fucking wiped her eyes. My mouth dropped open. She sucked in a shaky breath. "Drake, I see what you mean about the melody, but those lyrics are probably the best you've ever written."

I couldn't speak. I stared at her, my mouth hanging open.

"That line, 'I wanted to kiss you when you walked in. But you just said hey.'" She shivered. "Devastating."

"Um, thanks?"

Then she turned into the mega-millions businessperson. "But you're right, the melody isn't doing it justice. Let's work on it."

I didn't leave her cabin until 9:00 p.m. I texted Zeke to apologize and see how things were going, but he told me he had things under control and I should get some rest. Fuck, yeah.

I opened my text thread with Finn.

ME:

> Heading back to the cabin. I have the rest
> of the night off! What are you up to?

FINN:

Waiting for you

I broke into a jog.

MAPLEWOOD MATTERS BLOG, SATURDAY 9:53 A.M

MM has verified that our perpetually single Dr. Hunnicutt has spent a few nights this week at a cabin on Zeke Knight's property. Unfortunately we are not privy to which cabin, but until Wednesday, the only one occupied was that of a certain young musician. In addition, this week the younger member of the good doctor's household has been staying with the elder generation of Hunnicutts or with school friends on those same nights.

Might we have an announcement of official coupledom on the horizon? Time will tell.

\

CHAPTER 17

FINN

Friday, the third day of the festival

After I got Drake's text that he was on his way, I tossed my tablet onto the coffee table and stood up. But before I could even get my scrub top over my head, he opened the door and walked in.

"Dammit, I was going to be naked for you!"

He smiled. "It's not too late." He set his guitar down at the end of the couch, then came over to me. He seemed happier, less stressed than he'd been at the end of the days the rest of this week.

He kissed me, then pulled back. "Did you get dinner?"

"I did. You?"

"Yeah. I was in Poppy's cabin. She helped me work out the issues I was having with the melody on a new song." He was almost glowing with satisfaction. Was this what he looked like when he was pleased with his work? I'd seen glimpses of it when he'd told me about some of the festival stuff, but this was sexy as hell.

"Yeah? The friends one you played for us on D&D night?"

He dropped his gaze to my chest, and his mood dimmed.

"Um, no. I mean, I played that one for her too, and she wants to record it. But this is a different song. You haven't heard it."

I scrunched my forehead and ducked to catch his gaze. "What's the matter?"

He looked toward the kitchen. "It's, uh, kind of about us."

"Okay?"

His face turned a dull red. "Um...."

Oh, shit. "Is it about sex? Because you should write what you want. I'm not prudish or anything, even if people guess it's about me."

He shook his head, dropping his arms from my sides to cross them over his belly. My eyebrows must've been meeting my hairline. "Drake? What is it? Is it called 'Finn Hunnicutt Is a Selfish Lover' or something?"

That got him to look at me. "What? No!"

I made a *go on* gesture.

He huffed out a breath. "I wrote it when I was angry because you hadn't contacted me."

Oh.

"So it's called 'Finn Hunnicutt Is an Asshole'?"

He laughed. "No. Nothing like that." He sighed. "Let me play it for you. Poppy's planning to sing it tomorrow night at the festival, so you might as well be prepared."

Now I was concerned. What the hell had he written?

He got his guitar out of the case and sat at one end of the sofa. "It's called 'Friends with Benefits'." He paused. "Keep in mind, this song might've been based partly on us when I started writing it, but you'll see it's not actually us in the end."

Well, thank fuck for that. I sank down on the other end of the sofa. He played a haunting, sad melody, singing about someone who'd started out casual with a guy but had developed feelings. Feelings that were decidedly not returned.

The more he sang, the worse I felt, even though, as he'd

said, the ending of the song was absolutely different from where Drake and I were now. Still, it was a punch to the gut to hear he might've thought I hadn't returned his feelings.

When he finished, I blinked back tears. "Is that how I made you feel? You thought I didn't care? Because I cared. I cared from the beginning. I was just scared, and I didn't mean to make you think... to make you feel like *that*." I waved a hand at his guitar.

He set it aside and scooted over to put his arms around me. "You didn't. Don't ever think you did. The song's an alternate reality where I imagined what could have happened."

I nodded but leaned into his hug. "You're so fucking talented. The song's beautiful, even though I could live without hearing it again. But, shit, Drake, all of Poppy's teenage emo fans will eat it up, and it'll top the charts. I hope you'll be rolling in royalty money."

He chuckled. "I hope so too. I need a new amp."

A little before noon on Saturday, I drove into the compound and parked next to Zeke's house. Charlie and Kirk piled out and ran over to greet Dolores and the chickens. Drake had left before I'd woken, and I'd gone home to help Charlie prepare for his performance tomorrow at the amateur music competition. Both of us had wanted to spend the rest of today at the festival. The boys were almost jumping out of their skin they were so excited to meet Poppy after her show.

I got out of the car but stopped moving before I shut the door. A large man I'd never seen before stood a few feet away. His gaze flashed between me and the boys. He was wearing a jacket even though it was warm today.

"Who are you?" I moved away from the car, putting myself between the boys and the stranger. Charlie and Kirk went quiet. I hoped they'd stay where they were.

He raised an eyebrow at me. "My name's Del. I'm head of security for Poppy."

Oh. Right. Charlie and Kirk ran over. "Poppy's here? Can we meet her?"

I put my hand up. "Boys, Drake'll introduce you after the show tonight. You can't bother Poppy here; this is a private space for her so she can relax."

"Oh. Yeah, sorry." Charlie nodded in understanding.

Del smiled at him then looked at me. "You're Finn Hunnicutt, yes?"

"Yes. I—we—have permission to be here."

"I'm aware. Your car was here overnight."

My face turned red, and Charlie and Kirk hooted and laughed.

"What's going on, Del?"

The boys shut their mouths and practically stood at attention at the woman's voice. I turned to see Poppy herself walking toward us, trailed by a thirty-ish dark-haired man. She didn't have any makeup on, her hair was in a ponytail, and she wore an old Jake Lord t-shirt and joggers.

Del gestured at me. "This is Finn Hunnicutt, Mr. Derryberry's... friend." He looked at the boys. "I didn't catch your names."

"I'm Kirk Barbour. And I'm a big fan, Poppy, but we didn't mean to bother you."

"That's okay, Kirk." She walked closer to stand next to Del. "And what's your name?"

"I'm Charlie Hapwell. It's so cool to meet you."

She glanced between me and the boys, obviously waiting for an explanation, but I stayed silent. It wasn't any of her business how we were related. Still, she was being nice to us, so I broke the silence. "Drake has been letting us park here and go to the festival through the gate." I pointed in the direction of the festival grounds.

She nodded. "This is my husband, Mac." She put her hand around her husband's arm, then she looked between me and the boys again.

Oh. Got it.

"Hey, boys, you want to go ahead to the festival? If you see Drake, tell him I'll be there in a few."

Poppy smiled. "We'll put your names on the list to go backstage tonight, if you like."

Charlie and Kirk puffed up like they'd won the lottery, but they kept a lid on the fanboying. A minute later they'd run off toward the gate to the festival grounds.

After they were out of sight, Poppy disengaged from her husband's arm and put her hands on her hips. Her expression turned hard. "You're Mr. Friends with Benefits."

I reared back. Shit. "Um, we're boyfriends now." Had Drake not told her about us? I'd thought they were close.

She gave me an unimpressed stare. "So he said."

I frowned back. "What's the problem?" She might be an uber-talented multi-millionaire, but I was Drake's boyfriend, dammit.

Her lips twitched, then she burst out laughing. "I'm sorry. I was trying to do the shovel talk, but I can't."

I scrunched my eyebrows together and looked between Del and Mac for help. They were staring at Poppy as if she'd lost her mind.

"Poppy, honey, why don't you let Del handle any intimidating that needs to be done." He grimaced and turned to me. "Not that you need intimidating."

"Noted."

Poppy rubbed her face. "Finn, really, I'm sorry I tried that. Drake will probably kill me."

"No need to apologize. I'm glad Drake has such a good friend." I stepped away from the car and shut the door. "Speaking of Drake, I'm supposed to meet him at the festival. I imagine I'll see you later tonight. Good luck with the show."

I nodded to Del and Mac as I walked past them, heading for the gate. I was almost at the bend in the path when I heard Mac say, "I hope Drake won't be too pissed when he finds out what you did, or else you'll be writing all your own songs from now on."

I chuckled. Drake wouldn't hear about Poppy's awkward little attempt at protectiveness from me, but I was betting Mac would rat her out. I was still grinning as I entered the festival grounds. Drake was easy to spot, even with the size of the crowd. He'd taken to wearing his straw cowboy hat each day to help the vendors find him more quickly. But right now he was talking to a twenty-something girl who looked less like a vendor or band member and more like a festival-goer.

As I got closer, she showed him something on her phone. "I'm so happy I ran into you!"

Drake leaned in, then he clapped his hand over his mouth. "Oh, my god!"

"Right?" She glanced at me briefly as I neared, dismissing me as unimportant.

"Hey." I wanted to put my arm possessively around Drake, but he hadn't seen me approach and I didn't want to freak him out that some rando was hugging him.

He glanced up. "Hey!" He smiled, putting his arm out to pull me in for a kiss. The girl's eyes widened. Drake gestured. "This is Katie. She has a photo of me and her backstage at one of my first concerts with Melodious Moon." He smiled at her. "Would you please show Finn here how cute I was back then?"

Her face told me exactly how cute she thought he was now, but she obediently held her phone out for me to look at.

"Holy crap! How old were you?" Both of them had to be maybe eleven or twelve years old at most. Drake was dressed in some sort of sequined jumpsuit and stage makeup. Katie looked much more wholesome in a Melodious Moon t-shirt over a denim skirt. They had their arms around each other, and both were holding their free hands up in the classic rock and roll gesture, with pinky and forefingers extended.

He frowned. "Ten or eleven, maybe?"

"And you know this is you and not Dirk?"

"Yeah. My dad always made all of us twins have different hair so the fans could tell us apart."

No matter what the kids wanted. Got it.

Drake looked wistfully at Katie's phone.

"Hey, Katie. Um, Drake can't exactly give out his phone number, but if I gave you mine would you text me the photo?"

"Oh, sure!" She set the photo up to be sent and then handed me her phone to enter my phone number.

"Thanks so much, Katie. It really means a lot." Drake patted his pockets. "Do you want me to sign something for you since you're here? Take a selfie?"

I slapped my hand on my forehead. "We need to get Alex over here so you two can recreate the photo! He can do a cute then-and-now thing with it."

Katie looked confused so Drake explained who Alex was while I called him. He said he'd be right over.

Drake entertained Katie with tales of what his siblings were currently up to, though I was mostly sure he completely fabricated the story about Hunter and Heath being on a wellness retreat in the Indonesian jungle.

When Alex arrived, I showed him the photo Katie had

texted me. He instantly understood what I wanted. "Yes! That'll be fantastic." He took down Katie's name and contact information so he could send her a copy of the new picture. Then he positioned Katie and Drake in front of a huge sign advertising Poppy's concert and he had them take the same pose they'd been in for the original photo.

Drake also took a selfie with Katie, and he gave her a big hug as she left. He was smiling when he turned back to me and Alex. "That was fun." He glanced in the direction Katie had gone. "It's weird because I don't really have a ton of great memories from the Melodious Moon years, but I looked happy in that picture."

I texted it to him, then gave him a half-hug with a kiss on the temple. "I'm glad she found you."

I heard the unmistakable click of Alex's camera. I glared at him for interrupting a nice moment, but he shrugged, smiling. "I was documenting a new great memory for Drake."

Drake beamed at him. "Thanks, Alex."

I sighed and hugged Drake again. "Thanks, Alex."

Poppy's concert was incredible. It was also packed to the brim with festival-goers, and I was more than grateful for the back-stage passes. Charlie, Kirk, and I stood in the wings and got an insider's view of what went into putting on a concert. This wasn't even a tenth of her full arena show, but there were still costume changes, pyrotechnics, lasers, and choreography.

Drake stopped in to check on us about halfway through, but there was some issue with the plumbing in one of the restrooms, so he couldn't stay.

After the concert was over and Poppy had kindly taken

selfies with the boys and autographed their backstage passes, I texted Drake.

ME:

We're ready to head back to the car. Are you still working?

DRAKE:

Yeah. I'll be here for another hour, maybe more. Go on home.

ME:

Okay. But that means I won't get to see you until the competition tomorrow. I'll have to spend the morning listening to Charlie practice and making sure he's not panicking.

DRAKE:

He'll do great, and I understand. I'll miss sleeping next to you though.

ME:

Tomorrow night.

DRAKE:

I can't wait.

I was exhausted when I finally got to bed around 1:00 a.m., but every time I closed my eyes, I found myself reaching out for Drake. My bed was familiar and definitely more comfortable than the one in Drake's cabin, but he wasn't in it. It'd taken me less than a week to get addicted to sleeping next to him. It wasn't even sex I was craving. I needed Drake within touching distance.

Fuck. He'd said he'd stay after the festival, but for how long? I couldn't leave Maplewood, not with my clinic and Charlie. If Drake wanted a future with me, he'd have to move here. Would he even be open to considering it?

Addy's cryptic text that "someone" was already working

on keeping Drake here floated through my brain. But I couldn't rely on rumors about nameless people. I had to find the balls to ask Drake to stay, to give our relationship a real chance.

I hoped Charlie didn't mind leaving early for the festival tomorrow.

MAPLEWOOD MATTERS BLOG, SUNDAY 10:32 A.M

Wasn't Poppy's performance last night a-mazing? This blogger is planning to spend the entire day listening to all of her albums, in order. We were all stoked to hear her give a shout out to Drake Derry, our very own – if only temporarily – songwriter, who penned that phenomenal Friends with Benefits song she sang during the encore. If you happen to have a video of it, please post it in the comments below.

MM will not be speculating whether the song is based on any real-life relationship Drake may have been or is currently involved in.

Rumor has it that while the young musician in question was not in attendance at the concert, he procured backstage passes for our Dr. Hunnicutt and a couple of lucky teenagers.

We're all wondering if the good doctor will be asking Mr. Derry to stick around after the festival is over. MM speaks for all Maplewoodians in saying, "Please stay!"

CHAPTER 18

DRAKE

Sunday, the final day of the festival

The only thing happening at the festival today was the Maplewood Amateur Music Competition, which didn't start until 5:00 p.m. And, even better, I was a judge, so I got to sit down the entire evening.

The gates opened at 4:00, so I had most of the day off. And, wow, did I need it.

I'd told Nova and Zeke I'd take care of the chickens and Dolores this morning, so I got up at a decent hour to do that and to grab Mabel's bowl from the stump in the woods. Poppy and Mac, along with the band and assorted roadies, were loading up their vehicles to leave when I came back.

After I'd said goodbye to them, I shucked off everything but my underwear and got back into bed. It was a shame Finn couldn't have stayed over, because we'd have had plenty of uninterrupted time to make love. At the very least I wished I could've seen him last night before he'd had to go home. But Charlie needed his support today, and I understood. I didn't have a place there.

Still, I wanted one.

Fuck, it was so easy to imagine getting up every morning with Finn, having breakfast with Charlie before he went off to school. My chest ached with how badly I yearned for that.

A family. Finn and Charlie. And if I stayed in Maplewood, I could visit Zeke and Nova. Check on the chickens and future baby chicks. Play D&D with Alex, Andre, Mickey, Sam, and Jason.

Or I could go home to Texas, where I had Steve and his husband Baz. And occasionally Dirk.

I grabbed my phone from the nightstand.

ME:

> I'm staying in Maplewood. For real I mean. If Finn wants me to, of course. I haven't told him yet.

DIRK:

Wow. That's huge. And no way would he be stupid enough to say he doesn't want you.

ME:

I think you're right.

DIRK:

I'm pissed you didn't let me meet him first though. [winky face emoji]

DIRK:

Shit, I hope my next movie pays enough so I can buy a house there.

ME:

You'd do that?

DIRK:

Dude, we're twins. I might have to spend some time with Steve and Baz, but you're my home.

I blinked back tears. Dammit, I'd cried more this week than in the last five years combined.

Okay. I was staying. As long as Finn wanted me to.

Suddenly I wasn't that tired anymore, and lyrics were bouncing around in my brain. I threw back the covers and got out of bed.

I had a song to write. Maybe two.

FINN:

We're at the festival. Charlie's scheduled to go on at 7:30. But you probably knew that. Where are you?

ME:

The amphitheater. We're getting the tables set up for the judges.

FINN:

Wanna go somewhere and make out instead? Charlie and Kirk are hanging out with Kirk's parents.

ME:

Fuck yes

ME:

Meet me behind the Honey Spot booth

FINN:

On my way

As soon as Finn walked around the corner to the back of the booth, I grabbed him and shoved him against the plywood wall. There was a dumpster a few yards away, but it didn't smell too bad and at least no one could see us. He grinned and put his arms around me. I tipped my bowler back on my head and went in for a kiss, reveling in the feel and smell of him.

He broke away, panting. "It's good to see you."

I mouthed his Adam's apple. "I missed you last night." My hat collided with his jaw and fell off somewhere behind me.

"*Mmmm*. Same." Tilting his head to give me better access, he slid his hands into the back pockets of my jeans and pulled our groins together. Fuck, that was hot.

Reluctantly I left off my exploration of his neck. "I think we'd better stop here, or else we'll get arrested for public indecency."

His grin was unrepentant. "Worth it." His smile dropped and he lifted a hand to tuck a lock of hair behind my ear. "Can you stay over at my place tonight?"

I nodded. "As long as there isn't some emergency keeping me here late."

"Good. Look, um, I wanted to ask you." His gaze fell to the open collar of my button-down, and he swallowed. I tensed, bracing for whatever it might be. "Um, I know Maplewood isn't exactly what you're used to; it's not trendy or metropolitan or anything. But, would you consider staying? Like for at least a few months so we can see where things go between us?"

My heart started beating double time. "I—" I cleared my throat. "I'd like that." I smiled into his eyes, and he gave me a shy smile back.

"Good. Me too. I mean, I'd like that too." Then he stopped talking and just stared at me, still smiling but as if he didn't have any idea what to do next.

I threw my arms around his neck and kissed him.

The door at the back of the booth slammed open, and Ever King stepped out with a large black trash bag bursting at the seams. He stopped when he saw us. "Uh, hey?"

Shit. Finn and I broke apart. "Sorry, Ever. We'll get out of your way." My face had to be bright red. Ever owned the Honey Spot, and he was competing in the amateur contest. I'd spoken to him several times this week.

"Hi, Ever." Of course Finn knew the guy.

"Hey, Finn. I heard you two were seeing each other." He shrugged then headed for the dumpster. "As long as you keep your clothes on, I don't care what you're up to back here."

I took the opportunity to snatch my hat off the ground, and I occupied myself with dusting it off while Ever finished his garbage run.

As he walked back, he said, "Oh, Finn, tell Charlie good luck at the amateur competition." He grimaced. "Though I heard the Rocktogenarians are playing 'Uptown Funk'. Kian and I don't have a prayer of winning against them." He glanced at his watch. "Speaking of, I'd better get to the amphitheater." The door slammed shut behind him as he went inside.

"Fuck." Finn glanced toward the amphitheater. "Charlie's scheduled to go on right after the Rocktogenarians."

I groaned. "Sorry. Zeke made the schedule. He said he did it randomly, but it's hard to know what that means in his mind."

He sighed. "Charlie'll be fine. He told me he's not expecting to win; he just wants to do it for his parents and for the experience." He put his arms around me again and smiled. "Back to what we were discussing before we were interrupted...."

I raised an eyebrow. "Were we discussing anything though? I remember us using our mouths for other things."

"Yeah, yeah. But this is important."

"Okay?"

"Yeah, um, I don't know how long Zeke's cool with you staying at the compound, but...." He trailed off and his eyes searched mine.

"But?"

He inhaled deeply then said, "But I'd like you to stay with me and Charlie for as long as you want to."

I blinked, a slow smile curving my lips. "Yeah? Is Charlie okay with it?"

His face went slightly red. "I, uh, haven't asked him. But I will! I just wanted him to get through the competition first. I'm sure he'll be fine with it."

I pressed my lips together. He probably would be. But Charlie had only lived with Finn for a couple of months. I didn't want to suddenly make their entire home life dynamic all about me. My gut said we should ease into it.

So instead of jumping up and down in celebration and shrieking, *Yes!*—which is what I really wanted to do—I gave him a long, tender kiss. "That's sweet of you. But I think I should stay at the compound for the next couple of months at least. Let's take it slow for Charlie and for us. I'd like to see how things go when I don't have the festival taking all of my time."

His face lit up. "I heard that *at least*. No matter how long it takes you to move in with me and Charlie, you're staying in Maplewood permanently and you know it."

I pushed him away, my bratty side coming out to play. "I know no such thing. We haven't even been on a date yet. What if you can't hold up your end of a conversation for that long? What if you have a bad habit I can't stand?"

He picked me up and spun me around. "You're staying!"

Okay, that was more like it. Except I lost my hat again.

Finn put me down and leaned over to grab the bowler, which appeared unharmed. He dusted it off and carefully placed it on my head, tapping the crown to make sure it was secure. "There you go."

I kissed him once more, putting my hands on his waist. His skin beneath the t-shirt was warm, and I could feel his diaphragm moving as he breathed. My heart felt like it would burst out of my chest.

"I haven't talked to Zeke about it yet, but he doesn't have anyone scheduled to use the cabins this summer." I shook my head. "Which is a waste of a perfectly good revenue opportunity if you ask me."

He chuckled. "Noted. Hey, maybe your brothers can come visit in June. The Pride festival is my favorite." He winced. "Sorry. Nothing against the music festival, but it doesn't have a parade with drag queens."

"I'll keep that in mind if I end up being involved with it next year." I slid one of my hands around to the front of his t-shirt to smooth it across his chest. He pressed his lips to mine, smiling against my mouth.

My phone chimed with a text, and I groaned as I pulled away. "They're probably looking for me so we can go over the judging rules again."

"I don't regret a thing." He released me but grabbed my hand. "I'll walk back with you. Charlie and Kirk were going to hang out with Kirk's parents and watch the other acts."

There was a decent-sized crowd already forming, even though we still had over twenty minutes before the first performance. Finn scanned the crowd, then waved. "I'll be over there until it's time for Charlie to head backstage. Have fun judging!" He kissed me on the corner of my mouth before weaving away through the crowd.

I watched him go with what I was sure was a silly smile on my face. I was staying. He wanted me to stay. Fizzy excitement swirled through my body as I made my way to the area in front of the stage they'd roped off for the judges.

I could see Zeke with Roy, who was acting as our emcee, and the other judges. I'd met most of them already, but not all. A woman with long, multi-color hair was standing next to

Zeke. Was that...? "Oh, my god!" I ran the rest of the way and hopped over the rope barrier. "Mona!"

She whirled around and gave me a huge smile. "Drakey!" She held out her arms and I collided with her, spinning her around as we laughed. Her sparkly red dress ballooned out as we twirled.

"I can't believe you're here!" Not letting go of Mona, I turned to Zeke. "Did you arrange this?"

He gave a weird little shrug, almost looking embarrassed. "I thought I'd do something nice for ya, since you've been working so hard on the festival. I had Jake call your twin to see if he wanted to be another judge, but he had movie stuff to do today and couldn't get here on time. He suggested we ask Mona." He tipped his head in her direction.

"Well, thank you. I'm grateful."

Mona spoke into my ear. "I'm here for a couple of days. I'm dying to meet this boyfriend of yours."

I wiggled my eyebrows and whispered back, "Things just got real. I told him I'm going to stay."

"Yes!" She jumped in the air with a fist raised high. I got another hug and a kiss on the cheek. "Congratulations!" Then in a swirl of sparkly skirts she went into professional mode. "Sorry for delaying things, gentlemen."

The others assured her there was no problem. Zeke merely grunted and started pointing. "Drake, you know Roy from Harmonic Circus. And Bastian Hall from Hall of Fame is our other last-minute addition to the judging panel."

I waved at him. "Thanks again for filling in on Thursday."

"We had a blast, and I'm looking forward to seeing all your local talent tonight."

Zeke carried on. "This is Dmitri Fairchild, the violinist." I nodded at him. "And you know Pan MacLeod from Satyr's Kiss."

"Good to see you again." I waved at him.

"Hey, Drake. I was sorry we didn't get to hear you play on Thursday."

I smirked. "You got to see Hall of Fame. I think it's a fair trade." Everyone laughed, and Zeke slapped Bastian on the back, causing him to stumble forward.

Zeke held up a stack of rating sheets. "Y'all pay attention. All of the acts are listed here, and you'll mark your rating after each one finishes. We'll tally up the ratings at the end and announce the top three winners."

I held up my hand. "I have to abstain from voting on the 7:30 p.m. act, Charlie Hapwell. I'm dating his... family member."

Everyone nodded. Zeke waved at the tables where we were supposed to sit. "Let's get settled. Roy's gonna introduce us and kick everythin' off."

Roy went over to the stage to make sure the first act was ready to go, and the rest of us sat down. Zeke had put our names on the backs of our chairs. I was on one end, with Mona beside me, and he was on the other.

The crowd had almost doubled in size. I honestly hadn't expected the competition to be this well-attended, but maybe having some famous musicians as judges was part of the draw.

I hoped Charlie wasn't nervous about performing in front of this many people. It was one thing to stand on a stage in front of rows of empty seats. Facing actual people was completely different.

TEXT CONVERSATION, SUNDAY 4:57 P.M

DRAKE:

How's Charlie doing?

FINN:

Seems okay. He's a little wound up, but that's to be expected.

DRAKE:

Good. He's got this.

CHAPTER 19

FINN

Sunday, the final day of the festival

I slid my phone back into my pocket. "Drake was checking on you."

Charlie rolled his eyes, but he smiled. "I'm fine."

"That's what I told him." I glanced over at Kirk, who was occupied talking to his parents. We were sitting on the hill behind the amphitheater's rows of built-in seats. "Listen, I asked Drake if he would stay in Maplewood after the festival."

He whipped his head around to stare at me. "He already said he'd stay for a couple of weeks. You mean he'll be here longer?"

I nodded, my smile breaking through despite my best efforts. "He wants to give our relationship a shot."

Charlie's grin was everything. I was already over the moon about Drake staying, but to see Charlie's happiness about it? I was floating with joy.

He threw his arms around me, which was slightly awkward due to our seated position, but I wasn't complaining. "He should come live with us."

I chuckled. "That's what I said. But he feels like he'd be intruding on our time together."

He gave me another eye roll, then released me from the hug. "We'll wear him down."

I was still laughing when Roy walked onto the stage and asked for everyone's attention. "Welcome to this year's Maplewood Amateur Music Competition!" We all clapped, and I felt Charlie stirring beside me, like he wanted to jump up and cheer. "If this is your first time joining us, I'll just go over the rules very quickly. Participation is limited to people who live within fifty miles of Maplewood as their primary residence and who have either never been a professional musician or who make less than a certain dollar amount per year as a professional musician. You can see our website for details. All proceeds over and above the operating costs for next year's festival will be donated to the Maplewood Foundation and the Vermont Bee Conservancy. Now let me introduce our panel of judges."

I leaned forward, waiting for Drake's name to be announced. We were a good distance from the stage, but he was readily identifiable by his hat, seated at one end of the judges' table.

"Our first judge is Zeke Knight, founder of the Maplewood Music Festival." He paused for the applause to die down, then he introduced the lead singer from Hall of Fame, who'd apparently asked to be a judge so he'd been added to the panel at the last minute. Next was Dmitri Fairchild, who I knew from way back. Then he called out Pan MacLeod from Satyr's Kiss. Roy again waited for the applause to fade. "We have another surprise addition to the judging panel. Please welcome singer-songwriter Mona Derry!

Charlie and I exchanged a shocked glance. Drake's sister was here? He'd told me their relationship was cordial but not terribly close. It was wonderful that she'd come to support him. I tried to make out her face when she turned around to wave at the audience, but all I could see was her long hair, which was dyed blue, green, pink, and purple.

Charlie nudged me. "Bet you didn't think you'd be meeting the family so soon."

I nudged him back, smirking. "I'm not the only one."

"Oh, fuck."

Roy held up his hand for silence. "And also please welcome Drake Derry, songwriter and musician." Everyone clapped and cheered, Charlie and I loudest of all. Drake turned around and lifted his hat to the audience. Roy chuckled. "Drake arrived last week and has been helping Zeke with the details of putting the festival on. We're all hoping you come back next year, Drake."

More cheering. Drake shouted something at Roy, but I couldn't make it out. Roy laughed, and when he could be heard again, he said, "Drake wants us to show him the money." Everyone laughed. "But, according to Maplewood Matters, you might stay for other reasons." The crowd roared and whistled, and I ducked my head, though Kirk and Charlie were pointing at me, so it probably didn't do any good.

Roy clapped his hands together. "Okay, that's enough, people. Young love has to bloom in its own time, or some such claptrap." My face burned as everyone chuckled. "Let's welcome our first act, Ever King and Kian Lass."

We all applauded, and Ever and Kian came out with their cello and guitar. While they played, I kept half my attention on Charlie, but he seemed relatively calm. We had over two hours before he was to perform. I hoped he could keep from overthinking and freaking himself out.

An hour or so later, Kirk's parents offered us some of the sandwiches and snacks they'd brought, but Charlie refused, saying he didn't think he could eat.

At last it was time to head down to the stage. Kirk's mom

kissed Charlie on the cheek for luck, and Kirk gave him a bro hug. Charlie picked up his guitar case, and I carried his amp. We made our way down the hill to the right side of the stage. The current act, the Rocktogenarians, would finish in a few minutes, and then it would be Charlie's turn. Luckily the festival provided a roadie-type person who helped everyone get set up with their mics and other equipment if they had it, so all Charlie had to worry about was playing his song.

The Rocktogenarians were indeed playing "Uptown Funk". And they were playing the hell out of it. Charlie had said he didn't expect to win, but I hoped the ladies didn't intimidate him. Not that I'd ever ask. Right now my job was to look confident and proud of him.

Charlie's spine was straight and his walk was steady as we went down the final steps to the area next to the stage. Fuck, those women were loud. Charlie's acoustic guitar would be a welcome relief after this.

Roy greeted Charlie and handed him off to the roadie, who I didn't recognize. He was around Zeke's age, so maybe they were buddies from back in the day. Charlie told him he just wanted a microphone for his singing, and his acoustic amp would do the rest. He took his guitar out of the case, and I traded him his amp for the case.

"You'll be amazing, Charlie. I'm so proud of you." I gave him a quick half-hug, since his arms were full.

"Thanks, Finn." He smiled at me until his eyes went over my shoulder, and his face went pale and slack.

I turned. From this angle, the crowd appeared to extend to the horizon. Only the darkening sky was visible beyond the people sitting at the top of the hill. I had no idea how many attendees there were, but the number was at least equivalent to a high school football game.

Charlie looked like he might be sick. His eyes kept scanning the crowd, who were getting to their feet and singing along with the Rocktogenarians' final chorus. The noise was deafening.

"Charlie?" I put my hand on his shoulder, since there was no possible way he could've heard me.

He met my eyes and shook his head. "I can't do it." I had no trouble reading his lips. He closed his eyes for a long moment, then he opened them again and extended his hand for the guitar case.

The Rocktogenarians finished their song and were bowing their way through a standing ovation.

Charlie grabbed for the guitar case, but I pulled it away. "Charlie, you were so excited about this." I was yelling to be heard over the applause. "What's the worst that could happen?"

He glared at me. "I'll throw up all over the stage. That's the worst that could happen." He seemed to decide I wasn't going to hand him the guitar case, so he started walking toward the steps with his guitar on its strap over his shoulder and his amp tucked under one arm.

Oh, shit. "Charlie, wait!" The crowd was quieter now, and the Rocktogenarians were removing their equipment from the stage.

I put my hand on his arm to stop him. "Are you sure? Did you try visualizing how you'll feel tomorrow if you don't play tonight?"

He gave me an incredulous look. "I don't need to visualize it! I'll feel fucking relieved."

Dammit, he'd been so excited. Everything in my gut said Charlie would regret not performing, but I wouldn't force him to do it.

Though that didn't mean I wouldn't try to change his mind.

Roy appeared. "What's going on?"

Thank fuck. Roy was his teacher. He'd have some magical words to bolster Charlie's confidence.

Charlie firmed up his quivering lips and jerked his head at the crowd. "I'm sorry, Mr. Griffin, but I can't do it. I can't be onstage with all those people staring at me. It's too much."

Roy nodded sympathetically. "I understand, Charlie. Public performance isn't for everyone."

Okay, so Roy was *not* interested in changing Charlie's mind. I ran my hand through my hair and spun around, searching for someone, anyone to help.

I didn't have to look very far; Drake was right there. He smiled reassuringly and patted my arm. "I've got this, Finn. You can leave it to me."

I blinked. When was the last time someone had told me that? I'd felt so alone since Charlie had come to live with me. Floundering along without a clue as to whether I was doing things right or making them worse. And maybe Charlie wouldn't listen to Drake either, but even having him take over, having him try, was such a comfort. I put the guitar case down and rubbed my watering eyes.

Drake, having zero idea that not only was I falling in love with him, but he'd just cemented his place in my life forever, edged in front of me to speak to Charlie. "What if you weren't alone?" He reached out and rubbed Charlie's shoulder. "Crowds are fucking scary. I get it. But it's easier if somebody's up there with you."

Charlie hesitated, seeming conflicted. "You'd do that?"

"Of course. Remember how much fun it is to play together? It'll be like that, only with people dancing in their seats at the same time."

Zeke and the other judges, including Drake's sister, crowded around. Roy looked between Drake, Charlie, and the others. "Charlie is apprehensive about playing in front of such a large audience. Drake has volunteered to go on stage with him, but he doesn't meet the qualifications for being an amateur musician, and he's not a Maplewood resident."

Charlie and Drake's faces were identical in their disappointment.

Dmitri cleared his throat. "While rules are important, so is being supportive of our friends and neighbors. It's not like we're hosting *American Idol* here. What if we let everyone know that because Drake's a professional musician, Charlie's not eligible to win, but we're still allowing him to perform?"

Zeke nodded. "I like it. And we've got the resident thing taken care of too."

I frowned. Had Drake already told Zeke he was staying? Nope, not based on the way he was raising his eyebrows.

Zeke waved his hand toward Drake. "I'm retiring this year. Movin' to the beach where it's warm. Jake and I—Drake's friends with Jake Lord." This was an aside to the other judges. "Jake helped me get you here so's I could see if you'd be a good fit to take over the festival, and you are. You'll take over the compound too, so there you go." He made a *ta-da* gesture. "Resident."

TEXT CONVERSATION SUNDAY, 11:21 P.M

DRAKE:

What the fuck, Wesley? You thought it'd be better to manipulate me into going to Vermont "to help your friend" than to tell me I was effectively going on a week-long job interview?

WESLEY:

Can I call you to explain?

DRAKE:

No.

CHAPTER 20

DRAKE

Sunday, the final day of the festival

I stared at Zeke, struggling to absorb all the ramifications of what he'd just said. He and Wesley had decided I might be the right person to take over the festival—and the compound —so they'd engineered my coming here as some sort of test?

"If Drake will go on stage with me, I'll play."

My attention snapped back to Charlie. Fuck. Focus on Charlie first, murder Zeke and Wesley later.

I found a grin from somewhere and said, "Can you go ahead and get set up onstage? I'm gonna see if I can borrow Agnes Peabody's sweet Les Paul Gibson." I managed to keep my Texas drawl to a minimum, but it was close.

Finn was regarding me with a concerned expression, but I gave him a wink and a wave as I jogged over to where the Rocktogenarians were packing up the last of their stuff. No way had Finn known about what Zeke had been planning. He hadn't even known who I was when I hit town.

"Agnes!" I came to a stop next to her. "Hey, I hope this isn't too much to ask, but could I please borrow your Gibson for, like, five minutes?"

Her sharp eyes flicked between me and Charlie, who was grimly walking up the steps to the stage with his guitar and amp. Roscoe, Zeke's roadie buddy, was waiting to help him get set up.

"Charlie needs some moral support? Of course you can borrow her, my dear. Her name's Janis."

"Thank you so much. I'll be careful with her."

She scoffed. "Janis would prefer to be played hard and long."

I grinned, for real this time. "Then that's what she'll get."

She helped me adjust the strap and handed me a sparkling blue pick that matched the guitar. Then she plugged in the amp and handed it to me to carry up the steps. "Knock 'em dead, Drake."

"I'll do my best."

When I got to the stage, Charlie was dithering around, pretending to fiddle with his amp. I nudged him. "Go tell everyone who you are and what you're playing. Get the song started. I just need a minute and I'll play in, okay?" He gulped but nodded. "Remember, this is going to be fun!" He made a good effort at matching my smile.

Roscoe walked over and pointed at the front of the stage. "I set up a second mic for ya."

"Thanks, Roscoe." He nodded and headed offstage. The amp was battery-powered, so I just needed to turn it on. I knelt next to it, holding Janis out of the way. Charlie reached the mic, and the lights went out except a single spotlight.

Charlie's shaky voice echoed through the amphitheater. "Hi. Um, my name's Charlie Hapwell and, uh, you probably know Drake Derry." Some moderate cheering broke out. "I want to dedicate this song to my parents. Noelle and Jin Hapwell, and, uh, Finn Hunnicutt."

The audience clapped, and I barely kept myself from spinning around to gawp at him. Holy shit, that was big. I was so happy for Finn. Smiling, I leaned down to power on the amp. My bowler fell forward, landing on its crown.

Charlie strummed the first chords and began to sing. He was tentative at first, but then his voice became stronger.

I looked at my hat. I'd been planning on joining Charlie on "Can You Feel the Love Tonight", using the Gibson to add chords while Charlie did the fingered notes. But since I was here, I might as well go big and help Charlie honor both his mom and his dad. Plus, I'd promised Agnes I'd give Janis a workout.

I let Charlie get to the chorus, then I stood, making sure I was at the edge of the spotlight. Positioning Janis in front of me, I held my bowler up high, my left arm outstretched at a sharp angle to my shoulder. I tucked my chin into my bicep and let the hat tumble down my arm and land on my head.

The crowd roared. I'd done well with the timing; Charlie was about to start the second verse. I walked up behind him and picked out the unmistakable intro to "Smooth".

Charlie's head spun around, but he turned back to the microphone almost instantly, continuing to pluck out the melody for his song while I sang the first verse and chorus for "Smooth". I stepped back and he didn't hesitate to continue singing "Can You Feel the Love Tonight". I was so proud of how he was taking it in stride, because we'd never practiced this.

I stepped forward and back to let him know when I was coming in and out, and then at the end I joined him on the final chorus of "Can You Feel the Love Tonight". He gave me a delighted grin.

We held the final note, and the crowd cheered and whistled their approval. Charlie grabbed my hand, and we bowed to the audience.

Roy walked out onto the stage and took Charlie's mic.

"Another round of applause for Charlie Hapwell and Drake Derry!"

Charlie and I bowed again, then we went to grab our amps and leave the stage.

"Oh my god, Drake! That was incredible! I can't believe you did the mash-up!" Charlie practically floated down the steps.

"You were amazing, Charlie. I knew you'd roll with it." I smiled to see Finn waiting for us. He caught Charlie in a hug, so I took the time to return Janis to Agnes. "Thank you so much. Janis has a wonderful sound."

Agnes beamed. "You gave her the picking she needed!" A faint scent of weed wafted from Agnes' general direction, and I smiled. No wonder she was cracking jokes tonight.

Finn was waiting when I turned around. He wrapped me in his arms and kissed me, nudging my hat up when it got in the way. "Thank you. I didn't want Charlie to miss out on the experience, and you—" He got choked up.

"I enjoyed every minute of it." I kissed him again. "I should probably get back to judging before the next act."

He barked out a laugh. "No need. They found a substitute." He turned us so I could see the judges' table, where fucking Dirk was sitting in my chair with a shit-eating grin on his face.

"What the fuck?" Finn let me go and I ran over to embrace my twin. "How are you here? I thought you had to be on set?"

"Pure FOMO. Plus we got done early today, and I'm driving back tonight. Introduce me to your boyfriend."

I glanced at Zeke, but he waved me off. I took that to mean they had the judging under control. He and I would be having a long conversation later.

Mona waved but seemed intent on watching the next act, so I'd introduce her to Finn tomorrow. I pulled Dirk with me over to where Finn and Charlie were waiting. "Guys, this is my brother Dirk. Dirk, this is Finn and Charlie."

Finn held out his hand for Dirk to shake, and Charlie copied him.

I gestured toward the top of the hill outside the amphitheater. "Let's go outside so we can talk."

We all headed up the stairs. Kirk and his family waved at Charlie, who turned his puppy dog eyes on Finn. "Can I stay at Kirk's house tonight? I promise I'll come home and change before school tomorrow."

I could tell Finn would rather have kept Charlie close, but he merely said, "Sure. Leave your guitar and amp with me and I'll take them home. Give me a hug." Charlie did so, and I heard Finn mutter, "I love you, and I'm so proud of you."

Charlie came over and gave me a big hug. "Thanks, Drake. You were right. That was a hell of a lot of fun. I'm gonna try to get Kirk to play with me next year." With a wave at Dirk, he spun around and trotted off.

Dirk smiled at Finn. "Your kid's pretty talented, especially for how short a time Drake said he's been playing."

"Thanks. I'm very proud of him."

Dirk glanced toward the parking lot. "Look, I'm sorry I can't stay longer, but I do have to be on set at 6 a.m. tomorrow. Finn, I won't give you the shovel talk, because Drake can take care of himself. I'll try to come back and spend more time with you guys later this summer."

I poked him in the side. "You'd better. By the way I bought a painting for you. It's by this fantastic local artist. You're going to love it."

He brightened. "Thanks! I can't wait to see it. That'll give me an incentive to come back even sooner."

"Thanks for coming, Dirk. It was good to see you." We hugged, and I felt myself tear up for what felt like the hundredth time today. I'd known he and I were going our separate paths for a while now, but it suddenly seemed so much more real.

I was distracted from my introspection by the feel of Dirk's ribs under his t-shirt. "Bro, what the fuck? How much weight have you lost?"

He groaned as he stepped back, and I chuckled when Dirk wiped his eyes at the same time I did. "You don't want to know."

I scowled. "You said there was all this food available."

"Not if you've got a sex scene tomorrow."

"Dirk."

He waved me off. "It's fine. Filming will be over in a couple of months, and I can catch up on my eating then. But for now I've got to be mostly naked for the camera, rolling around with my mostly naked costar." He made a face, and I echoed his expression. Dirk was gay like me, and he was playing a straight character.

"That'll be a big test of your acting abilities."

He tilted his head back and forth. "The director said the kissing scenes were hot, so I'm hoping this'll just be more of the same."

I shook my head, smiling. "It's so weird to think of you as an actor. But you need to go. Drive safe, and I'll talk to you this week."

"You know it." With a wave at Finn, Dirk turned and made for the exit.

"You okay?"

I nodded, tearing my eyes from where Dirk had disappeared to look at Finn. "Yeah. It's so strange to feel us evolving into different lives after being joined at the hip for so long."

He wrapped his arms around me. "It wasn't the same at all for me and Addy. Maybe because we weren't identical, I don't know. But we always had our own interests and our own friend groups."

I hugged him silently for a moment. "I need to talk to Zeke tonight. But not here. I'm gonna go wait for him at the compound."

He rubbed my back. "I can hang out in your cabin."

"You have work in the morning."

He met my eyes. "Waking up early is worth it if I get to spend time with you."

I leaned back in his embrace and goggled at him. "That was terrible. Truly awful."

He laughed. "I mean it though. We've barely had any time together the last few nights."

He was right, and I did want to spend the night with him. But I didn't think I'd be very good company until after I'd had it out with Zeke. "You go home. I'll come over once Zeke and I have talked."

"Okay. But if you're too tired, let me know and I'll come to you. You've had a long week."

I tipped my hat back and kissed him. Gah, how did I deserve someone so sweet?

Before we left, I texted Mona that I'd catch up with her tomorrow. Finn walked me back to the compound since he'd parked there.

He drove home, and I stopped at the cabin to pack some clothes for the morning, then I put those in my SUV. Nova's car was in the lot, so I went into the house. She was in the kitchen. "Hey, are you feeding Mabel? I can take care of it."

She set Mabel's bowl down on the counter and frowned at me. "Aren't you exhausted?" She looked at her watch. "Did the competition end early or something? I left after you and Charlie finished."

"No. I didn't stay." I leaned my hip against the kitchen table and crossed my arms. "Did you know about this plan to have me take over the festival? And this place?" I spread my arms out to indicate the compound.

She flinched. "Shit. Uh, yeah. Sorry."

I crossed my arms "Why aren't you taking it over? Or at least the compound?"

She was shaking her head before I finished my question. "Nope. No way. I'm never getting involved in the music industry, and Uncle Zeke knows it." She went to the fridge and pulled out a plastic container of something and a head of cabbage. "He's my great-uncle, in case you didn't know. On my father's side. Way back in the day, right after my dad graduated high school, Zeke got him a job at a record label. Just an entry level position, but my dad rose through the ranks, yada, yada, yada."

I went to help her prepare Mabel's meal. She handed me a knife and the head of cabbage.

"Anyway, he met my mom at some fancy party. They hooked up a few times, then she got pregnant with me. They got married, but Zeke's the one who ended up raising me. My parents essentially got addicted to the parties, the drugs and booze. When I was six years old they did some cocaine that turned out to be laced with some nasty toxic stuff. They didn't survive."

"I'm sorry. That's awful."

She sent me a faint smile. "Thanks. I'm pretty sure you can empathize somewhat with how the industry can change your parents into people you'd never recognize."

"Oh, yes."

"Right. So even though Zeke did something positive with his industry experience—creating the music festival foundation and all that—I've never been able to even consider participating in it myself." She shrugged one shoulder. "I grew up in this house and on this property, but Zeke knows I'm good with not inheriting it. He's leaving me everything else." She grinned. "When he said he wanted to move somewhere warm,

I told him to buy a beach house. *That's* the kind of inheritance I want."

She handed me Mabel's bowl and put the chopping board into the sink. "I hope you'll take Zeke up on his offer. And even though I don't want the property for myself, I do have some ideas for updating it and making some money off of it, instead of letting those cabins sit vacant most of the year."

I eyed her with interest. "Yeah? I've been thinking about that too."

"Good. We'll do lunch soon and discuss. Are you sure you want to take Mabel's dinner?"

"Yeah. I'm waiting for Zeke to get home. We're gonna have a conversation."

She sighed and pulled her keys out of her pocket. "All I can say is, he meant well. But I'm not the one in your shoes."

I grabbed the flashlight Zeke kept by the back door and followed her outside. Talking to Nova had calmed me down a little, but I was still fuming about being manipulated as I headed down the path to Mabel's stump. I was sure Nova was right, and Zeke *had* meant well. But, fuck, couldn't he—and Wesley, let's not forget—have treated me like an adult and told me about the opportunity to take over before I left Texas?

Something rustled in the trees up ahead on the right. Shit. "I'm coming, Mabel. Or whoever that is. Please don't eat me instead of what's in the bowl. I'm sorry your dinner is late." I sped up, but my clogs weren't made for jogging on uneven ground in the dark. "You know, Mabel, maybe you can provide some perspective here. I mean, I want to stay in Maplewood, right? I'm not giving up Finn either way. And I did enjoy running the festival, and I could do a lot with the compound. I guess what I'm saying is, I'd be a fool to turn down what Zeke's offering. But he sure pissed me off the way he went about it."

I made it to the clearing, hurrying to place the bowl on the stump. "Here you go." I looked around but couldn't see much of anything, even with the flashlight. "Enjoy your dinner. I'll let you know what I decide." I heard more rustling, so I hotfooted it out of the clearing and back down the path.

I slowed as I neared Zeke's house. He'd probably be home by now. I was tired, and I was sure he was tired too. It'd be easier to put this conversation off until tomorrow, but I needed it done. I would most likely take Zeke up on his offer —or was it a demand?—but I deserved some groveling from him for all the scheming behind my back.

Wesley could grovel to me tomorrow.

Zeke was waiting for me on the back porch. When I climbed the steps, he said, "You want a glass of somethin'?"

"No thanks." I sat in the chair next to his, which happened to be the one with the cushion Aragornette had destroyed. It was still comfortable. "Zeke, do you understand why I'm pissed?"

He heaved a huge sigh. "Yep. And I shouldn't have sprung everything on ya in the middle of the competition, and in front of everyone else."

I gripped the arms of the chair, trying to disperse my tension. The public announcement was the least of my concerns. "Take me through the thought process of not telling me why I was really invited here."

He rubbed his chest. "I was in a hurry. My health ain't what it used to be, and the doctor said running the festival is too much stress. No way I'd be able to wait and vet someone during next year's festival. Nova's the only family I'd consider givin' it to, but she's too smart to want it."

I snorted. True.

"An' I didn't wanna sell to some big corporation. Right now bands and artists beg to be in the lineup. It's a fuckin' honor to be invited. Some music label or satellite radio company would've sucked the soul out of the festival and turned this property into luxury condos or somethin'. I called around to a bunch of my friends to see if they knew anybody who was smart and hardworking but kind of looking for their calling. Jake brought you up right away."

I wasn't sure if I should be embarrassed or flattered that when Zeke mentioned needing an aimless drifter, Wesley's mind had immediately come up with me.

"Anyways we were both worried you'd say no right off if we made this trip sound like more than a one-shot, temporary thing.

That was a valid concern, I could admit. I might have still done it, but living in Vermont and running a festival wasn't anything I'd have considered as a career path before I experienced it for myself.

"I can't afford to buy you out."

"Not a problem. Festival grounds and the festival itself are all owned by the nonprofit that runs it. You'll have a board position and be president of the nonprofit. Which, by the way, comes with a nice salary."

"President!" I sputtered. "I don't have a college degree. In fact I only have a GED. I didn't even go to regular high school."

He shrugged. "You think I went to college? Most of the day-to-day shit is done by the directors. If you have questions, there's plenty of people to ask for advice. And it's not like I'll be livin' on another planet, even if I move to the beach."

I had severe reservations, but if Zeke could do it, there wasn't any reason to think I couldn't. "What about the compound? Do you own that?"

He glanced around fondly. "Yep. We'll do a rent to own contract, with the rent being the work you'll put in maintaining the property. If you make it big with one of your songs, you can pay me cash to make it yours faster. And when I die, it'll be yours free and clear."

Holy shit, that was incredibly generous. "How do you know I won't get tired of it and fuck off? Leave you high and dry?"

He shrugged. "I don't. All I have is Jake's word that you're trustworthy, plus the work ethic you've shown this past week. I'm pretty confident if you decide you don't want the festival or the compound anymore, you'll work with me to find someone who does."

Well, shit. I'd absolutely do that. Even if Finn dumped me tomorrow, I wouldn't have it in me to leave Zeke in the lurch.

"Okay. Thanks for telling me all this. I'm gonna need some time to think about it."

He eyeballed me. "You're lyin'. You want it. You just wanna make me wait as some kinda payback."

I stood up. "Do you blame me?" I walked calmly down the steps and crossed the parking lot to my car. Zeke didn't respond.

I fired off a text to Wesley before I started the car. He responded immediately, wanting to talk. Ha. Not tonight.

Finn had left the front door unlocked for me, and he was already in bed, reading something on his phone. "Hey. How are you? Do you want something to drink?" He set his phone on the nightstand as I walked over to him.

"No thanks." I dropped my backpack next to the bed before bending down and hugging him. Why did Finn's hugs always make me feel like I was home? "Thanks for waiting up. I need to shower real quick."

He kissed me. "Take your time. I'll be up." He cupped my face, running his thumb over the scruff on my jaw. "I'm glad you're here." Damn, the warmth in his hazel eyes was making my chest feel all hot.

"Me too." I leaned my cheek into his hand.

"Did you talk to Zeke?"

"Yeah. I'm making him wait til tomorrow to get my answer though." I winked.

He grinned wide and put both arms around me again, hugging me tighter. I pulled back and he let go. "Shower. Be right back." Picking up my backpack, I went into the bathroom.

I took as quick a shower as I could. I'd thought about doing a very thorough clean, but it was almost midnight, and I was wiped. We had tomorrow night for that. My whole body went all fluttery, and I grinned at myself in the mirror like a fool. We had tomorrow because I was staying.

I didn't bother putting on any clothes. I walked out of the bathroom naked, my dick already standing at attention. Sure, I was exhausted, but I was also twenty-two years old. My dick was in charge.

Finn did a double take when he saw me, which gave me a warm glow of pride. I hoped he never stopped looking at me that way.

He threw back the covers, and I slid onto the mattress.

"Hi." Finn rolled on top of me, slotting himself between my legs and giving me a slow, sweet kiss. I made a *Mmmm* sound and bucked my hips up into his. He smiled against my mouth. God, when he did that it made me feel like I was something special, like being with me made him so happy.

I gripped his hips and thrust up against him once more.

"Uh uh. I want to take my time with you. You deserve it."

"Babe, I want that so bad, you have no idea. But I'm running on fumes here. My stiffy's the only thing keeping me awake.

He chuckled. "Okay. Message received."

"Tomorrow night, though."

He kissed my neck, then licked his way up to my earlobe. I shivered, and he smiled against me. Fuck, that was hot. He blew a breath into my ear. "Are you sure you won't move in here?" He tweaked my nipple, and my hips shot up without me telling them to.

"Torture will get you nowhere." My eyes rolled back in my head when he replaced his fingers on my nipple with his lips.

After a moment he lifted his head. Ignoring my wail of protest, he brought our lips together in a hot, wet kiss. He finally moved his dick against mine, driving his pelvis into me. I vaguely wished we had some lube, but Finn moved just so, trapping the tip of my dick between his abs and mine, and I came, shuddering against him.

I woke a few minutes later when he ran a damp washcloth down my belly. "Fuck. Sorry. Did you get off?" I struggled to sit up, wanting to check.

"Oh, yes. No need to worry about me."

"Good." I flopped back onto the mattress.

He tossed the washcloth into the bathroom before sliding into bed and pulling me close.

I smiled against his skin.

TEXT CONVERSATION MONDAY, 11:46 A.M

DRAKE:

Hey, I already told Dirk and Mona. I'm staying in Maplewood.

STEVE:

You think Dirk didn't text me last night?
Also, Baz and I are keeping your rabbit.

DRAKE:

Thanks. I was worried about how she'd handle being separated from the others.

STEVE:

And I'm coming to visit when you least expect it.

DRAKE:

Is that some sort of threat?

STEVE:

Yes.

EPILOGUE
DRAKE

October

"I'm not saying you didn't see Mabel the other night. What I'm saying is that all of the so-called 'evidence' the Cryptid Night group gathered—at least what I saw—was easily explainable."

I snickered to myself as Finn tried to walk a line between his disbelief in Mabel and Charlie's obvious certainty that he'd seen her twice now.

Charlie opened his mouth to argue more, so I nudged him. "Look over there! That booth has stuffed Mabels!" I pointed at the sign next to the display of green leaf-covered stuffies.

Charlie and Kirk both made *Oooh* noises and ran through the Maplewood Fun and Fright Fest crowd to get to the booth in question.

"This is a fucking weird-ass town." I watched fondly as Kirk and Charlie inspected the toys.

Finn put his arm around my shoulders. "Then what does it say about you, since you fit in so well here?"

I elbowed him. "Even worse, what does it say about you, since you were born here?"

He pulled me against him, his beautiful eyes sparkling. "Ah, but you chose to be with me, so it's really on you."

I felt my grin fade, and I swallowed. My heart pounded, and I felt a little faint. But I gritted my teeth and straightened my spine. "I love you."

Finn gaped. The sound of the crowd was an irritating buzzing in my ears as I held my breath waiting for his reply.

"Here? You picked *here* to tell me that?" He let go of me and raked his fingers through his hair, making it stand on end.

Looked like I wasn't getting any declarations in return. I put my hands on my hips and glared at him. "I was having a fucking moment, you jerk! Never mind. I take it back." I threw up my hands and started to turn to go... somewhere.

"Drake, wait!" He caught my arm and pulled me into a hug. My Deadman top hat hit him in the face, and he pulled it off my head. "I'm sorry. That wasn't how I wanted to respond."

"Yeah? It wasn't how I wanted you to respond either," I muttered into his shoulder. "I know you love me, you asshole."

I felt his chest vibrate as he chuckled. "I've been trying to find the right time to tell you. I'm sorry. You surprised me, and I didn't react well."

I grunted in agreement, but I did put my arms around him.

He pressed a kiss to the top of my head. "Can I have a redo? Please?"

I huffed. "Fine."

He pulled back slightly so we could see each other, then he gently cradled my face in his warm hand. He leaned forward so his mouth was next to my ear. "I love you too."

I smiled, my chest feeling fluttery. I let him kiss me, but I broke away before it could get heated. "That was better." I raised an eyebrow. "Would you mind explaining why you complained when I told you the same thing?"

He winced before wrapping me in another firm hug. He stroked his hand down my back like he was petting Charlie's kitten. "I'm *sorry*. My immediate reaction was to throw you down and make love to you, but I can't do that here. If I could do it over for real, I'd tell you I loved you too, and then I'd kiss you like my life depended on it."

I smirked, my bratty side coming out to play. "Okay. Go for it."

Laughing, he pulled me against him even more firmly, though that might have been for warmth instead of romance, since he was only wearing his scrubs and a light jacket. He cupped my face again. "Drake Derryberry, I love you." He touched his lips to mine and started to bend me back over his arm.

"*What?* Finally!"

We broke apart and turned to see Charlie grinning at us and carrying a stuffed Mabel. Kirk was behind him, keeping his eyes on anything other than me and Finn.

Finn made a growling sound. "Did you need something, Charlie?"

"Nope! Did Drake say it too?" He turned his puppy eyes on me. "Does this mean you'll finally come live with us?"

When I hesitated, Finn chimed in. "Yeah, Drake. Will you finally come live with us?" He didn't let go of me, but again, that might've been for warmth.

I groaned. "Okay, look. Last week I put up an ad for a caretaker. I know you need to be near the clinic for emergencies, but somebody has to care for Dolores, Mabel, and the chickens, plus the cabins."

Charlie frowned. "Why can't Zeke do it? He hasn't left yet."

"No, he's helping out sometimes, but he's gone a lot. He's visiting a bunch of places to decide where he wants to retire to." Though Nova and I both suspected he'd just wanted to retire, period. We figured he was having second thoughts about actually moving away from his friends and Nova. Either way, I still needed to hire a caretaker before I could move in with Finn and Charlie. My new family, I thought with wonder.

Charlie huffed. "Fine." He got the sly look on his face that usually meant he was plotting something. "Kirk's staying over tonight."

Finn nodded. "Great. Um, I thought I'd stay at Drake's place."

The boys whooped and high-fived each other. Charlie had learned early on that if Finn wasn't on call and I was hanging out with them, he could get Finn to stay at my place by inviting Kirk or his other friends over. No doubt they'd play video games on the big TV in the living room all night.

We swung by Finn and Charlie's house—soon also to be my house—to drop the boys off and pick up clothes for Finn. As we were getting ready to leave again, Charlie handed me the stuffed Mabel. It looked like the love child of Gumby and the Jolly Green Giant. "Here. Can you please put this out with Mabel's food? I've been thinking about her a lot, and it must be lonely being the only one of your kind out there."

My mind ran through how, if Mabel did exist, she had to have had parents. I shoved that unsettling thought aside and smiled. "Of course. That's nice of you. I'm sure she'll appreciate it." And if she didn't take it, I'd hide the stuffie and pretend she did.

Zeke was in Burlington for the night again—the less I wondered about those trips, the better—so I made Finn go with me to drop off Mabel's food and her stuffed likeness. I held it up so he could see it. "What if this doesn't look like Mabel at all? What if she gets offended?"

He gave an exasperated huff. "I guess we'll just have to hope she leaves it where she finds it and we never try to give her anything again."

I stuck my tongue out at him. When we put the bowl and the stuffie on Mabel's stump, I took a photo and texted it to Charlie. "There. In the morning it'll be gone." I rolled my eyes at Finn's impending protest. "One way or another."

He put his arm around my shoulders as we walked back toward the cabin. "I feel like we're telling a seventeen-year-old that there's a Santa Claus."

We came out of the woods into the lighted area by Dolores' pen. I tapped my chin thoughtfully. "You know what I've heard about Santa?"

"Uh, no?"

I grinned. "He has a secret stocking." At least that song was good for some jokes. Finn groaned, so I elbowed him in the ribs. "If you catch me, I'll show you mine!" I took off toward the cabin as fast as my clogs would allow.

"Wait, *what?*"

He hadn't taken the bait, so I slowed and walked backward. "Come on. You know 'Santa's Secret Stocking' isn't about something you hang by the chimney, right?" We'd sanitized the hell out of the lyrics so we could play it when kids were present.

He frowned and still didn't speed up. "I thought it was either a condom or he wore, like, fishnets."

"So the internet would have you believe." I wiggled my eyebrows. "But it's *secret*. And, as the lyrics say, *he puts his favorite treasures inside*." I patted my ass before turning around again and running for the cabin.

"What? Are you—" He didn't catch me until we got to the bedroom.

"Why do I have to come? It's not like you don't know what you'll find."

I ignored Finn's whining and continued dragging him by the hand down the path to Mabel's stump. He hadn't appreciated me waking him up after I'd fed Dolores and the chickens. But this was for Charlie, so I wanted Finn to witness whether the stuffed Mabel was still there or not.

"Okay, get your phone out." More grumbling, but he did as I asked, and we entered the clearing.

"Holy shit!" I rushed over to the stump. The stuffed Mabel was gone. And in its place—"It's beautiful." Reverently I bent over to examine the wreath. It was oval, a little over seven inches on the longer length, and made of evergreen twigs. Or boughs. What was a small bough called? They were exactly like several of the shrubs along the edge of the clearing.

Finn snorted. "You did that. You replaced the stuffed toy with that thing." He waved dismissively at the wreath.

I straightened up and rounded on him. "Putting aside for a moment that you're accusing me of lying, do I look like someone who knows how to make a wreath?"

There. He knew he'd stepped in it. "Sorry. It's early and I just woke up. I let my skepticism get the better of me. I don't think you made it." He rubbed his face with his free hand.

"Apology accepted. I'll make sure you have coffee first, the next time we exchange gifts with Mabel." I gasped. "Christmas Eve!"

He wasn't paying attention. "But it's far more likely to have been a human—maybe an unhoused person living in the woods—who made that than Mabel."

"Well, Charlie will disagree with you. Take the picture so he can see it."

He did, and I handed him the empty food bowl before picking up the wreath. I held it up in the air to admire it. "I love living in Maplewood."

He sighed before putting his arm around me and kissing my temple. "I love you."

I turned in his arms. "I love you too." I kissed him, then I tried to put the wreath on his head.

He ducked away, releasing me to get some distance. "No! You don't know what's on that!"

I held it up to look at it. "Leaves? Or do you think Mabel has some sort of disease?"

He brushed a hand over his hair. "I was thinking more like spiders. Can we go get coffee now?"

I sighed. "Fine." I took my cowboy hat off and settled the wreath around the crown. "It's like it was made to be there." I smiled in satisfaction as I settled the hat back on my head.

Finn exhaled loudly in exasperation. "Let's go back to the cabin. I can have coffee, and you can text Charlie. This'll make you his favorite for the next month at least." We started down the path again.

I put my arm around his waist. "Do you think Charlie will love me someday? You know I already love him."

He stroked a hand down my back. "He thinks of you as part of the family. He loves you, but it might take him a while to say it."

I tapped my hat. "I'll just say it to him over and over so he'll get used to it."

Finn stopped walking. He put his hands on my shoulders

to make me face him. "I can tell you right now, I'll never get used to hearing you say it to me."

I nodded, tearing up suddenly. Dammit, I hated it when that happened. "I love you, Finn Hunnicutt."

He kissed me, soft and sweet. "I love you, Drake Derryberry."

Thank you for reading *Can You Feel the Maple Tonight*! Curious about Drake's background and family? Read *What's Santa Got to Do with It*!

Be sure to check out the other books in the Love in Maplewood series!

Winter Wishes and Coffee Kisses by Ana Ashley
Love Me Like It's Real by Rhys Everly
A Touch of Maple by Amy Aislin
Bee-tween the Music by Chantal Mer
Pride By the Book by Jeff Adams
Scoop Me Up by Riley Long
The Great Maple Mistake by Beck Grey
Something Cryptid This Way Comes by Susan Scott Shelley
Don't Clause a Scene by Lee Blair

ALSO BY BIX BARROW

BENT OAK, TEXAS

Holding On to a Hero (Will, Cole, and Jason's story)

Heart Me Up (Craig and Foster's story)

Head Over Feels (Felix and Malcolm's story)

What's Santa Got to Do with It (Steve and Baz's story)

We Don't Need Another Santa (Phillip and Lucas' story)

I Touch Hoses (Keson and Wesley's story) – Related novella

Last Mango in Palm Springs (Ford and Zachary's story) - Related novella

Voices Harry (Mitchell and Harry's story) – Free when you go to www.bixbarrow.com and sign up for my newsletter!

WONDERFALL

Seer (Cal and Greg's story)

Medium (Shane, Ellis, and Rory's story)

Wonder (Simon and Reno's story)

SINGULAR MAGICS

Unprecedented (Manny's story)

LOVE IN MAPLEWOOD (MULTI-AUTHOR SHARED WORLD)

Can You Feel the Maple Tonight (Drake and Finn's story)

ABOUT BIX BARROW

When Bix Barrow got an idea for her first book, it ended up turning into her second — and thus the first two stories in the *Bent Oak, Texas* series emerged. An aspiring author for most of her life, it took a foray into the MM romance genre to spark the humor, suspense, and blazing banter Bix now weaves into her novels. Accompanying her on her writing exploits are her two dogs and multitude of cats (six at last count). An avid traveler, Bix has started to view her expeditions as interviews for her future home. Born and raised in Texas, she is eager to move somewhere with fewer politicians, hurricanes, and flooding.

Join Bix Barrow's Boom Boom Room on Facebook for sneak peeks and fun conversation!

Sign up for Bix's newsletter and get a free novella! www.bixbarrow.com

facebook.com/bixbarrowauthor

instagram.com/bixbarrow

bookbub.com/authors/bix-barrow